"Ple

"There is a l
trust, Susannah, but I suggest you begin to earn it by
being honest with me about tonight! What have you to
do with the intruder?"

"Nothing! Nothing at all, I swear it! Now please let
me go!" she gasped, glancing at Anjuli's door again.

He could feel her warmth through her flimsy wrap,
and he could smell the faint fragrance of flowers that
seemed to cling to her hair. Both were affecting him
more than he wished. "I wish I could believe you, Susannah," he breathed, conscious of arousal stirring
through his body.

She was so aware of him that it was as if a current
of electricity were passing through her. "Please let me
go, Gareth," she whispered, but her entire being ached
to say the opposite. *Hold me close, make love to me,
stay with me until dawn. . . .*

Coming next month

SAVED BY SCANDAL
by Barbara Metzger
"One of the genre's wittiest pens."–*Romantic Times*
Abandoned at the altar, Lord Galen Woodbridge decides to
stir up a scandal–by wedding the London songstress Margot
Montclaire. But in saving his pride, he never planned on
losing his heart....
0-451-20038-1/$4.99

MISS TIBBLES INVESTIGATES
by April Kihlstrom
Pamela Kendall is in love with her childhood friend Julian,
who pines for an altogether different girl. But as luck would
have it, her mother's former governess, Miss Tibbles, is
visiting–and she knows the best way to avert a disaster of
the heart....
0-451-20040-3/$4.99

CASSANDRA'S DECEPTION
by Gayle Buck
While pretending to be her twin sister, Cassandra
Weatherstone finds passion in the arms of a refined young
suitor. But being true to her heart means being exposed as
an imposter. And is any love strong enough to survive such
a scandal?
0-451-20037-3/$4.99

To order call: 1-800-788-6262

Counterfeit Kisses

Sandra Heath

A SIGNET BOOK

SIGNET
Published by New American Library, a division of
Penguin Putnam Inc., 375 Hudson Street,
New York, New York 10014, U.S.A.
Penguin Books Ltd, 27 Wrights Lane,
London W8 5TZ, England
Penguin Books Australia Ltd,
Ringwood, Victoria, Australia
Penguin Books Canada Ltd, 10 Alcorn Avenue,
Toronto, Ontario, Canada M4V 3B2
Penguin Books (N.Z.) Ltd, 182–190 Wairau Road,
Auckland 10, New Zealand

Penguin Books Ltd, Registered Offices:
Harmondsworth, Middlesex, England

First published by Signet, an imprint of New American Library,
a division of Penguin Putnam Inc.

First Printing, May 2000
10 9 8 7 6 5 4 3 2 1

*For Susan Layton, my sister-in-law
and the namesake of my heroine.*

Chapter 1

The astonishing business of the tiara, its many would-be thieves, and how the abominable Duke of Exton became—quite literally—the butt of much amusement, began on the last night of 1803. London was wet and windswept, and as darkness fell over Pall Mall, a long line of sedan chairs and hackney coaches was to be found outside the exclusive Union Club. Inside, the card room was particularly crowded and hot, but instead of the customary low murmur of male voices, there was virtual silence as the cream of London's gentlemen pressed around a green baize table close to the seasonally decorated fireplace.

One of the few sounds was the snoring of Hercules, a plump bulldog slumbering by the armchair of its balding master, "Bull" Barker, who was as stout and jowled as his pet, and as wheezy. Bull had just awakened from a postprandial doze and was reaching for his tenth measure of the club's famous whisky punch when he observed the intense interest around the table. He called across to Lord Faringdon, an acquaintance some twenty years his junior. "I say, Jerry, what's goin' on?" he asked, easing himself forward very gingerly in his chair in order not to put any further strain on the seams of his too-tight silk breeches.

The younger man, small and spruce in bottle-green silk, came over a little reluctantly, for they had had differences of late. "It seems His Grace of Exton has decided time's up for the country whippersnapper," he replied, holding a lighted spill to his slender clay pipe. "Maybe now we'll find out why Exton has been concerning himself so much with a nobody from the sticks."

"I think I already know. Well, part of it, at least," murmured Bull, studying the three men seated at the table, their faces illuminated by a shaded candelabrum. Only two of them were still in play; the middle-aged, soon-to-be-married Duke of Exton, who had been careful to sip water all night, and a little-known

Lincolnshire squire barely in his twenties, by the name of Stephen Holland. The latter was now so tipsy that it was doubtful he could stand up, let alone think clearly about how best to play his hand. The third man, Sir Gareth Carew, was a soft-spoken Welshman of thirty-two, whose courage, wit, and blond good looks made him the darling of the ladies. Tonight, after throwing in his hand sometime earlier, he had remained at the table to watch.

Jerry looked curiously at Bull. "If you know anything about all this, you're the only one here."

Bull smiled and leaned down to pat Hercules, who rolled over. "I find it hard to credit that you of all men have not guessed."

"Me? Why?" Jerry moved warily away from the bulldog, which was renowned for its unattractive digestive problems.

"Because it concerns the toast of Drury Lane herself."

"Fleur Fitzgerald?"

"The very lady. For an age now she has been refusing you and Exton, who between you are as rich as Croesus, then along comes hard-up young Holland, and bingo! Into her bed he leaps."

"I don't believe you!" Jerry's fingers tightened so furiously on the stem of his pipe that he snapped it in two. He leapt back as the bowl fell to the carpet and scattered its lighted contents over his elegantly buckled shoes. "Damn it!" he breathed, stamping on the sparks.

Bull chuckled. "For the life of me I can't see what fascination the woman has. If she were a rose, I'd describe her as overblown."

Jerry was appalled. "Overblown? Bull, she's a voluptuous divinity, and I've wanted her for so long that I can hardly sleep at night! Now you tell me she's surrendered to that . . . that rustic *nincompoop*?" He scowled across the room at Stephen Holland.

"I fear so."

"But why? What on earth can such a paltry fellow offer her?"

"Not money, that's for sure." Bull gave a sly grin. "Perhaps he's a leading man."

"Eh?"

"You know, large part."

Jerry, sensitive to his own shortcomings in that area, was not amused.

Bull's brows drew together. "I have the oddest feeling that the names Holland and Fitzgerald have a past connection. I seem to recall a legal feud of some sort. Oh, it must be a hundred years ago."

Jerry gave him a sour look. "I knew you were old, but not *that* old."

Bull drew a long breath. "Most amusing. It so happens that I'm interested in old legal disputes. Anyway, I'll remember, just give me time. . . ."

Hercules stirred and made a very rude noise that was heard throughout the room. Jerry had to move hastily to the other side of the chair. "Damn it all, Bull, do you have to bring that flatulent cur in here?"

"Just because your vicious chimpanzee has been banned from Grillion's."

"Bonaparte is not vicious," Jerry replied stiffly. Until the humiliating debacle at Grillion's, London's newest and most exclusive hotel, the chimpanzee had always gone everywhere with him, guaranteeing that he would be the center of attention. Now Bonaparte was banned from the hotel, and from numerous other establishments, including the Union Club.

"Bonaparte *is* vicious," Bull insisted. "He bit Hercules on the backside and caused a near riot."

"Damn brave ape to get anywhere near your beast's backside," Jerry muttered, flicking his perfumed handkerchief in the air. Bonaparte had been blamed for the entire episode, even though Hercules had bitten him first. Now all chimpanzees, monkeys, and anything else of vaguely simian appearance were banned from London's most fashionable hotel, while disgusting canines were still welcomed through the hallowed portals. It was a damned injustice!

Conversation lapsed as the two men resumed watching the play, then Jerry's brows drew together. "I'd lay odds Exton is cheating, but I'm damned if I can figure out how. It must be marked cards."

Bull nodded. "I share your suspicions, and so, if I'm not mistaken, does friend Carew." He nodded toward the third man at the table. "Our blond Welsh friend is a past master at not seeming to be paying particular attention, but I can tell you he's watching Exton like a hawk. One slip, and Carew will have him!"

At that moment there was a stir, as Stephen Holland played

a very foolish card. Beads of perspiration immediately broke out on the unfortunate young man's forehead as he fingered the few gaming counters he had left. He was twenty-two years old, with a freckled face, chestnut hair, and blue eyes, and he wore a purple velvet coat and a white brocade waistcoat, both of which had seen three winters. The modest pearl pin in his neckcloth would not have been given a second glance by the other gentlemen present, nor would the unremarkable gold signet ring on his finger. He was a hunting, shooting, fishing Lincolnshire squire who had only come to London to sell some land to raise a dowry for his twin sister's arranged marriage, and he hadn't been able to believe his luck when Fleur Fitzgerald, one of the most beautiful and sought-after women in the capital, had bestowed her favors upon him. She had woven such a seductive spell around him that he had very swiftly become enslaved. But, as he had been informed very bluntly last night, such irresistible pleasures would continue only at a high and very particular price. What a gull he had been! He should have been immediately suspicious of anyone by the name of Fitzgerald! But he was a bumpkin governed by a lower portion of his anatomy than his brain! And as if yesterday had not been bad enough, today he had fallen in with the likes of the Duke of Exton. Oh, if ever a man wished he had never left the simple pursuits of Lincolnshire, that man was Stephen Holland.

Opposite him, the square-jawed face of Delavel Harmon, fifth Duke of Exton, was inscrutable. He was stocky, with cold, pale eyes, and an upturned, flattened nose that resembled a snout. His powdered wig boasted a ribbon to match his bright-rose silk coat, and from his cuffs there spilled lavish frills of fine lace. Numerous valuable rings cluttered his stubby fingers, a diamond-studded pin glittered in the folds of his lace neckcloth, and a thin smile played upon his lips as he glanced down at the card Stephen had played.

He wagged a reproving finger and murmured, "Foolish boy."

Stephen gave a weak smile and closed his cards together before reaching for his glass of punch. The third man at the table immediately pushed the glass out of reach. "You've had enough, my friend," Sir Gareth Carew advised.

Stephen flushed, but didn't argue. If only he had the gumption to just get up and walk away from the table—but he didn't. The amount he had lost tonight simply did not bear thinking about. What was he going to say to his sister, Susannah, who had arrived in London that very day to order a gown for her forthcoming marriage? As for lavishing anything on Fleur in the hope of keeping her sweet and avoiding her ultimate demand . . . he closed his eyes wretchedly.

Gareth sat back again. Stephen might be too much in his cups to play sensibly, but if the young fool was going to lose, it should be fairly, not because his opponent wasn't dealing from the top of the deck. Too many cards were going Exton's way, but Gareth had yet to see how he was doing it. The Duke of Exton's suspected sleight of hand slipped his mind for a moment as he glanced at the holly-swathed longcase clock in the alcove by the fireplace. He was tired of kicking his heels in London. How much longer would it be before Lord Hawkesbury's expected instructions arrived? When the Secretary of State for Foreign Affairs had first approached him more than two years ago because of the number of friends and connections he had in St. Petersburg, he had needed much persuading to go there to see what information he could garner for London. But he had proved rather good at it, and he enjoyed the danger, so he had been sent back several times since then. Now another such an assignment was imminent, and the suspense of waiting was driving him to distraction. He had come here tonight only for something to do but had found the deep and intense play very intriguing indeed.

Another stir from the crowding gentlemen brought Gareth's attention swiftly back to the table. The duke had put down a card that gave full warning of the strength of his hand, so Gareth intervened again, firmly clasping Stephen's sleeve. "You're over your head, my friend, so leave the table now," he advised quietly.

The duke heard and sat forward. "Keep out, Carew. This has nothing to do with you." His voice was harsh and grating.

Gareth's cool green eyes swung toward him. "He's not in your league, and you know it."

Stephen shook his arm free. "I can look after myself."

"Maybe you can in the depths of Lincolnshire, but not here," Gareth replied.

"By the law of averages I have to win sometime, and—"

Gareth interrupted. "In cards there's no such thing as the law of averages," he said, feeling like clipping the young idiot around the ear.

The duke gave a cold laugh. "You heard him, Carew. Look, isn't it about time you wandered off to foreign parts again?"

"Foreign parts? I really don't know what you're talking about," Gareth murmured. Damn Hawkesbury's indiscretions to his wife. Dinner table chitter-chatter had a lot to answer for. His expeditions to St. Petersburg were supposed to be covert!

The duke looked at Stephen. "Get on with it, man."

With a rush of sadly misplaced confidence, Stephen pushed his last gaming counters forward. "I'll see you, sir," he said, laying down his hand of tens and sixes.

Chapter 2

As Stephen placed his cards upon the table, the clock began to strike midnight. The faint jangle of bells drifted in from outside as 1803 slipped away and 1804 began; this was the one night when church bells could ring, for usually they were only to sound as a warning of French invasion. No one at the Union Club took heed of the joyous pealing, however, for at that moment the duke, with gloating triumph, spread his hand upon the green baize. Aces and queens. Gasps and exclamations rippled around the gathering.

"You lose, I think, Holland," the duke murmured, gathering Stephen's final few counters.

As Stephen reached for another glass of whisky punch and swallowed it in one gulp, the duke's eyes glittered as brightly as his diamond pin in the candlelight. "Of course, I'm prepared to give you the chance to win it all back," he said softly, then waved a languid hand at the gleaming pile of counters before him. "My bride-to-be, whom you all know I adore with all my heart, has a great liking for rubies, and I wish to give her an appropriate wedding gift. So I wager all this against the Holland tiara."

Light dawned throughout the room, and suddenly there was a buzz of conversation as everyone at last realized why the unfortunate Stephen had been of such interest. Bull Barker brought a triumphant hand crashing down upon the arm of his chair. "Of course! *That's* why the names Holland and Fitzgerald seemed connected."

Most of the gentlemen present knew the story of the Holland tiara, which had once belonged to Queen Henrietta Maria and was famed for its twenty-five perfectly matched rubies. One hundred years ago it had come into the possession of the Hollands, but their enemies, the Fitzgeralds, had laid false claim to it. The

Hollands won the case in court, but the Fitzgeralds, although disgraced at the time, had not conceded defeat and had sworn never to rest until the tiara was theirs. Fleur's interest in Stephen Holland was suddenly explained. The room was a hive of talk. No one could believe two and two hadn't been put together before, but then, the Hollands *had* faded from prominence over the past century, rarely leaving their country estate as their financial fortunes diminished. Selling the tiara would have solved a great deal of their difficulty, but it was a precious heirloom and they were far too proud to part with it. Now it seemed they were going to be forcibly deprived of it, unless Stephen found the grit to get up from the table. One thing every man present *did* know for certain, however: If the Duke of Exton won the tiara, it wouldn't be going to his unfortunate fiancée, Lady Jane Bancroft, for whom he felt nothing, but to Fleur Fitzgerald, for whose surrender he had lusted so long.

Gareth suddenly understood everything as well. So *that* was the branch of the Holland family to which Stephen belonged. La Fitzgerald's interest was suddenly as clear to see through as a window. As was Exton's hypocritical mention of his bride-to-be. A nerve twitched sourly at the corner of Gareth's lips. He liked Lady Jane, although he did not know her well. She was exceedingly plain, but of matchless lineage, and Exton had chosen her for those very qualities. The duke had a pathological dread of one day wearing a cuckold's horns, and he wouldn't have married at all if he hadn't needed an heir. So he had selected the plainest wife he could, in the belief that no lover would ever be interested in her. Of course, while he would demand absolute faithfulness from her, she would certainly not enjoy the same restraint from him, for Delavel Harmon was one of the most profligate men in England.

The room quietened again as attention centered upon Stephen, who had yet to respond to the duke's challenge. Seeing the indecision on the young man's face, Gareth placed yet another warning hand on his sleeve. "Listen, you numskull! If you want to stay out of debt, and keep your family's heirloom, you *must* end play now," he breathed urgently.

A modicum of intelligence began to flicker through Stephen's inebriated fog of self-pity. The tiara was Fleur's price too, as she had informed him only too bluntly last night. He had learned that if it hadn't been for a chance remark of his that first night in the green room, she wouldn't even have glanced at him. But she had suddenly realized that he was the Holland who possessed the tiara, and so he had become of intense interest. Until that moment she had almost given up trying to trace it, for a century earlier the Hollands hadn't lived in Lincolnshire but on the other side of the country, in Cornwall. Now her Fitzgerald aspirations had been ferociously reawakened, and she was prepared to go to any length to claw back a piece of jewelry that even the very law of the land insisted had never belonged to her family.

Devastated by the harsh truth about the woman he loved, Stephen had begged time to consider her demands, but he knew in his heart that he couldn't submit to such terms. The tiara meant too much to his family, especially his sister, Susannah. It was bad enough that he had already lost so much ill-afforded money, but how on earth would he tell Susie if he forfeited the tiara as well? He and Susie were the only remaining Hollands, and the tiara was an important symbol to them both. Pride, courage, and common sense at last marched into Stephen's haze; the Duke of Exton and Fleur Fitzgerald could go to hell!

"Well?" the duke pressed impatiently, his fingers drumming on the green baize. "What's it to be, Holland? Are you too craven for another duel with the goddess of fortune?"

Common sense marched out again. "No man calls me craven!" Stephen cried, leaping to his feet, and swaying from side to side so alarmingly that Gareth was obliged to steady him.

The duke was as smooth as silk. "Shall we say just the turn of a single card this time? One card, highest wins, aces low. What d'you say?"

Gareth looked wearily at Stephen. "For once in your idiotic life, do the sensible thing and say no," he advised again.

But Stephen had already taken the duke's bait. "Very well, sir, one card!" Gareth groaned inwardly and seized the pack before Exton could. "A new deck is necessary, I fancy," he said. If the others *were* marked, that would put a stop to it.

The duke made no protest. "By all means, Carew. I wouldn't dream of doing otherwise."

Gareth reached angrily for another pack of cards. Exton *knew* he was going to win, just as he had known all night, but how in God's name had he been doing it? Clearly not with marked cards. Gareth reluctantly shuffled the new deck and placed it neatly on the green baize. Stephen reached out immediately and turned the top one. The ten of diamonds. Not good, but not bad either. The odds were slightly in his favor.

Time stood still as the duke reached out, but the moment his fingers touched the topmost card, the heavy frill of lace at his cuff tumbled forward over his hand, just as it had throughout the evening, only this time it happened in such a way that everyone present realized what had been going on. The oldest trick of all, cards hidden up a sleeve, and done so dexterously that not a single man present had seen! A pin could have been heard to drop, then the wind outside sucked fiercely down the chimney, the fire flared, and the leaping flames dazzled for a moment. As they died back to their former glow, the duke's card lay upturned. The king of diamonds. Stephen stared at the winning card, then at the duke's conveniently lacy cuff. At last he understood he had been cheated, but it was too late.

The duke exhaled with cold triumph and rose from the table, beckoning to one of the club's footmen to collect his winnings. Then he looked down into Stephen's eyes. "I will expect the tiara to be delivered into my hands within two days. Two days, do you understand?" He turned to leave, and everyone parted before him. At the door he paused to survey them all. "Oh, by the way, a Happy New Year to you all," he declared genially, then went out to take a hackney coach to the Theatre Royal, where he happened to know there was a backstage junket taking place that was planned to go on until dawn.

As the door closed behind him, Hercules the bulldog fired a two-gun salute, which everyone present thought singularly appropriate.

The Duke of Exton drove through the rainswept darkness to Drury Lane and entered the Theatre Royal to find a noisy celebration in progress. Everyone was welcoming the New Year, and the crush was considerable. He soon found Fleur Fitzgerald—he had only to look for the greatest concentration of eager gentlemen. Sure enough, she was seated on a gold-and-white-striped sofa in the center of the candlelit stage, holding court like the queen that she was.

The duke paused in the wings to gaze upon the object of his desire. Fleur Fitzgerald was an Irish beauty with a soft Dublin brogue that could turn a man's heart over. She was over thirty

now, although no one knew how far over, and she was still the
most breathtakingly beautiful creature Delavel Harmon had ever
seen. Her thick, glossy hair, worn flatteringly loose in a tumble
of girlish curls, was the color of a raven's wings, her complexion was pale and pure, and her large eyes were the darkest brown
imaginable. She had full, pouting lips, and her figure was a
voluptuous hourglass loosely clad in delicate wine-red silk that
plunged perilously low over her magnificent bosom. Fleur never
felt the cold, or so she claimed, and even though it was not all
that warm in the theater, she scorned to wear a shawl; thus her
shapely charms were revealed in all their desirable glory. A fan
wafted prettily before her face, and she was smiling at something an admirer was saying.

She seemed to sense the duke's presence, for her fan suddenly
became still and her melting brown eyes met his through the
throng. She dismissed her eager admirers with a wave of her
fan, and as they drew resentfully away, she beckoned to the
duke.

"I trust you will have a very happy New Year, Your Grace,"
she said, her voice almost lost in the continuing noise of the
celebrations.

"Oh, I believe I will," he replied, his gaze drawn to the irresistible curve of her wonderful breasts. She wore nothing beneath that flimsy silk, nothing at all. . . .

Fleur smiled a little. "Lady Jane must be eagerly making her
wedding plans."

"Eh? Oh, yes, I believe she is."

Fleur's dark eyes missed very little, and she patted the sofa
beside her. "Do join me, my lord."

He obeyed, still unable to tear his gaze from her exquisite
body.

"Now why, I ask myself, have you come to see me tonight?"
she asked softly.

"The Holland tiara now belongs to me," he said without further preamble.

Fleur's lips parted. "To you?"

"Your boy lover has no head for whisky punch and no idea
at all how to play cards."

Fleur rose to her feet, and suddenly clapped her hands loudly.
The party came to a confused standstill, and then there were
protests as she told them all to leave. But no one defied her, for

her word was law. When she and the duke were entirely alone, Fleur turned to face him. "The tiara belongs to *me*," she said then, her brown eyes hard and shining.

The duke lounged back on the sofa. "The Fitzgeralds lost their case a hundred years ago, and now *I've* won the tiara from that idiot Holland. It is mine to dispose of as I wish, Fleur."

"*I'm* the only one with a true claim to it," she declared grandly.

He shook his head. "If you truly believe that, then you're a fool. And I know you're not a fool. Your family has merely been smarting since losing their lawsuit, whining about the injustice they suffered. Except it wasn't an injustice. They had no right whatsoever to that tiara."

She flushed. "If you've just come here to insult me—"

"You *know* why I've come here," he interrupted quietly.

"You think the tiara is the key to my favors?"

"Well, isn't it? Why else would you bed a callow youth like Holland? For his skill as a lover? I think not."

"If you have a proposition, I suggest you state it now."

"Become my mistress, and the tiara will be yours." Suddenly he removed a costly emerald from his finger and held it out to her. "Here, take this as a token of my sincerity."

She gazed at the ring. The emeralds were very fine, very fine indeed. With a slow smile, she took it and slipped it onto her thumb, for it was too large for any of her fingers.

The duke seized her hand and pressed it ardently to his lips. "I will give you jewels to dazzle you, Fleur. The Exton collection is the finest in England and—"

"And should be at the disposal of Lady Jane Bancroft when she becomes your wife," Fleur interposed.

"Jane will wear what I say she can, and she will *never* wear the tiara."

Fleur stepped a little closer. "That tiara means everything to me," she said softly. "I grew up with the story ringing in my ears of how the Hollands took it from us, twisted the evidence in court, and ruined my great-great-grandfather's health and reputation."

It was strong liquor and a villainous streak that ruined your great-great-grandfather's reputation, the duke thought, but he smiled and said. "To have the tiara, all you have to do is give yourself to me."

She met his eyes for a long, long moment. "Very well," she

said then, for all the world as if she were accepting a mere invitation to dine.

He got up joyously and went to take her in his arms, but she held him away. "Oh, no, my fine duke, not so quickly. First I must have the tiara."

He gazed at her in angry confusion. She had surrendered to Holland without such a condition; why not to him? "You have my *word* that the tiara will be yours," he said.

"Your word isn't good enough."

His gaze froze. "Holland was welcome enough between your sheets."

"I was foolish then. I am not foolish now."

His lips pressed thinly together. He didn't appreciate being dictated to, not even by the fragrant Fleur. "As you wish," he said. "Holland will have the tiara for me in two days' time, but I fear that I must then go to Exton Park. I will be out of town for several weeks."

"I can wait," she replied, then stepped even closer to press cool lips to his cheek. "We have a bargain, my lord," she said softly before walking off the stage in a whisper of silk.

The duke gazed hotly after her. Her refusal to submit immediately had heightened his desire but had also incurred his resentment. A crafty light entered his small eyes. She would learn that he wasn't to be trifled with. Oh, indeed she would. . . .

Chapter 3

While the Duke of Exton was propositioning Fleur Fitzgerald on the stage of the Theatre Royal, a hackney coach was splashing west out of London, en route to Stephen's rented house in Kensington. New Year's bells still caroled, and the blustering rain stung the coachman's face. The capes of his greatcoat flapped like wild things, and he cursed under his breath as the horses faltered through a deep puddle that stretched across the rutted road.

Inside the shabby vehicle, Gareth was doing his best to prevent Stephen, now almost senseless with drink, from falling off the seat onto the soaking straw on the floor. Though seriously impaired, Stephen was still conscious enough to unfairly blame Gareth for events at the Union Club.

"Exton cheeded," he declared thickly, his blue eyes glazed in the light from a passing streetlamp. "You—*hic*—sh-should've stopped me, Pengower."

"My name is Carew," Gareth corrected. "Pengower is my estate."

"Well, worrever. Is'still your faul'. . . ."

"I did my damndest to keep you in check." Gareth was tired of this half-baked Lincolnshire ninny, but in the absence of anyone else to see the tiresome fellow safely home . . .

"F-Fleur doesn't love me, y'know. Sh-she tole me she only wanned the tarara. Oh, she's so—*hic*—cruel. . . ."

Gareth exhaled slowly. Fleur Fitzgerald was an avaricious, calculating, heartless *chienne,* as this poor saphead now knew only too well. Exton was bound to be the next in her bed, and if ever two souls deserved each other, it was *that* pair!

"The tararara's bin in my f-family for a long time," Stephen went on. "If you were a tr-true friend, you'd've . . ."

"Damn it, I'm not your friend, I've never clapped eyes on you before tonight!" Gareth snapped.

Stephen flinched. "It was your faul'," he insisted churlishly, then took a long, shuddering breath. "I feel sick," he muttered.

"Use the straw," Gareth replied, carefully moving his legs out of harm's way.

But the urge to throw up subsided, and Stephen gave a careworn sigh. "M-my sisister expec's to wear it—hic—at 'er weddinin-din-nin . . ." He gave up trying to say the word.

"Your sister?"

"S-Susie. Sh-she's my twin, y'know. She only arrived—hic—today. It's an arranged m-match. H-he's takin' her to Begnal, y'-know."

Begnal? Where in tarnation was that? Scotland? Gareth pondered Miss Holland. Was she a hunting, shooting, fishing female? he wondered with a shudder. She was bound to be if she was this dolt's twin. The carriage suddenly drew to a standstill, and he wiped the misty glass to look out. They had reached Stephen's address, a three-story semidetached property built of brown brick with stone facings. A lighted lamp was fixed beside the green front door, where a Christmas wreath shuddered in the wind. The only lighted window was that of a bedroom on the second floor, where the curtains had twitched aside the moment the coach arrived. A young woman in a nightgown looked down. She was a mere silhouette against the light behind her, and as he watched, she drew sharply back and the curtains fell back into place.

Gareth climbed reluctantly down. Needles of icy rain dashed his face, and the wind snatched his voice away as he bade the coachman wait. Then he hastened up the shallow flight of steps to knock loudly on the door. It opened almost immediately, for a manservant had been dozing on the hall chair, waiting for Stephen's return. The man was taken aback to see an unknown gentleman "S-sir?" he inquired.

"Assist me with Mr. Holland. He's more than a little in his cups," Gareth said, immediately turning back to the coach. The man followed him, and together they managed to ease Stephen down to the pavement, but hardly had they done so than the young woman who'd been at the window hurried out. She had hastily donned a cloak, and the flapping hood was raised over her hair. Her face remained in shadow as she gasped on seeing her brother's condition. "Oh, Stephen! How could you!"

Her voice was raised because of the weather. Or perhaps she

always shouted like that, Gareth thought, picturing her riding bareback over the Lincolnshire Wolds like some latter-day Fury.

The drunken man had stirred at little on hearing her. "S-Susie? Iz not my faul'—*hic*—t-truly iz not."

"What isn't your fault?"

"The tarara-ra . . ."

"The tiara?" She turned quickly to Gareth, who still couldn't see her face because of the flapping of her hood. "May I know who you are, sir? And what has happened?"

"Sir Gareth Carew of Pengower," Gareth murmured, inclining his head as elegantly as he could with Stephen's arm flung tightly around his neck. "Miss Holland, I'm afraid your brother has been playing cards with the Duke of Exton and as a consequence has gambled away the Holland tiara," he said bluntly, for there wasn't a gentle way to break such news.

Before she had a chance to reply, her brother stirred himself again. "It waz Caroo'ze faul'. He—*hic*—egged me play on when he-he knew Exton-non-non was cheeding. He-he's Exton's c-cat's-paw."

Gareth exhaled angrily. So that was all the thanks he got for trying to look after this country muffin!

Susannah believed her brother. "What have you to say, Sir Gareth?" she demanded angrily.

"Miss Holland, your idiot brother deserved everything that happened to him tonight. He drank himself silly, refused to heed advice, and insisted on accepting every wager the duke chose to place before him."

"Stephen would not lie, sir," she said coldly.

"Believe him if you wish, madam. That is your prerogative," Gareth replied frostily. He was tired, cold, becoming increasingly wet, and had had enough of all things Holland.

"*Did* you know the duke was cheating?" she pressed.

Gareth wasn't about to endure any more. "Oh, but of course I did! I was in Exton's pocket all the time, helping him to slip aces where no aces should be!" he replied sarcastically and stepped purposefully past her into the house, forcing Stephen and the footman to stumble along with him. Once in the mock-marble hall, he dumped Stephen unceremoniously on the only chair, then without another word strode out, intending to quit Kensington before he forgot he was a gentleman and expressed an even more acid opinion of the strident Miss Holland and her doltish sibling! God help her unfortunate husband-to-be!

Susannah called scornfully after him: "Take a message to your crony the duke, Sir Lackey. Tell him I will not rest until the tiara he stole with your assistance has been restored to my family." With that, she retreated inside and slammed the door.

Gareth was so angry he could have cheerfully forced his way in after her and throttled her! Just who did she think she was? Plague take Lincolnshire and its tiresome rustics, he thought savagely as he climbed back into the hackney coach to return to his residence in Hanover Square.

He seethed with rage all the way from Kensington, and glowered out the window as the carriage entered the elegant Mayfair square, where terraced red-brick town houses stood sentinel on all four sides, their exclusive grace evident even in the wildness of the winter night. As Gareth alighted at his door, the New Year's bells seemed to mock him. *Sir Lackey, Sir Lackey, Sir Lackey.* He paid the coachman, who drove off immediately as Gareth paused to glance toward the railed garden in the center of the square. The lamps that were placed at regular intervals all around it were shuddering in the wind, and the trees had suffered so much that several branches had fallen. What weather, he thought, and tugged his top hat low for the short dash to the house, the door of which had already been opened by a footman. But then a carriage drove up at speed and halted. Gareth's pulse quickened as he recognized Lord Hawkesbury's crest on the lacquered door. At last!

But it wasn't the Secretary of State who alighted. Instead Gareth saw Hawkesbury's right-hand man, Daniel Trask. "How timely of me to arrive just as you crawl home," Trask said, wrapping his cloak around him and accompanying Gareth into the house.

The footman closed the door behind them, and the dismal night was banished. The servant relieved both men of their outdoor clothes, then Gareth ushered his visitor into the study. "Cognac?" he inquired over his shoulder as he went to the decanter. It was Trask's favorite tipple. Too favorite, on occasion.

Trask shook his head. He was a lanky man with hollow cheeks and straggly gray hair that was just too short to be tied back. His eyes were watery and of a nondescript color, and his nose very large and hooked. "Where have you been, Carew?" he asked. "I inquired at the Union Club and was told you'd left an age ago.

You're supposed to leave word of your whereabouts at all times," he added reproachfully.

"Forgive me, but on this occasion it just slipped my mind. I was attending to the safe return home of a drunken, obnoxious, moaning example of the Lincolnshire squirearchy, whom in the end I wished I'd tipped into the nearest ditch," Gareth replied, his annoyance resurging as he recalled the accusations leveled at him in Kensington.

Trask raised an eyebrow. "A sore topic, evidently."

"Very."

"Then let us change it to another. You are to leave immediately for St. Petersburg."

"And about time too! The suspense of waiting has been irritating in the extreme."

"Then consider the irritation at an end. My orders are to get you on your way without delay. By the way, I trust you're taking your man Hector Ambleforth with you?"

"Naturally."

"Good, for his, er, qualities will probably be particularly useful this time. I'm reliably informed that there are some very high, very small windows to be entered. However, you'll learn more when you're aboard ship. A vessel awaits in the Medway, and her captain has detailed information." Trask pointedly took out his pocket watch. "With all due respect, time and tide are not known to wait."

Gareth said no more, but hurried from the room, calling loudly for Hector, whose swift appearance on the staircase denoted a certain amount of eavesdropping. He was a small, wiry man in his forties, with a wizened face and ears that stood out like vase handles; such looks could not have been more appropriate for someone who had once made his living as "the Human Monkey" at Astley's Amphitheatre. He could swarm up and down a seemingly sheer wall without any effort and wriggle through openings that even a child might find difficult; such agility made him indispensable on these furtive visits to Russia

By noon on that first day of 1804, Gareth's ship was many miles out to sea, scudding northward through gray whitecapped waves. It was to be three long years before he and Susannah Holland met again. Circumstances would be very different then, but sparks would still fly. Oh, how they would fly.

Chapter 4

It was December 1807, and the Bengal sunrise was particularly splendid as the heavily laden barge glided away from the fine riverside mansion at Chinsura, taking Susannah, now the widowed Mrs. Richard Leighton, on the first part of her long voyage home to England. Once the rust-colored sail was set, there would be little for the small crew to do, for the current of the Hooghly river would carry the flat-bottomed vessel downstream to Calcutta, some twenty miles away to the south.

Peacock cries filled the air, seeming to say good-bye as Susannah, clad in mourning for her late husband, made herself comfortable on the piled cushions beneath the vessel's palm-frond awning. She carried her little pet monkey, Chatterji, who clung to her fearfully because he hated water. Her luggage was piled all around, and she was accompanied by her Hindu maid, or ayah, Anjuli, who had claimed to be thirty ever since Susannah had known her but was most likely ten years older. Anjuli was the only one of her huge army of servants that she was taking with her. The rest lined the riverbank now, waving and sobbing as their memsahib departed for the last time.

Susannah waved back. She had chestnut hair and blue eyes like her twin brother, but unlike Stephen, she loathed hunting; nor was she particularly fond of horses or boisterous gundogs. Slender, pretty, and spirited without being hot-tempered, she liked to walk, read, and paint watercolors, so she certainly wasn't a Fury in any way—unless one counted a fierce determination to take back the tiara that had been purloined from her family. In that respect at least, she was just like Fleur Fitzgerald, except in Susannah's case, the cause was justified.

A black pagoda parasol shaded her from the slanting morning sunlight, and she wore a veiled black straw hat and an unbuttoned spencer that revealed the intricate black beading on the

bodice of her gown. Everything was the work of a tailor in Calcutta and had been copied from the latest fashion journals as
they arrived from England; of course, after a voyage that sometimes took more than six months, the illustrations were already
out of date. In London, what was à la mode one week could be
considered hopelessly unstylish the next. Still, in Bengal she was
definitely bang up to the mark!

Anjuli was weeping now that the moment of parting had come.
The ayah, a dark-eyed, dark-haired woman who was always
graceful in a white sari, wore bangles that clinked as she waved
farewell to everything she had ever known. Her future, like Susannah's, lay in England.

Susannah gazed at the grand brick-and-stucco house that had
been her home. It had a portico supported on fine Doric pillars
and was surrounded by an elegant verandah, where all her lovingly tended plants still flourished. Peacocks strutted on the close-
cut lawns that stretched down to the riverbank, and fountains
splashed in the little English garden that had been her pride and
joy. Behind the house there was jungle, shrill with noise, and
beyond that, almost lost in the luminous haze of early morning,
there were distant purple hills.

On arriving in this fabulous land, she had never expected to
leave so soon—and certainly not as a rich widow. She had always been largely ignored by her husband, an employee of the
East India Company, who had squandered most of his income
on polo ponies and painted mounts of an entirely different nature. Then had come the stroke of luck that had made him a
truly rich man. One day, on his way back from a Calcutta bawdy
house, he had rescued the favorite son of the Nawab of Bengal
from drowning. The nawab's gratitude had been expressed in a
gift of magnificent diamonds, some of which Richard had used
to purchase this fine estate at Chinsura.

After that, his fortune seemed to increase of its own volition,
leaving him to indulge himself so much that his wife seldom
crossed his mind. Some of his friends had not forgotten her,
however, and had made it clear that she need not spend her
nights alone, but she had remained a faithful wife. Richard lived
extravagantly in Calcutta, while she remained quietly at Chinsura, running the house and tending her garden. Thus it had
seemed set to continue, until three months ago, while playing
polo at one of the nawab's palaces, a pretty face and golden sari

in the crowd distracted him. His pony swerved, and that was the end of Richard Leighton.

Susannah trailed a hand in the river, where blossom offerings floated. She was her own mistress now, no longer beholden to a philandering husband whom she had never loved and who had never loved her. Not even obliged to return to her brother's care, for a widow was able to do as she pleased. Not that she could have returned to Stephen, anyway, for after the debacle of the tiara, he had had to sell up in Lincolnshire and had gone to America to seek his fortune. She wasn't even sure where he was in America, because letter writing was hardly his forte.

Chatterji the monkey trembled in her arms, and she cuddled him closer. She adored him and could no more have left him behind than she could have flown across the Hooghly. He was exceedingly vain, mischievous, and light-fingered—or should that be light-pawed?—and his funny little ways made her laugh. Fear of water may have silenced him for the time being, but it was because of his constant chattering that she had called him Chatterji, a Bengali name that to her English ears seemed singularly appropriate.

A choked sob from Anjuli made her turn. The ayah was watching Chinsura pass out of sight around the curve of the river, and the finality of it all had become a little too much. Susannah put a comforting hand on the woman's bangled wrist. "It will be all right, Anjuli. You'll be safe with me, and I know you'll be happy in England."

"But, memsahib, everyone tells me how cold it is there. They say the land freezes for months on end, and the people have to grow fur to keep warm," replied the ayah in the lilting Bengali accent that sounded oddly like Welsh.

Susannah had to laugh. "Fur? No, Anjuli, they may *wear* fur, but they do not grow it. You should not listen to such tales."

"Tails? Yes, that is another thing, memsahib. The punkah coolie swears that some Englishmen have tails as long as that rascally Chatterji's."

"The punkah coolie is wrong, Anjuli. Besides, you know that Leighton sahib did not have a tail, nor do I, or any of the English people you have seen, come to that. It's all nonsense."

"Yes, memsahib, if you say it is so, then it is so." The ayah remained unconvinced. "Then there is your food."

"Food?"

"It is so *bland,* memsahib! How will I manage if there is no curry?"

Susannah smiled. "You may curry whatever you wish, Anjuli. I'm sure you have brought sufficient spices with you to supply every kitchen in the realm!"

"Spices are essential, memsahib."

Susannah looked kindly at her. "Anjuli, if you are truly afraid to come with me, I will understand. I will release you at Calcutta, and you will be able to return to everyone at Chinsura. Is that what you wish?"

Anjuli was horrified. "Leave you, memsahib? Oh, no, that is not what I wish at all. My place is at your side, and never will I desert it. It is my duty to protect you and see that no dishonorable sahib comes near."

"You will find it hard work, I fear, for England is full of dishonorable sahibs," Susannah replied, thinking of the Duke of Exton, Sir Gareth Carew, and even Stephen, whose reluctantly confessed affair with Fleur Fitzgerald could hardly be applauded. "Anyway, dry your tears now, Anjuli. I am proud to have you with me, and I will do all I can to see you are happy. And Chatterji, too, of course," she added, as the monkey suddenly jumped from her arms to the ayah's lap, where he rattled her bangles, which always fascinated him, as did all bright things.

Anjuli smiled. "It will be good, this new life," she declared with sudden resolve and gave the delighted monkey an ivory bangle inlaid with tiny pieces of colored glass. He immediately began to gibber delightedly and temporarily forgot his fear of water as he leapt all over the barge, waving his trophy aloft.

At last he put the bangle on his head like a crown, then settled comfortably on a cushion to sleep. Susannah gave him a wry smile. "So, sir, you have your crown, and soon I will have my tiara again." Oh, yes, she hadn't forgotten the tiara, or the warning she had so haughtily instructed Sir Gareth to deliver to the duke. Events of that New Year's Eve had probably faded entirely from the minds of those two gentlemen, but she remembered everything, including the part played by Fleur Fitzgerald.

The sun was high in the sky when the barge reached the crowded quays of Calcutta. The busy port, which was also the capital of India, stood at the highest navigable point of the Hooghly, and had grown up around Fort William, the headquarters of the

East India Company in Bengal. There was a forest of masts on the wide water and a great deal of noise, which frightened Chatterji so much that he clung to Susannah as the barge at last nudged alongside the merchant vessel *Rajah*, which was soon to weigh anchor for England.

The above-deck cabin allotted to Susannah was on the starboard side, which would be in the shade for most of the voyage. On the outward voyage, when she and Richard had been much more lowly, all they had warranted was a stuffy cabin below the deck. How different now, she thought, as she flung off her black-veiled hat, unpinned her hair, and shook her long chestnut curls free. While Anjuli began to unpack the luggage they would require for the coming voyage, Chatterji leapt from place to place, inspecting everything. He soon found the gimbal-mounted candles, which provided endless fun as he swung on them.

As the *Rajah* set sail, Susannah stood on deck to watch until Calcutta passed out of sight, and the navigation of the lush green delta that lay between the port and the ocean got under way. She was asleep in her cabin when they reached the open sea. Oven-hot offshore winds began to blow, carrying the fading scent of spices as India was left behind.

Nearly six months later, in May 1808, the *Rajah* made landfall off the south coast of England. Tropical skies had given way to racing northern clouds, and because the English spring had been very late that year, the heavy rain felt icy to Susannah and Anjuli. Heaving whitecapped waves thundered ashore, and the distant spires of Portsmouth were barely visible through the spray. Anjuli was filled with dismay. All she had heard was true. England was a terrible place, and in such cold, the people surely *must* grow fur!

Chatterji was also appalled by the cold. He wrapped himself in Susannah's warmest scarf and sulked as he huddled close to the stove that had been brought in to warm the cabin. He missed India and felt neglected as Susannah sat on the window seat beneath the cabin window sewing something small and red. She was no longer in mourning but wore a warm rose woolen gown she had had made before leaving Chinsura. Knowing that she would find England much cooler than Bengal, she had ordered a complete wardrobe in suitable materials, and now she was very glad indeed of her foresight. She had also ordered several warmer saris for Anjuli, who at the time had declared that silk was all she would ever wear. Her determination to adhere to this had soon waned once the *Rajah* reached the turbulent waters of the Bay of Biscay

Susannah finished what she was doing. It was a little coat for Chatterji, who was clearly also in need of warm clothes. She clicked her tongue to call the monkey, who shuffled crossly toward her, the scarf still clasped tightly around him. "Here you are, my friend," she said, gently relieving him of the scarf. He protested, but she managed to slip the tiny new garment on him. "What do you think?" she asked, showing him his reflection in her hand mirror.

Chatterji gazed at himself delightedly, and swaggered to and fro, the better to view his new finery. Then he stopped with a frown. Something was missing. He turned toward her, tapping the top of his head and chattering loudly. She understood, and laughed. "You want a hat? Very well, I'll make you one. No, better than that, I'll make you a little turban. I believe I've got a little piece of cloth of gold that will be ideal. I'll just go and see."

She left the window seat and went to a valise she had hidden away very carefully behind all the other luggage in a corner of the cabin. She immediately found the cloth of gold, but as she took it out, she remembered something else. The valise had a false bottom, beneath which lay a very important package about one foot square and three inches deep. She took it out and opened it. Inside lay a paste replica of the Holland tiara, perfect to the very last ruby. It had been made by a Calcutta jeweler who'd followed a drawing she had executed from memory, and the result was very accurate indeed. To the casual glance, maybe even a relatively close inspection, it *was* the Holland tiara. And if she had anything to do with it, one day soon—without anyone being the wiser—it would be exchanged for the real thing. Only the Hollands had any true claim to the tiara; cheating dukes certainly did not, nor did scheming actresses who chose to perpetuate past lies. The thought of the duke's eventual discovery of the substitution was Susannah's prime reason for going to such lengths. She imagined the moment when he realized he had been deceived. The cheat would be cheated. It was far better than simply robbing him. Oh, to be there when it happened! But since that could not be, simply *knowing* it would happen was reward enough.

Smiling, she put the package back in its hiding place. She knew from London newspapers that up to at least a year ago, the original tiara had still been in the possession of the Duke of Exton, whose duchess, the former Lady Jane Bancroft, had worn it to an important St. James's Palace reception for an emissary from Constantinople. The duchess attended the reception on her own, and the tiara attracted attention because it was the first time she had ever been known to wear it. As a salacious aside, one newspaper also reported that within days of this, the duke had been given his congé by Fleur Fitzgerald, "with whom he had enjoyed an intimate friendship lasting since January 1804."

It was good to know that the predatory belle of Drury Lane had been denied the tiara. Reading between the lines, Susannah guessed it was only when the duchess wore it that Fleur finally realized *she* was never going to be the proud owner. His Grace of Exton had promptly been sent packing. As for Sir Gareth Carew, no scandal appeared to attach to his name, which Susannah had only read once, when he was reported as "having recently returned from abroad."

She pushed the valise back into its corner, then got up to wave the cloth of gold at Chatterji. "Here you are, sir, this will make a very fine turban indeed!" The monkey leapt into her arms, and she resumed her place at the window. The English shore was almost lost in flying spume, but she could just make it out. Soon, very soon now, she would set about retrieving her family's stolen property.

Anjuli came in a moment later. The ayah knew nothing of her mistress's secret plans because Susannah had never confided in her. Anjuli did not even know that her maiden name was Holland. It wasn't that Susannah did not trust the ayah, just that she rather superstitiously believed that if one confided a secret plan, that plan would fail.

Chapter 5

On arriving in London, Susannah took rooms at Grillion's Hotel in Albemarle Street. Her sumptuous balconied accommodation overlooking the fashionable street was a far cry from the leafy elegance of Chinsura, and an even farther cry from the small rented house she and Stephen had so briefly occupied in Kensington.

Although homesick for the warmth, color, and hurly-burly of India, Anjuli soon set about shielding her memsahib from unworthy fellows. Any impudent fortune hunter—and there were a lamentable number of them—whose eyes lit up on the arrival of a wealthy young widow was immediately confronted by a veritable Bengal tiger. Nary a one dared to find out if the tiger would pounce.

Had the hotel been aware of Chatterji, he would have been ejected immediately, for the ban imposed in 1803, only months after the establishment first opened, was still very much in place. The spat between Lord Faringdon's chimpanzee and Bull Barker's bulldog had not been forgotten, and a notice refusing admittance to apes of any description was very prominently displayed at the hotel entrance. The ban wasn't one that Susannah had any intention of observing, so she smuggled Chatterji in and out in the white fur muff she had used when walking on deck during the cold latter part of the voyage.

Chatterji may have been forbidden the main part of the hotel, but he was given the run of the suite of rooms, and both Susannah and Anjuli were very careful indeed to keep the door firmly closed at all times. Only once did he manage to get out, and they never discovered how he accomplished it. The first they knew of it was when they were returning from a walk and saw him in his rajah finery on the ornamental pelmet above the dining room door. They could only watch in dismay as he lowered himself by his tail to snatch the wig of an elderly bishop. While the outraged man of the cloth caused a most ungodly uproar, the cheeky monkey slipped away to stuff the wig into a coal scuttle, then disappeared back to Susannah's rooms.

Susannah and the ayah searched in vain for the way the monkey had escaped. "It's almost as if he just opened the door," Susannah said with a laugh, and they thought no more of it. Chatterji was given a severe talking-to about the wig but remained unrepentant. While Susannah's finger wagged sternly at him, he sat boldly on her bed sorting through her jewelry box, holding up the shiniest gems so they flashed pleasingly in the shaft of cool spring sunlight slanting through the window. Every now and then he stood up on his hind legs in order to glimpse himself in the dressing table mirror across the room. "Vain" was not the word to describe the look on his face as he preened and posed in his new clothes. Realizing that her efforts were like seeds falling on stony ground, Susannah abandoned the telling-off, but she wondered if in future a threat to the monkey's coat and turban might prove a useful curb.

For that first week in London, Susannah had many things to do, such as discussing her estate with a solicitor, opening a suitable account at Coutts's Bank, and commencing a halfhearted search for a town house, it not being her intention to stay long at Grillion's. She made it her business to discover which firm of solicitors acted for the Duke of Exton, and soon determined that it was Messrs Godber, Stanridge, and Cowper, of Collingridge Street, Mayfair. Mr. Godber himself dealt with the duke's affairs, but Susannah had to be content with the junior partner, Mr. Cowper. From him, however, she learned something that made her secret plan to exchange the tiara much more urgent. The duke was negotiating to sell her heirloom to the Ottoman emissary, Abbas Ali, who had recently returned to conduct further negotiations with the Foreign Office. The tiara was desired for a favorite concubine and within a month might be whisked away to a harem in Constantinople, never again to be seen by outside eyes. Susannah was horrified. She had only a few weeks in which to act, and she didn't really know where to begin!

The first thing to do, she decided, was find out all she could about all her adversaries' present circumstances and whereabouts. She soon learned that everyone was in town. The Duke and Duchess of Exton were at their grand mansion on the south side of Berkeley Square, and Sir Gareth Carew had recently returned from yet another sojourn abroad and was at his residence in Hanover Square. Fleur Fitzgerald, no longer quite as leading as before, was appearing in a pantomime at the New Theatre, Sadler's Wells. Pantomimes were usually beneath the dignity of the beau monde, but since the opening of the season on Easter Monday, Sadler's Wells had become astonishingly popular with the upper echelons of society. This was attributable not to Fleur but to the amazing clown, mime, actor, and acrobat Grimaldi, who was appearing alongside her. Because of him, it was all the vogue to drive out to the semirural venue on the edge of Islington village to the north of London—and because of him, Fleur Fitzgerald's waning career had waxed again.

The actress's private affairs remained of intense interest to the *on dits* columns of certain newspapers. She had taken various lovers since dismissing the duke from her bed, but the latest gossip had it that she was now the mistress of Lord Faringdon, who had been obliged to sell his beloved chimpanzee, Bonaparte, before he was allowed to enter her bed. Clearly his lordship could not have *two* chimpanzees in his life, thought Susannah.

But private mirth at Fleur's expense could not be permitted to cloud the issue, because the exchanging of the tiaras was now a pressing matter. Then, only two days after learning from Mr. Cowper about Abbas Ali's imminent acquisition of her family heirloom, luck chose to smile upon Susannah. It was the first truly warm morning since she had been in London, and she couldn't resist the urge to go for a walk in Green Park, which lay not far from Albemarle Street. She always found walks conducive to clear thought, and she hoped this one might prove inspirational.

London in May was always beautiful, with fresh young leaves, lovely blossoms, and myriad flowers everywhere, and she felt in almost buoyant spirits as she left the hotel with Chatterji concealed in the white fur muff. She wore a royal-blue pelisse and matching gown that suited her well, and the spring sunlight glinted on the thick chestnut ringlet that tumbled over her left shoulder. Her beige straw hat was tied beneath her chin with the widest blue-satin ribbon Chinsura could provide, and apart from the muff she carried a reticule. She didn't feel quite as modish as she would have wished, but her Indian tailor had not let her down very much. When she had succeeded in her quest, she would treat herself to a fine new London wardrobe.

The weather had brought many people to the park, not all of them desirable. Some quarrelsome street urchins, who had no business being in the park at all, were sailing roughly carved toy boats on the small reservoir owned by the Chelsea Water Works and were making so much noise that more genteel folk kept well away from them. Chatterji chuntered as he peered at the boys over the edge of the upturned muff. He thought they were quite mad for actually *choosing* to play with water and was telling them so in no uncertain monkey terms. Susannah knew what he was saying and smiled. "You're wasting your time, Chatterji. They can't hear you above all the racket they're making."

She had been strolling in the park for some time when she noticed a theater poster fixed to a lamppost. Resplendent in Oriental lettering, it extolled the delights of the pantomime *Jan Ben Jan, or Harlequin and the Forty Virgins* at the New Theatre, Sadler's Wells. The ticket agent was at Old Slaughter's Coffee House in St. Martin's Lane in the city, and almost before she knew it was in her mind, Susannah had hurried from the park to hire a hackney coach from the nearest rank. At the coffee house she was told that although some weekday seats were still available, it would be most inadvisable for a lady alone to purchase one, because that was when the lower elements attended. She should consider only a Saturday seat in a private box, but unfortunately they had all been taken. However, the owners of boxes often sold seats they did not require to a certain bookshop in Bond Street, and if she were to go there . . .

By now quite determined to see Fleur Fitzgerald onstage, Susannah returned to Grillion's to take a light luncheon, then walked the short distance to Bond Street, which ran parallel with Albemarle Street. There was a jeweler's shop on the corner, and as she passed the doorway, a young woman—a lady's maid, by the look of her simple gray dress and blue linen cloak—came hurrying out with a package under her arm. She and Susannah collided, and the package fell to the pavement.

Susannah bent quickly to retrieve it, fearing that whatever it contained might have broken. To her relief there were no suspicious tinkling sounds, so she handed it back to the maid. "There, all is well, I think," she said with a smile. "Thank goodness it isn't fine porcelain."

The maid, a pale-faced city creature with brown hair and eyes set deep beneath prominent eyebrows, did not reply but bobbed a nervous curtsy and hurried on ahead. Susannah thought no more about the incident as she continued to search for the bookshop. At that very moment, if she had but known it, Gareth was strolling pensively toward her. She was intent upon the shops, and he upon the traffic in the street, so neither of them knew as they passed within inches of each other.

Chapter 6

Gareth, on his way to an appointment with his tailor, had taken a very circuitous route from Hanover Square in a vain effort to fend off the ennui that always seemed to beset him these days. He wore a superbly cut charcoal coat, close-fitting cream breeches, and a mustard brocade waistcoat, with a topaz pin in his neckcloth. He swung a cane rather irritably in his gloved hand. He was *bored!* His last excursion to St. Petersburg had been exciting and dangerous, with more narrow escapes, chicanery in high places, last-minute problems, and tangles with beautiful women than he cared to recall. He and the inestimable Hector Ambleforth had had many a tight scrape. Now he had nothing to do again, except visit his damned tailor!

The cane paused. No, that wasn't strictly true, for that morning something certainly had aroused his interest: the delivery of a disturbingly conciliatory overture from the Duke of Exton. To any man of wisdom, an approach from Delavel Harmon could only be a matter of grave concern; therefore the advent of a social invitation was very unsettling indeed. What was his motive? The possibilities were legion, none of them comforting. Why would Exton invite him anywhere? They had barely spoken *before* New Year's Eve, 1803, and certainly hadn't since!

Gareth paused to look in a printshop window where, as coincidence would have it, there was a savage caricature of the duke and Abbas Ali, both armed with immense scimitars, fighting over the Holland tiara. Gareth's mind went back to the night the duke had acquired the tiara, and to the other persons affected by what had gone on at the Union Club. Had Stephen Holland managed to rebuild his fortunes in America? he wondered. And had the outspoken Miss Holland married and gone to Begnal, or wherever it was? He prayed it was somewhere suitably disagreeable, for he would *never* forgive her intolerable insults. As for the equally deplorable Fleur Fitzgerald, well, the less said, the better. The actress was a schemer par excellence, but she had seemingly met her match in Exton! Stephen Holland, Miss Holland, and Fleur Fitzgerald—all three wanted the tiara. Now it would vanish into a Turkish seraglio. And good riddance.

The only person connected with the tiara for whom Gareth felt the least sympathy was the unfortunate Duchess of Exton, who had worn it only once, from all accounts. She was far too good for her husband, upon whose detestable head—with any luck!—she would soon put the horns he dreaded so much. Plain Jane's warmth and charm more than made up for her lack of looks, so much so that she had begun to figure in the betting books, and the wagers were no longer concerned with *if* she would take a lover, but when and who. So far, she had remained true to her vows, but everyone was sure that sooner or later she was going to make a cuckold of the much reviled Delavel Harmon. At least, that was what the beau monde hoped, with the singular exception of Bull Barker, who had a very tidy sum indeed riding upon her continuing marital fidelity. Gareth smiled, for this was one wager Bull was almost certain to lose.

Gareth's thoughts slid back to the duke. It would be good to know why that invitation had been made, and the one sure way to find out was to accept. Why not? It would certainly banish boredom! With a final smile at the caricature in the printshop window, he turned and strode across the street to his tailor's premises.

Meanwhile, with Chatterji still surveying the world from the perspective of the muff, Susannah at last found the bookshop and entered, with barely a glance at the shining town carriage waiting outside. The bell tinkled pleasantly in the gloom, where tightly packed bookshelves reached from floor to ceiling. In one corner there was a writing desk at which a very elegantly dressed but otherwise unremarkable young woman was engaged in writing a hasty letter, a lighted candle before her in readiness for sealing wax. A clock ticked somewhere, although Susannah could not see it, and at first she and the lady, who on second glance was clearly in a lather of nerves about something, appeared to be the only persons present. Then a plump young man in a fawn coat and bright-blue neckcloth straightened suddenly from behind the polished oak counter.

"Maybe I be of assistance, madam?"

Susannah smiled with relief. "Yes, I hope so. I seek a box seat for the pantomime at Sadler's Wells this Saturday."

"I'm afraid we have nothing, madam; indeed, there are no Saturday places available for the foreseeable future. Mr. Grimaldi is so very acclaimed that everyone wishes to see him," he replied apologetically.

"So it seems. Oh, dear, I was so hoping . . ." She didn't finish, for in truth her reason for wishing to go wasn't all that pressing. What did it matter whether or not she saw Fleur Fitzgerald perform?

A light voice suddenly spoke from the writing desk. "I believe I may be able to help." The lady quickly rose, in her hand the letter that she had just sealed. She wore an embroidered gray spencer over a buttercup silk gown, and her yellowish hair was tucked up beneath a straw bonnet. Her nervousness seemed to be under very tight control now; indeed, there was barely any sign of it as she approached the counter, upon which she laid her gloves, reticule, and the letter. She was about Susannah's age, with a rather flat face, pale-lashed hazel eyes, a wide nose, and a sallow complexion that was far from flawless, but when she smiled, she exuded charm.

"My husband and I are attending Sadler's Wells this Saturday," she said, "and we have a whole box to ourselves. Well, perhaps not entirely to ourselves—I believe he expects a gentleman to join us. Anyway, I gladly extend an invitation to you as well. It's the very best stage box in the house, with a prime view of the proceedings. Please accept." She pressed Susannah in a tone that was meant to be causal, but was actually filled with ill-concealed urgency.

Taken by surprise, Susannah didn't know what to say, and the lady hoped her startled silence denoted acceptance. "Is that settled, then?" she ventured, then suddenly noticed Chatterji. "Oh, a monkey! she gasped delightedly and stretched out a tentative hand to touch him. Chatterji didn't shrink away, for she wore rings that glittered most appealingly in what little sunlight came in through the shop's small-paned bow windows. The lady was quite ecstatic. "I absolutely *love* monkeys, they make me laugh so. *Do* tell me his name."

"He's called Chatterji," Susannah replied, and on hearing his name, the vain little creature put on his cloth-of-gold turban, straightened his red coat, and ventured importantly out of the muff.

The lady was transported, and her suppressed worry temporarily ceased to matter. "How delightful! A veritable little maharajah! You are most fortunate to have such a wonderful pet. How did you come by him?"

Susannah explained briefly about her life in India.

The lady was very interested. "And you've only just returned?"

"Yes, a week or so ago."

"So you have no friends here? No acquaintances?"

"None, I'm afraid." It was the truth, for Susannah's friends were all in Lincolnshire, and she had lost touch with them since going to Bengal.

"Surely you have family?"

"Only a brother who lives abroad now. There isn't anyone else."

"You are clearly in need of company, so I *insist* that you accompany us to the pantomime on Saturday," the lady declared firmly.

Susannah would have had to be rude to decline; besides, she did still rather want to see Fleur Fitzgerald. So she accepted. "You're very kind. Thank you very much indeed."

The lady linked her arm in a rather charming gesture of friendship. "I have bullied you into it, have I not? So I must redeem myself. Come, there is a tearoom just along the street, where they serve the most excellent cream pastries imaginable and where we can talk a while. Does Chatterji like cream pastries?"

Susannah had to smile. "I'm afraid he does, rather too much," she replied.

"I *must* see him eat one." The lady turned to gather her belongings from the counter, and the young man picked up the letter.

"Do you wish this to be delivered, my lady?"

"Er, no, I-I don't think I'll send it after all. Please destroy it."

The young man immediately began to rip the letter into pieces, but not before Susannah glimpsed the name upon it; Sir Gareth Carew. Shaken, she watched as he bore the fragments away.

The lady ushered her outside, then paused to speak to the coachman in charge of the carriage at the curb. Susannah glanced at the fine crested monogram on the carriage door, an ornate *H* surmounted by a griffin's head. She already knew the lady was titled, but exactly *who* she was remained a mystery. As did her relationship to Sir Gareth Carew. Susannah now felt on her guard with her new acquaintance.

But the lady's identity was soon revealed, for on reaching the door of the tearoom, she paused with a rather self-conscious smile. "How silly of me, we don't even know each other's names."

"I am Mrs. Richard Leighton," Susannah said, waiting with bated breath.

"And I am the Duchess of Exton," the lady supplied, smiling warmly as she opened the tearoom door.

Chatterji's antics with the cream bun sent the entire tearoom into raptures, and being a rather conceited monkey, he wasn't averse to putting on a show. His pastry wasn't so much eaten as messily dissected, and by the time he eventually finished it, his fur and little red coat were a disgrace. It was, declared the duchess, like watching the great Grimaldi himself, who had commenced his career with a performance as just such a naughty monkey. Her anxiety was a thing of the past as she laughed at Chatterji; indeed, she laughed so much it was hard to remember how worried and almost distressed she had been when Susannah had first seen her in the bookshop.

As Chatterji entertained everyone in the tearoom, Susannah endeavored to assess her new friend. The former Lady Jane Bancroft spoke of the duke only when she was obliged to, so clearly the marriage was not one forged in paradise. Was that why she had been writing such a hasty letter to Sir Gareth Carew? Was the Welshman her lover? It would certainly explain the letter.

Soon it was time to leave the tearoom because Jane had an appointment at an art gallery. One of the waitresses did her best to clean the cream-daubed Chatterji and, in order to spare the white fur muff from being spoiled beyond redemption, provided a large napkin in which to wrap him. When he had been inserted in his hidey-hole once more, Susannah and Jane emerged into the Bond Street sunshine, and after making arrangements for Saturday, the two new friends went their separate ways.

As Susannah walked slowly back to the hotel, she could hardly believe that fate had played so very neatly into her hands.

Chapter 7

On Saturday, at half past four in the afternoon, the Duke and Duchess of Exton's carriage drew up outside Grillion's. The curtain at Sadler's Wells did not rise until six, but the journey out to Islington would take well over an hour, for the London streets were still crowded. There was an unexpected chill in the air, as if winter were making a final bid to postpone summer, and Susannah descended to the hotel lobby wearing an indigo velvet cloak over her best sky-blue taffeta evening gown. The gown possessed a train that was longer than the latest mode, but she hoped it would not seem too out of date. She was more confident about her hair, for pretty Grecian knots were still very much the thing, and there could be no quarrel with the fine strings of river pearls that Anjuli had skillfully looped through it.

One of the hotel footmen escorted her out to the waiting carriage. The duke wore the formal black attire that was essential for all theaters, but his partiality for bright colors was evident even now in the garish vermilion lining of his coat. This lining would not have been visible had it not been for the flourish with which he had flicked his coattails upon sitting down. He did not alight to assist Susannah into the vehicle, nor was there any courtesy in the way he deigned to move his legs to one side so that she could take her seat. This, and the fact of his snoutish nose, put her unavoidably in mind of an ill-tempered hog—and by the end of the evening she would not have had reason to change her opinion.

Jane was visibly on edge again, just as she had been those first minutes in the bookshop, but as the carriage pulled away she strove to sound relaxed. "Delavel, this is Mrs. Leighton, of whom I've spoken with such pleasure. Mrs. Leighton—Susannah—this is my husband, the Duke of Exton.

The Holland tiara shone invisibly before Susannah as she met his gaze without flinching. "Your Grace," she murmured politely, but although she inclined her head with all due deference, what she really wanted to do was kick him ferociously on both shins. It would be easy to do, for he was directly opposite her and the carriage was confined. Oh, to be wearing a pair of hobnailed boots, she thought behind her innocuous smile.

He grunted at her. "Madam," he said shortly and looked rudely out the window as the carriage drew away north out of Albemarle Street, then turned east into the throng of vehicles choking Oxford Street.

Jane wore shell-pink silk, which did little for her, and a bright-red boa, which did even less, as it drained her already sallow face. Orderly yellow curls edged her face, and a ruby necklace graced her throat, but on her head, instead of the tiara Susannah had secretly hoped for, there was a gold satin opera hat that sported tiny bells at its four corners. Her arms were sheathed in white gloves, there was a fan over her wrist, and she carried a sequined reticule containing her opera glasses and the various other essential items a lady could not be without for an evening at the theater.

She gave Susannah a smile that was too bright. "You said in the tearoom that you feared your wardrobe wasn't quite à la mode, but you really do not need to worry. You look quite splendid."

"Thank you," Susannah replied gratefully.

Jane smiled again. "But you are very mean not to bring Chatterji."

Susannah smiled. "He would be quite a disruptive influence, I fear, so I've left him with Anjuli."

"Anjuli?"

"My ayah, er, my maid."

"Oh, well, I do trust I will be permitted to see him again soon," Jane replied, and then gave a rather awkward laugh. "How I'd *adore* to see him with Minette. Wouldn't you like to see that, Delavel?"

"See what?" The duke hadn't been paying any attention.

"I was saying that I'd love to see what Chatterji and Minette make of each other." Jane smiled at Susannah again and explained, "Minette is my white poodle, and she is as naughty as

Chatterji." A thought suddenly struck her. "Susannah, what are your plans for the next few weeks?"

"Plans? Well, I have none in particular, except to find a suitable house." *And retrieve Holland property misappropriated by your curmudgeonly husband.*

"Do you like the country?"

"The country? Why, yes, of course."

"Good." Jane looked tentatively at her husband. "Delavel, may I invite Susannah to come with us to Exton Park? And her ayah, too?" Exton Park was the duke's great Gloucestershire estate near Cirencester in the beautiful Cotswold Hills.

The duke seemed caught off guard, but after a moment he nodded. "By all means, if that is what you wish, but it cannot be for very long."

Jane was surprised. "But I was hoping to stay there for the rest of the summer."

"That won't be possible. I'm only going back to attend to a few estate matters and to personally collect the tiara." He gave a hard little smile. "With the price the Turk is paying, it wouldn't do for anything to happen to it."

"No, of course not," Jane agreed. "But—but what has that to do with me?"

Something in her tone made Susannah look swiftly at her, but already the duke was continuing. "When I return to town for the actual transaction, I wish you to be with me, Jane."

"With you? Oh, but—"

"You are not to remain in the country if I am in town, not even if you have a thousand Mrs. Leightons with you."

Their eyes met, and Jane lowered hers. "I will be delighted to return to London with you, Delavel," she murmured.

"I'm pleased to hear you say it, my dear. And in the meantime, of course, Mrs. Leighton will be more than welcome to stay with us. Or perhaps she has no desire to sample the rural delights of the West Country?" Had he announced that her presence was not required, he could not have been more obvious.

Jane looked earnestly at Susannah. "Do say you will come, for I would adore to have your company. Exton Park is so huge and Delavel always so busy that I sometimes feel I rattle there like the only pea in a colander."

"Of course I will come," Susannah replied, ignoring the duke's ill-concealed displeasure.

Jane clapped her hands delightedly. "Excellent! We leave the day after tomorrow."

The New Theatre, Sadler's Wells, stood on a high ridge north of London, near the village of Islington. Built among avenues of tall poplar trees, with the New River of the Chelsea Water Works flowing alongside, it had been established since 1683, but until this season had never achieved the standing of either the Italian Opera House or the Theatre Royal. Grimaldi and the pantomime had changed all that, however, and the carriage soon joined a long queue of other fine vehicles. They all passed slowly through an elegant iron gate and drew up one after the other at the door.

Once inside the glittering, candlelit horseshoe-shaped auditorium, it was immediately clear that tonight all two thousand seats would be filled—well, almost all. Apart from all the usual private boxes, there were four that aspired to be called stage boxes. They were divided into upper and lower on either side of the curtain, and the Duke of Exton's was on a level with the stage. The noise was tremendous, the laughter and babble easily drowning the Mozartean efforts of the orchestra. A rather rowdy gathering of young gentlemen infested the pit, rattling their snuffboxes and tapping their canes.

Practically the only quiet place in the entire building was the Extons' box, which also happened to be far from fully occupied. At least eight people could have used it with ease, but there were only four of the elegant crimson velvet seats. Four? It was then that Susannah remembered Jane had mentioned a gentleman probably having been invited as well. Who was it? she wondered. Then she was distracted as Jane dropped her opera glasses a second time. The duchess's unease had intensified so much now that they were at the theater that she would undoubtedly have dropped them again had not her husband stirred himself to growl that it would be better if she held them more firmly. At this her fingers clenched so tightly over them that Susannah did not doubt her knuckles were as white as her gloves.

The duke's vermilion coat lining clashed most horridly with his crimson velvet chair, and his heavily ringed fingers drummed on the gilded arm like a quick-marching army. Once or twice he inspected his closed fob watch, as if he thought the curtain to be overdue for rising, but instead of opening it to see what time it was, he simply put the watch away again. He began to make Susannah feel nervous too, and if it hadn't been for her determination to pursue the tiara, she knew she would definitely have been seeking a suitable excuse to cry off the invitation to Exton Park.

There was still no sign of the other guest when the curtain rose at six o'clock precisely. A ballet opened the program, followed by *The Milkmaid's Adventure,* which Susannah knew from the poster in Green Park would bring both the great Grimaldi and Fleur Fitzgerald onstage for the first time. Grimaldi came first, of course. He was astonishingly accomplished, with an extraordinary ability to make people laugh or cry, and his every movement had the audience rapt, but at last Fleur stepped out as the eponymous milkmaid. Susannah immediately saw why men like Stephen, the duke, and now Lord Faringdon were so hopelessly beguiled, for even though the actress was no longer in the first flush of youth, her beauty still shone. She was feline and graceful, and her shapely figure and legs were shown off quite brazenly by her flounced costume. The milkmaid, who spent the entire time wandering in a forest inhabited by a wild man played by Grimaldi, was supposed to be a frightened virgin of tender years; as played by a woman like Fleur, she was a knowing doxy. Richard would have adored her, Susannah thought, but then he had a taste for trollops.

The duke's gaze did not waver from Fleur from the moment she appeared. Did he still desire his ex-mistress? Susannah wondered. If so, it was clearly not mutual, for the actress ignored him completely, seeming far more interested in someone in the wings, to whom she tossed flirtatious, almost kittenish glances. Susannah couldn't see who it was because the wings were quite crowded, mostly with players, dancers, and stagehands. Intrigued, she leaned across to beg the use of Jane's opera glasses, and the moment she trained them on the gathering at the side of the stage, she saw a tall, shadowy gentleman standing behind the others. Sure enough, when Fleur next glanced toward him, he inclined his head. Susannah, wondering who he was, willed him to step forward a little so that some of the light from the stage lamps would fall upon his face.

She was so intent upon the gentleman that she gave a start when applause suddenly broke out. *The Milkmaid's Adventure* was at an end! Fleur and Grimaldi were kept onstage for a considerable time because the audience was so enthusiastic, but at last the painted curtain began to descend, signifying the intermission. Susannah just managed to see Fleur hurrying toward the gentleman, and for a split second his face was revealed. It was a face that was imprinted upon Susannah's memory, for it belonged to Sir Gareth Carew!

Chapter 8

The lamps were turned up in the auditorium, and a shrill babble of conversation broke out as the audience set about refreshments and visiting acquaintances in other boxes. Susannah's mind was racing. Because of the letter in the bookshop, she had presumed that Sir Gareth was Jane's lover; now it seemed more likely that he was Fleur's! Just who was with whom?

As she leaned across to return the opera glasses to Jane, she saw that the latter's agitation now verged on panic. Jane's hands trembled, and her tongue passed nervously over her lips as she plucked constantly at her delicate fan. Beside her, the duke was an ominous presence, like the blackest of storms waiting to break. They were both anticipating something—he with calculated cruelty, she in a state of trepidation close to collapse.

There came a tap at the door of the box, and Jane started like a frightened rabbit. So did Susannah, but it was only a theater footman bringing a tray of iced champagne and sugared almonds. As he placed the tray on the small table at the rear of the box, Susannah realized there were four glasses. She glanced at the empty chair.

The duke rose to pour the champagne, and Susannah immediately leaned across to whisper to Jane, "What on earth is wrong? Can I help?"

Before Jane could answer, there was another knock at the door of the box. Jane's face had a hunted look. "Please, will you pretend you know the gentleman who is about to join us, Susannah?" she begged.

"But—"

Jane glanced desperately toward the door, which the duke was on the point of opening. "*Please,* Susannah," she breathed. "I would not ask if it were not important!"

"Who is the gentleman?" Susannah asked, although she was sure she already knew the answer.

"Sir Gareth Carew. Susannah, I want you to pretend to be a former love who is still very smitten with him."

Susannah stared at her. "I-I beg your pardon?"

"Will you do it for me?" Jane's eyes were anguished.

The duke ushered Gareth into the box. "Ah, Carew, I'm glad you accepted the olive branch."

"How could I not?" Gareth smiled. He was immaculately turned out in close-fitting black velvet, lace ruffles, and white silk breeches, and Susannah had to concede that he was one of the most attractive men she had ever seen. It grieved her to think this, but there was no denying the effect his style and blond good looks were having, even upon her. When she had seen him close up before, it had been a wild winter night, with wind, rain, and anger to distort judgment; tonight she saw him under very different circumstances. She still loathed him, of course, for he was Sir Lackey, who had done nothing at all to help Stephen. Her glance lingered on his lips, so fine and curved as he laughed at something the duke was saying, and she loathed him still more because she was drawn to him.

The duke ushered him forward, first to Jane. "Now, then, Carew, I believe you know my wife." Susannah was conscious of the subtle intonation in the harsh voice, the eagle intentness in the pale eyes.

Gareth smiled down at Jane. "We are acquainted," he said, drawing her hand to his lips.

His Welsh accent was soft and caressing and his quick green eyes those of a man who had broken many hearts, thought Susannah, privately telling herself that such things probably indicated a philandering nature.

Jane looked faint. "Th-thank you, Sir Gareth." Again her eyes fled to Susannah, whom she clearly prayed was to be her savior.

Susannah knew she had to come to the rescue. She might not know Jane very well, but here was a damsel in distress, and Susannah Leighton must become Saint George in skirts! Gareth turned to be introduced to her, and to her relief she saw not a flicker of recognition in his arresting eyes. He had no idea at all that they had met once before. She rose from her chair in a flurry of sky-blue taffeta and hurried to him. "Why, Gareth! Oh, how truly wonderful to see you again!" she cried and stretched up to place an exceedingly warm kiss on his cheek.

She felt his astonishment, but after a moment's hesitation, he went along with her. "And how delightful to see you again too, er, *cariad*."

His thoughts darted. Who in God's own name was she? He could only suspect that she was part of the duke's present design, whatever *that* might be!

Susannah laughed a little reproachfully. "Why, Gareth, did that slight hesitation signify forgetfulness? Surely you haven't forgotten my name is Susannah?" She knew the name was unlikely to jog unwelcome memories, for Stephen always referred to her as Susie, and apart from that, when in London last, she had been known only as Miss Holland.

"How could I forget?" he murmured, but the glimmer in his eyes said, *We both know you're a complete and utter mystery to me, sweet lady.*

She went on quickly, giving a ripple of flirtatious laughter. "Oh, Gareth, I have to confess that you were not only my first love, but that my heart may still belong to you." She laughed again and tapped his sleeve playfully with her fan.

The duke was as astonished as Gareth. "Well, Carew, I was about to introduce Mrs. Leighton, whose late husband was with the East India Company in Calcutta, but it seems that introductions are not necessary."

Gareth's sharp glance missed nothing, and he could have sworn the duke was as mystified as he himself was. Maybe the lady wasn't part of any design after all. If not, then what was she up to?

Susannah turned her dazzling smile upon the duke. "La, how amazing this is. I return to England after all this time and find myself face-to-face with my first sweetheart," she declared, using the sort of teasing tone so often heard in drawing rooms.

Silent gratitude reached out in waves from Jane, who was suddenly lighthearted. "Come, Delavel, or the champagne will be too warm," she chided, giving her husband a flutter of her eyelashes. "And do bring the sugared almonds, for you know how I like them."

"Er, yes, of course." He turned to finish pouring the champagne and gave everyone a glass, then he presented his wife with the dish of sugared almonds before looking inquiringly at

Susannah and Gareth. "Clearly you are both well acquainted. May I ask how you met?"

"We were children together," Gareth replied, with angelic sincerity.

"Indeed?" The duke looked curiously at Susannah. "I didn't realize you were Welsh, Mrs. Leighton."

"I-I . . ."

Gareth smiled. "Why yes, of course she is."

Susannah gave a weak smile, hoping he wouldn't go too far and thus pull the wool *from* the duke's sharp little eyes, instead of over them.

Gareth looked deep into her eyes. "We were totally inseparable, weren't we, *cariad fach*?"

He *was* going too far, Susannah thought in dismay. She didn't know a single word of Welsh—or indeed anything about any of this!

Jane sat forward suddenly. "Delavel, I have had the most splendid idea. Would it not be wonderful if Sir Gareth were to join us at Exton Park as well?"

Susannah's smile fixed for a split second, as did Gareth's, but the duke seemed pleased with the notion. "Why, yes, indeed, my dear. What d'you say, Carew? We leave for the country the day after tomorrow."

Gareth raised Susannah's hand gallantly to his lips. "What man in his right mind would turn down the opportunity to spend pleasant hours reminiscing with his first love?" Suddenly he relieved her of her champagne glass and drew her hand over his sleeve. "You'll never believe it, but old Meredith is here tonight. You remember him, surely? We almost set fire to his hay barn."

"I—Yes, of course I remember," she answered, looking daggers at him.

Gareth was undeterred. He glanced apologetically at Jane and the duke. "I trust you will not mind if I whisk Susannah away for a few minutes? I promise to bring her back in time for curtain up."

Before she knew it, Susannah had been ushered out to the narrow, poorly lit staircase behind the box. There Gareth caught her hand and hurried her upward, past the identical box on the level above and then into the lofty area known as the flies, from where the pulleys, scenery, curtain, and other tackle were operated. There were no stagehands there at the moment, because they too had hurried off to enjoy the intermission, so Garth was able to speak as he wished, without fear of being overheard.

He turned to Susannah, his smiling charm replaced by cool suspicion. "Now, then, perhaps you will tell me what all this is about?"

Chapter 9

Susannah looked at Gareth in some exasperation. "Perhaps *I* can tell *you*? Sir Gareth, I was rather hoping it was going to be the other way around."

"So you have no idea what Exton's up to?"

"I would have thought that was your province, sir."

"My prov—? What do you mean?"

"Well, Jane, I-I mean the duchess, invited me, but you are here at the duke's invitation, are you not?"

"Yes."

"Then I presume you and he are friends."

Gareth laughed. "Friends? I would as soon sup with the devil."

So the former cronies had fallen out, had they? Susannah thought.

Gareth went on. "Delavel Harmon and I are certainly not bosom companions. In fact, I would go so far as to say the opposite is more the case. But what of you, Mrs. Leighton?"

Color flashed into her cheeks. "What are you suggesting, sir?"

"I'm not suggesting anything, madam. I'm merely trying to ascertain what is going on. However, I confess you do arouse my curiosity. It isn't every day that a woman I do not know, a complete stranger in fact, kisses me and declares me to be her enduring love."

"No? The speed with which you went along with the thing made me wonder if it was a regular occurrence," she replied dryly.

His green eyes flickered in the mixed light shining up from the stage. "One should never spurn a kiss from a beautiful woman," he murmured.

She flushed again. "Please do not misinterpret my actions, sir, for I only acted on Jane's behalf. There is something between you and her, is there not?"

"No, madam, there certainly is not!"

"Then there has been until very recently," she insisted, thinking that his transferred affections must be behind Jane's distress. Yes, that must be it! He had been Jane's lover, but was now in the process of taking Fleur Fitzgerald away from Lord Faringdon! And the duke *knew* of his wife's infidelity!

"I mislike the knowing gleam in your eyes, Mrs. Leighton, for it conveys a complete misinterpretation of the situation. There has never been anything between the Duchess of Exton and me. We are acquaintances, that is all."

Susannah searched his face. He sounded completely sincere, but then a practiced Lothario would, wouldn't he?

"I see you remain unconvinced, sirrah! The first time I met Jane, she was in a bookshop writing a very hasty letter to you, and to say that she seemed anxious would be put it mildly. Presumably the duke has found out about your liaison, because tonight, the closer the time came for your arrival at the box, the more agitated and distressed she became. Then when you actually arrived, she implored me to fling myself upon you and pretend to be one of your previous lovers. She wanted to fool the duke, and so, Sir Gareth, did you. Which is also why you went along with things. Your compliance had nothing to do with never spurning kisses from beautiful women, and everything to do with allaying the suspicions of a betrayed husband."

He looked at her as if she had gone mad. "Well, if that was a spur-of-the-moment explanation, it was really good, except that your deducing is somewhat flawed. I repeat, I am not and never have been the Duchess of Exton's lover."

"Then why did she write a clandestine letter to you?"

"I have no idea. Unless—" He broke off.

"Yes?"

"Well, there is one incident that might account for all this." He glanced at her. "Provided you are telling the truth, of course."

"Why would I lie?"

"I couldn't even begin to guess," he replied cynically. "Anyway, as I was saying, there is one explanation I can think of, and given the common knowledge that the duke's great bugaboo is the thought of wearing cuckold's horns, I think it's probably the nub of all this. A week or so ago, as I was leaving Hyde Park after a ride, the duchess passed me in her open barouche. Her glove dropped to the ground, and I rode after her with it. She seemed most flustered, indeed I almost wondered if she would have preferred me not to have returned it. After a few polite words, she drove on to join the usual parade in Rotten Row. It was then I saw the duke watching from the window of the Turkish emissary's house in Park Lane."

"The Turkish emissary?" Susannah's interest quickened.

"Abbas Ali. Rumor has it he's purchasing a tiara from the Exton collection, and I presume the duke was there to drive the hardest bargain he could. Anyway, with hindsight, I think the incident with the glove was open to misinterpretation, especially by a man like Exton, who lives in anguish that one day he will wake up and find he is the victim of infidelity."

"Is that really his fear?"

"Yes, it's well known, although clearly not by you."

"No. Well, I suppose that would explain it." She glanced at him. "Isn't it the Holland tiara that Abbas Ali wishes to buy?"

The tangent took him by surprise. "Mm? Yes, I believe it is." Suddenly he looked more closely at her. "We've met before after all, haven't we? I'm sure I know your voice."

Had mentioning the tiara jogged his memory? She shook her head quickly. "I think I would remember if we were acquainted, Sir Gareth."

"Yes, I suppose so." He ran a hand through his blond hair. "Look, I've told you the truth about my dealings with the duchess, so either you believe me or you don't."

"Maybe I do," she conceded.

"Hallelujah."

She raised an eyebrow and continued. "But maybe I *don't* believe that Jane's feelings for you are as innocent as they should be."

"What?"

"Perhaps the duke is right to fear her unfaithfulness. I think you've aroused her heart, Sir Gareth, and she is distressed because you are more interested in Fleur Fitzgerald." Susannah warmed to her explanation. "Perhaps that's what is concerning the duke as well! He knows not only that his wife is in love with you but that the former mistress he wants back is in love with you too!"

Gareth stared at her as if she had gone quite mad. "By all the saints, madam, you are a mistress of invention."

Susannah raised her chin defiantly. "Surely you aren't going to tell me I'm wrong about you and Fleur?"

"That's *precisely* what I'm telling you. I admit that there was a time when she set her cap at me, but I certainly did not respond."

"Oh, liar! I saw her making cow eyes at you throughout the performance, and then rushing to you at curtain down."

"You saw her making cow eyes at Jerry Faringdon, and rushing to *him* at curtain down," Gareth corrected coldly.

Susannah drew back slightly. "Lord Faringdon?"

"The very fellow. He's so small that even in his top hat he can get lost in a crowd." Gareth held out a hand to indicate the height in question. "Damn it all, woman, he's my friend, and I was only backstage because I happened to accompany him here tonight! Fleur Fitzgerald is of concern to *him*, not to me." Very much of concern to him, Gareth thought, for Jerry had that very evening confessed a fear that Fleur wished to end their relationship.

Susannah felt a little awkward, for now she came to think of it, she *had* seen another top hat low in front of him. "Well, maybe I was wrong . . ."

"Yes, you were—again," he said dryly. "An apology would be rather nice."

Apologize? After his contribution to the loss of the tiara? She would rather fling herself down onto the stage! But she knew the situation called for a tactical withdrawal, and so she forced herself. "All right, I'm sorry. I accept that you aren't Jane's lover, nor are you Fleur Fitzgerald's, and that the only thing that might have brought you to the duke's unwelcome attention is that incident in Hyde Park. Will that do?"

"It lacked true grace, but I suppose it will suffice." He folded his arms and studied her. "Right, that's me dealt with, so what about you?"

"Me? I don't understand."

"Tell me about yourself, Mrs. Leighton, for I vow I am all interest."

"There's nothing to tell. I have been widowed for almost a year and have just returned from India. I met Jane in a Bond Street bookshop, she invited me here tonight, and the rest you know."

"It's that simple?"

"Yes." She met his gaze squarely. *No, it's much more convoluted than that, Sir Lackey. . . .*

"Very well, Mrs. Leighton, I accept that to be the truth. Which brings us to the matter of how we intend to go on at Exton Park."

"We have already begun to play our parts, Sir Gareth, so we can hardly change character now. The duke believes us to be former lovers, and—"

"And that is how we will continue," he interrupted quietly. "I *was* going to ask you if you wished to cry off, in which case we could dream up some tale to keep one or other of us here in London, but since you clearly intend to proceed, then that is the end of the matter."

"I'm not in the habit of crying off anything, Sir Gareth," she said, thinking again of the tiara.

"Good."

"Good?"

"I am in need of something to keep the demon of monotony at bay, and this would seem to be the perfect thing."

She eyed him suspiciously. "I don't know quite what you are thinking, Sir Gareth, but if you imagine I am going to indulge in anything more than light pretense, you are going to be disappointed."

He smiled. "You almost make that sound like a challenge, Mrs. Leighton."

"It isn't. You may be sure of that."

"What a pity." Susannah Leighton interested him greatly, for she certainly wasn't quite what she seemed. Every now and then he detected a curious expression in her lovely lavender eyes, and he still had the damnedest feeling that he knew her from somewhere. But where? It would be rewarding to piece it all together.

Susannah wanted to steer the conversation away from the awkward matter of their supposed shared past. "Look, before we leave for Exton Park, I think we should engineer a meeting with Jane. She is, after all, the instigator of all this."

"A meeting *would* be useful," he agreed. "I suggest you arrange to drive with her in Hyde Park tomorrow. I will 'encounter' you, say, at noon by the eastern end of the Serpentine?"

"Very well."

"Mind you, I am more and more convinced that it is simply a demonstration of Exton's obsessive fear of having an adulterous wife."

"If you are right, then it's all the more reason why we should help Jane."

"I cannot disagree with that."

The stagehands returned by a back ladder, signifying the imminent end of the intermission. Gareth spoke again as he and Susannah turned to return to the box. "Let me do the talking about old Meredith."

"Meredith?" She had forgotten.

"The fellow I supposedly dragged you off to meet."

"Oh, yes. By the way, I'll have to leave all talk of Wales to you as well, for I don't know anything about it."

"You don't know about Wales?" He pretended to be horrified. "Oh, *cariad fach*, we'll have to do something about that."

"What does *cariad fach* mean?"

He laughed. "It means 'little sweetheart.'"

"Oh."

"We're fond former lovers, remember?"

"I'm unlikely to forget," she replied, as he opened the stage box door for her.

Chapter 10

Susannah remembered very little of the second half of the performance, although there were certain incidents—none of them to do with the actual program—that were very sharply etched upon her memory. Gareth, on the other hand, was such a past master at subterfuge that he was able to concentrate on both the stage and what was going on around them. Idle flirtation came easily to him, and he was the personification of romantic involvement as he leaned toward Susannah, sometimes putting his hand to his mouth to whisper something, sometimes simply speaking directly. He played his part as faultlessly and naturally as one of the actors, and more than ever Susannah knew he was a man who broke hearts.

The pantomime was well worthy of its acclaim. Jane, now much more relaxed, nibbled upon sugared almonds and laughed delightedly at Grimaldi's brilliance. The duke eyed his wife occasionally, and Susannah would have dearly loved to know what was going through his mind. For the main part, however, his attention was strictly upon the stage; upon Fleur Fitzgerald, to be precise.

It wasn't long before the actress espied Gareth in the Exton box, apparently paying a great deal of attention to the russet-haired lady in blue. Susannah was aware of the precise moment, for the actress faltered over her lines. It would have been barely perceptible to the rest of the audience, but Susannah actually felt the wave of jealousy emanating from center stage. From then on, she was in receipt of many darting looks filled with all the dislike of a woman who had suddenly perceived a rival. It was abundantly clear that in spite of being Lord Faringdon's mistress, Fleur still had a very strong interest in Gareth. It was also abundantly clear that the vain and arrogant actress could not understand what Gareth saw in Susannah Leighton. What

did such a carrot-haired creature have that the matchless Fleur
Fitzgerald did not? the looks asked. Susannah enjoyed the
woman's jealousy. Serve the *chienne* right, she thought, and wondered what the actress would have said if she knew exactly who
the lady in blue really was. What would everyone in the box
say, come to that!

Whether Lord Faringdon detected Fleur's revealing reaction
was hard to say. Gareth had pointed him out in an opposite stage
box, and every time Susannah glanced across, he was gazing at
his mistress with an unblinking devotion that verged on the canine. The duke's gaze was equally unblinking, although whether
it was one of canine devotion, Susannah wouldn't have liked to
hazard. Delavel Harmon's expression was never constant, sometimes seeming desirous, sometimes contemptuous—always disturbing.

Gareth leaned toward her suddenly and whispered low, as he
had throughout. "I rather think our host still hankers after La
Belle Fleur."

"Who in turn still hankers after you," Susannah whispered
back.

"Mm?"

"Oh, come now, sir, don't tell me a master such as you has
failed to notice interest shown by a member of the opposite
sex?"

Gareth's gaze moved swiftly toward the stage, where sure
enough, he immediately encountered Fleur's flirtatious glance.

"See?" Susannah murmured.

Gareth didn't respond, for his attention had gone past the actress to his friend in the box opposite.

Susannah followed his gaze. "Lord Faringdon will have to accept the inevitable, I fear," she said.

Gareth turned to her. "Maybe, but that makes it all the worse.
He *knows* she's cooling, you see, but he doesn't know it may
be because of me! Damn it, *I* didn't know, either."

"Well, she could cheerfully tear out my heart, you may count
upon that," Susannah murmured.

"Yours?"

"Because you are paying attention to me."

"Perhaps, for his sake, I should pay even more."

"What do you mean?"

Suddenly he put his hand to her throat, then around to the

back of her neck, where he slid his fingers into her warm hair. He drew her lips toward his and kissed her tenderly. Oh, it was a kiss to melt even the most hardened heart, and Susannah's certainly was not that. Her senses began to spin deliciously, and treacherous erotic thoughts slid beguilingly into her head. No! She mustn't feel like this! She drew back sharply. "You are too bold, sir," she breathed.

"Too bold to rebuff?" he murmured, meeting her eyes.

Her cheeks felt hot, and she resorted to her fan. "If you do anything like that again, I-I'll . . ."

"Yes?"

"Just don't do it."

"As you wish, *cariad.*"

"And don't call me that."

"Have a sugared almond."

"I beg your pardon?"

"A sugared almond." He held the dish out to her and smiled.

She wanted to hate him. She wanted to remember how much she had loathed him since the night the duke purloined the tiara, but as she gazed into those teasing green eyes, she knew that it was going to be very difficult indeed to hate him. How could one hate a man one desired? The realization shook her, and her hand trembled a little as she made much of selecting a sugared almond. She didn't even like the wretched things, but taking one was a distraction.

"Do you think that had the intended effect upon La Fitzgerald?" he asked suddenly.

Susannah struggled to bring her emotions under control. "I-I, er, don't really care. At least, I care about poor Lord Faringdon, of course, but she can go to perdition."

It was an unguarded remark, and Gareth looked intently at her. "That sounded rather personal. What have you against her?"

"Nothing," Susannah replied quickly.

"I'm not a fool, I can read you like a book."

"If you're that good at reading, how was it that you missed Fleur's redirected interest?"

"Don't change the subject, *cariad.*"

He could make that word sound like a caress, she thought, again having to struggle with her senses.

He smiled and held out the sugared almonds once more. "Have another one."

In that second she realized he really could read her like a
book. He knew he had stirred unwanted feelings in her, and he
was amused by the fact. This really wouldn't do! She had too
much to hide! She drew herself up very sharply indeed. The
next page he turned would be blank. And the one after that.

To her relief, his attention was drawn to the pantomime, and
she was able to compose herself properly. She would be very
much on her guard with him from now on. This Welsh breaker
of hearts wasn't going to add her to his list.

The remainder of the program seemed to drag by, but at last
the final curtain fell. There was much shuffling, scraping of
chairs and benches, coughing, and conversation as the audience
prepared to leave. As Gareth and the duke paused to observe the
gradual emptying of the auditorium, Jane gave Susannah a grateful smile. "Thank you so much for coming to my aid."

"Look, we really have to talk about this. Can we drive in
Hyde Park tomorrow?"

"Yes, of course."

"If we are at the eastern shore of the Serpentine at noon, Sir
Gareth will happen to ride past."

Jane nodded. "I will come to Grillion's for you in good time."
But then she gave a start as the duke stepped to her side.

"Where are you and Mrs. Leighton planning to go, my dear?"
he asked in a silky tone.

Jane gave a nervous laugh. "Oh, nowhere important."

"Where?" he repeated.

"Only Hyde Park. Susannah and I have arranged to drive there
in the morning."

His pale eyes slid to Susannah. "How very pleasant," he murmured.

Jane looked at him. "You don't mind, do you?"

"Of course not," he replied, taking a golden snuffbox from
his pocket and flicking it open.

Chapter 11

The following morning Susannah was awakened by a commotion in her dressing room and sat up with a start. Chatterji was jabbering furiously as Anjuli rebuked him with a stream of language the propriety of which did not bear close inspection. What on earth was going on? Susannah wondered, flinging back the bedclothes and hurrying to the scene of the disturbance.

Chatterji appeared to have turned criminal, for he held a gentleman's gold fob watch in his felonious paws. Anjuli was trying to take it from him, and a noisy battle was in progress, the determined monkey tugging one way, the outraged ayah the other. Susannah's sudden appearance in the doorway distracted Anjuli for a second, and with a triumphant shriek Chatterji gave an extra tug, won the watch, and leapt to the sanctuary of the pelmet, dislodging his prized turban in the process.

Anjuli was dismayed. "Oh, you villainous thieving monkey!"

Chatterji took no notice; indeed, he was cheeky enough to open the watch, which chimed a melody if a little knob was moved. He knew about such things, for Susannah's late husband had possessed a similar watch. The monkey bared his teeth in a broad grin as he put the watch to his ear.

The ayah was scathing. "Oh, you are very musical, you naughty fellow, but you are also a wicked thief!"

"Whose watch is it?" Susannah asked.

"I do not know. This terrible creature ran in with it in his paw when the maid brought your morning tea."

Susannah was dismayed. "But how did he get out in the first place? Was the door left open at all?"

"Oh, no, memsahib, of that I am most certain."

"This is the second time now," Susannah murmured, recalling the business of the bishop's wig.

"He was here in these rooms when I arose, memsahib, but I do not know when he got out. All the windows were closed, and I did not open the door at all until the maid came. It is most puzzling, most puzzling indeed."

Chatterji continued to play with the watch, making little crooning noises as it repeated its tinkling notes. From time to time his button-bright eyes darted down to the two women, then away again, showing that he knew perfectly well he had done something wrong.

Susannah glanced at the ayah. "I know I said it in jest before, Anjuli, but do you think it possible that he can open the door?" she asked.

"But, memsahib, he is so small a monkey, and the door so very big."

"I know, but what other explanation is there? We've already established that the windows and door were closed, and if he climbed up the chimney, there would be soot to show for it." She gave an exasperated sigh. "Oh, Chatterji, sometimes you are nothing more than a horrid little pest!"

"A pest who cannot resist bright, shiny things," Anjuli added.

"True." Susannah watched the aggravating little creature as once again he opened the watch to make it play. "Well, it will soon need rewinding, and he'll lose interest." The dainty melody died away as she spoke, but instead of discarding the watch as she had hoped, Chatterji wound it up again!

Anjuli gasped. "I believe he *can* open doors, memsahib!"

"I'd lay odds on it," Susannah replied. "Well, we have to return that watch to its owner without revealing who stole it in the first place. I have no desire to be ejected ignominiously because I've smuggled a monkey into the hotel. First, however, we must get Chatterji down from that pelmet."

"How memsahib? If we try to stand on a chair, he will merely leap down and go somewhere else. We could spend a very long time chasing him."

Susannah's glance went to the floor and the moneky's turban. "Vanity, thy name is Chatterji," she murmured and went to get her scissors from her workbox. Then she picked up the turban and snapped the scissors threateningly toward it. He affected not to hear her, but his gaze slid anxiously toward his beloved headwear.

"I'll cut it into tiny pieces," Susannah warned.

He turned his head away indifferently, with his nose in the air.

"Very well," she declared and turned away, pretending to snip the cloth of gold.

Chatterji gave a squeal and jumped down with the watch held aloft in a gesture of surrender. Susannah took it from him and let him have the turban, which he inspected closely for any sign of damage. Then he put it on and bared his teeth at her as if he were very pleased with himself.

"You may think it's amusing, sirrah, but I do not," Susannah muttered, giving the scissors to Anjuli to put away, then examining the watch. It had a richly engraved gold case encircled by two rows of alternating sapphires and diamonds—just the sort of thing Chatterji would find temptation beyond endurance. But then she realized she had seen it somewhere before quite recently. In fact, the Duke of Exton had used it last night! How on earth did Chatterji have it? The monkey hadn't been at the theater, so he could only have laid paw upon it here at Grillion's; and if that were so, it meant the duke must have come to the hotel since last night. A cold finger passed down her spine. Why would he do that? Did he somehow suspect who she really was?

Anjuli looked concernedly at her. "Is something wrong, memsahib?"

"No, not really. It's just that I recognize the watch. It belongs to the Duke of Exton."

The ayah nodded. "I think so too, memsahib."

Susannah was surprised. "You do? But why? You don't know the duke."

"I watched from the window when you left last night, memsahib. I saw the duke sahib look out of the carriage window, and then this morning, while you were still asleep, I saw the same sahib arrive on horseback." The ayah went to the window, from which she was just able to see down past the edge of the balcony to the hotel entrance. "His horse is still there, memsahib."

Susannah caught up her nightgown and ran to the window to look down at the fine bay thoroughbred. "Are you quite sure you saw the same gentleman who was in the carriage last night?"

"Most certainly, memsahib."

"I have to know why he's here! "Quick, bring my apricot muslin gown."

Within minutes Susannah was dressed and ready, her russet curls piled loosely on top of her head. With the watch in her reticule and a red-and-brown cashmere shawl over her arms, she hurried downstairs to search for the duke. She heard him before she saw him, for he was berating the maître d'hôtel in the vestibule, and she paused at the top of the stairs to look down. He wore a scarlet riding coat, instead of the tasteful pine-green that was considered de rigueur for gentlemen of fashion, and his neckcloth was a veritable explosion of black-and-white spots. His overpowdered wig was tied with a yellow ribbon, and he held his top hat in one beige-gloved hand. In the other he held his riding crop, which tapped impatiently against his shining top boots as he virtually accused the maître d'hôtel of personally stealing the watch.

Susannah deemed the moment right to make her presence known. She took the watch out of her reticule, then gave a tinkle of laughter. "Why, good morning!" she cried down to the duke.

The two men turned quickly, and the maître d'hôtel, who was looking a little ill, managed to give her a smile. "Good morning, Mrs. Leighton."

The duke said nothing, so she beamed a him as she descended the staircase. "What an unexpected and welcome coincidence to find you like this, for I do believe I have found something that belongs to you," she declared, and as she reached the two men she held the watch in front of the duke's nose. "It was right there on the staircase. It is yours, isn't it?"

He stared at it, then took it from her with a mystified nod. "Er, yes, it is, Mrs. Leighton. I am most grateful to you. On the staircase, you say?"

"Right at the very top."

The duke turned back to the maître d'hôtel. "I seem to have been dealt a stroke of good fortune, sir, but the fact remains that you have a pickpocket at work in this establishment."

The maître d'hôtel could only spread his hands and apologize for all he was worth; no, more than that—he positively groveled before the duke.

Susannah gave a horrified gasp. "A pickpocket? Oh, how dreadful! Did you see him?

"No, he was too clever for that. I came to call upon you, Mrs. Leighton, and thought I saw you in the dining room, but as I entered I distinctly felt someone snatch the watch from my fob. Yet when I looked around, there was no one there!"

Susannah's glance slid to the dining room door, and the convenient pelmet from which Chatterji had helped himself to the bishop's wig. If the duke had looked up instead of around, he would have seen the pickpocket very well indeed!

The duke gave the maître d'hôtel a sour look. "Does it not occur to you that if this lady found the watch at the top of the staircase, the wretched thief might at this very moment be going through the bedrooms?"

The maître d'hôtel looked positively faint. "I-I . . ." His mouth clamped shut, and he scuttled away as if someone had set light to his coattails. In a moment there were footmen and other menservants scurrying in all directions as a full-scale search was instigated. Susannah could only hope that Chatterji did not choose now to venture out on another of his unauthorized excursions.

The duke attached the watch to his fob once more. "Whoever the villain is, he must be an agile devil."

"Yes, indeed," she murmured.

"Anyway, Mrs. Leighton, as I mentioned a moment ago, I came here to speak to you. I would have sent a running footman, as I have to Sir Gareth, but since I had business close by in Albemarle Street, I decided to deliver the message to you in person."

"I do hope the visit to Exton Park is not to be canceled?" she inquired in dismay, remembering how very unwilling he had been when first approached in the carriage.

"No, but I fear the same cannot be said of your drive today with my wife. I have received urgent word from Exton Park requesting my immediate presence, so the duchess and I will be leaving at midday. I'm sure that given your, er, history, you and Sir Gareth will be pleased to travel down together tomorrow. You will have much to discuss."

Susannah summoned a dismissive smile. "Yes, we will." *More than you realize!* "I, er, trust the urgent matter at Exton Park isn't a cause for alarm?"

"Indeed no, just the usual tenant quarrels."

Tenant quarrels? They must be battles royal if they needed the hasty return of a landlord as important as the Duke of Exton!

"I trust you are not too inconvenienced by the change of arrangement, Mrs. Leighton?"

"Of course not. Besides, it has prompted me to do something I have been thinking about for some time."

The duke's pale eyes were penetrating. "Indeed?"

"Yes. When I was in India I used to paint a great deal, watercolors mostly, and while on my way to Green Park yesterday, I noticed an excellent artist's emporium in Piccadilly. It made me feel I wished to resume the pastime. I asked the hotel doorman if it was an establishment that could be recommended— for as you know, hotel doormen know all about such things—and he said it was considered the best in London."

"I would not know, but if you are taking up painting again, I promise there are excellent views at Exton Park."

"I'm sure there must be." She felt awkward exchanging such mundane pleasantries with him. He simply wasn't a man with whom one could relax in any way, because a thin veil of suspicion seemed to accompany his every glance and word.

"Well, I will not keep you any longer, Mrs. Leighton. I trust you and Sir Gareth will be able to make mutually agreeable arrangements for the journey tomorrow. Until Exton Park, *chère madame*." He raised her hand almost to his lips, then turned to walk away.

"Until then," she murmured, watching as the doorman hastily thrust the doors open for him. She would have gone straight back to her apartment had it not been that as the duke emerged onto the pavement, he was approached by a burly broken-nosed man who resembled a former prizefighter and who had clearly been waiting for him. For a split second she thought the man was a footpad, but as her lips parted to call a warning, she realized that the duke had expected the man to the there. She watched as they exchanged close words, then the prizefighter— for that was definitely what he was, she decided—touched his hat and walked away. The duke mounted his waiting horse and rode off.

Susannah returned to her rooms, which had escaped the mâitre d'hôtel's search because Anjuli had stoutly refused to allow anyone to come in. If the footman concerned had insisted on being allowed in to look for the fictitious pickpocket, he would have discovered Chatterji sorting busily through Susannah's jewelry. It was the monkey's favorite pastime, especially when the morning sun made even the most indifferent gem sparkle for all it was worth. He had forgotten the duke's watch as he sat on Susannah's bed with the open box, crooning contentedly and holding up a topaz necklace so that a rainbow of little reflections danced across the bedroom wall.

Susannah went to the window and looked down into the busy Mayfair street. The postponement of any private conversation with Jane was most frustrating. Now she and Gareth would have to wait until they got to Exton Park to find out why their aid had been enlisted. And in the meantime there was the journey. She sighed a little apprehensively, for the Welshman had a very strange effect upon her. Since that New Year's Eve she had always thought of him as being third only to the duke and Fleur Fitzgerald on her list of villains, but he wasn't fitting into the mold. Instead he perplexed her more than any man ever had before—and attracted her more as well. When he had kissed her . . .

She turned hastily away from the window, for it didn't do to recall how she had felt when he had kissed her!

Chapter 12

A little later, after sending word to Gareth requesting him to call upon her in the afternoon to discuss the situation, Susannah set off for the artists' shop. She wore her gypsy hat and a cream pelisse over her apricot gown, and she smuggled Chatterji out in her muff. The hotel doorman had noticed the muff on a number of occasions, and this time he felt moved to ask her why she required such a thing on a warm spring day like this. Keeping Chatterji's head down, she murmured something about having very cold hands after the heat of India, and she didn't stop to discuss the matter further!

The monkey was very much in evidence when she reached the shop. He had grown more bold each time he was taken out, and as she purchased paints, paper, and pencils, he caused quiet chaos behind her back. Wearing his turban and hat, he rummaged through a pile of prints, unsorted all the brushes so that they were in hopeless disarray again, and took particular delight in moving the little blocks of paint from drawer to drawer, until anyone trying to find a particular color would find it virtually impossible. It was just as well that the store was warm and rather dark, for not only did he soon become so sleepy that he sought the refuge of the muff but his monkey misdemeanors went unnoticed.

Susannah wondered how much painting she would do, for it required a state of relative calm, and if she was engaged in searching for the tiara, calm she definitely would not be. She was on the point of leaving the shop when to her surprise she saw Gareth peering in through the uneven panes of the bow window. He was dressed in a dark-gray coat and pale-gray breeches, and his top hat was tipped nonchalantly back on his blond hair, but she could tell that he was uneasy about something. After casting a surreptitious glance across the street, he removed his top hat and entered, coming straight to her. "Good morning, Susannah."

"Good morning, er, Gareth." She stumbled over the informality, for although she thought of him by his given name, and he clearly intended to use hers, she still found it very difficult indeed to address him with familiarity. "What an odd coincidence to meet you like this," she added, wishing her pulse hadn't quickened just that little bit and her cheeks gone more pink than they had been before.

"It is no coincidence. I went to the hotel, and the doorman directed me here."

"I suppose you wish to discuss the change of plan?"

"Mm?" He was glancing across the street again.

"The duke has to return to Exton Park earlier than expected and wished to inform us at the earliest moment. I sent you a note about it." She watched him in puzzlement. "You must know, because the duke said he had sent a running footman to you, and I can't imagine that both messages went astray."

He dragged his attention briefly back to her. "Yes, I know all about it. Something about urgent estate business."

"That's right." She was puzzled. "Why did you go to the hotel so early in the day? I knew I was going out, and so asked you to call later."

"Oh, I was passing."

That was a fib, she decided, wondering what was wrong with him. She gave him a bright smile. "You were fortunate to get only the duke's running footman, I suffered His Grace of Exton's personal presence."

"I'll warrant that was enough to upset your digestion." Gareth met her eyes, then looked outside again.

She wondered what was of such interest on the other side of the street. All she could see was the usual melee of traffic and pedestrians. "You do realize my ayah and I are expected to travel to Exton Park with you tomorrow?" she inquired.

"It's of no consequence."

"Thank you very much," she said dryly.

He gave a quick smile. "I didn't mean it to sound quite like that."

"I'm relieved to hear it." She noticed him glance across the street again. "What is so interesting outside?" she asked at last, her curiosity now thoroughly aroused.

He looked intently at her. "Look, Susannah, there is something you should know."

"What?"

"I'll tell you as we go."

"Go? Where?"

"For an amicable, nay, loving, stroll along the street."

Before she could protest, he took the package containing her artistic acquisitions and ushered her out of the shop. Once out on the pavement, he offered her his arm, then rested his hand over hers; to anyone who saw, it seemed a tender gesture. As they walked east along Piccadilly, toward Albemarle Street, the bright sunshine and noise of the street awoke Chatterji, who sat up blinking and adjusting his turban.

Gareth gave a start. "Good God, a monkey!"

"You didn't imagine I was carrying a muff because I was cold, did you?"

"I merely thought you were a little eccentric."

"You have such a gallant way with you."

He smiled quickly into her eyes. "So I'm told," he murmured. "Do they allow monkeys at Grillion's now? I thought such things had been banned since Jerry Faringdon's chimpanzee a few years ago."

"They are banned, but no one knows about Chatterji."

"Chatterji? What a singularly appropriate name," Gareth observed, glancing down at the monkey, who gibbered as he peered out of his luxurious nest.

"You said you would explain what all this is about," she reminded him.

"So I did. Don't be alarmed, but I'm being followed, and I now know that you are as well."

"Followed?" She turned to peer around.

"Don't be so obvious!" he reprimanded sharply, and she looked quickly to the front again.

"But how do you know? What makes you suspect?"

"It's my business to know such things."

"Your *business*?"

"It doesn't matter now, just take my word for it. The fellow following me was leaning on a lamppost opposite my front door first thing this morning, and he's been on my heels ever since I left the house, although he's at pains to conceal the fact."

Gareth stopped outside a pastry cook's shop. "Look at the reflection in the glass."

She obeyed, and so did Chatterji, who was always conceited enough to like seeing himself in mirrors. The monkey preened, taking his turban off, then putting it on again as he looked first one way and then the other.

Gareth was momentarily distracted by him. "The creature poses like a courtesan!"

"The creature is typically male," Susannah replied.

"I stand corrected. Now, then, to the glass again. Do you see the man standing outside the bootmaker's opposite? He's quite tall and broad-shouldered and is wearing a brown coat and a low-crowned black hat."

"I see him."

"Now look a little further along the street toward Green Park? Do you also see a man who looks as if he's seen the bloody conclusion of one prizefight too many? Actually, come to think of it, they both look as if they've had a great deal to do with the fancy. That's the noble art of fisticuffs," he added in explanation.

"Yes, I know what it means," Susannah murmured, staring at the second man in the glass. She recognized him. "Gareth, I've seen the broken-nosed man before. He spoke to the duke outside Grillion's today."

Gareth's breath escaped on a knowing sigh. "So they *are* Exton's creatures. I thought as much."

"But, why would—?"

He interrupted. "To test our story of being former lovers. Whatever Exton had planned for last night didn't go quite as he anticipated, and he's suspicious. The horns loom ever large in his imagination, so he still wonders if I am Jane's lover, and therefore if you are merely aiding and abetting us."

"Am I aiding and abetting you?" she asked suddenly, a lingering doubt returning.

"You don't still think I'm lying about it?"

"No, I-I suppose not." But her doubt didn't entirely go away.

"What a vote of confidence *that* was. Last night you also convinced yourself that I am bedding Fleur Fitzgerald. Perhaps you are still of that opinion too?"

"No." She regretted saying anything. "Can we forget I spoke?"

He smiled. "It would ill become me to decline such a request, so of course we can forget. I will just say that at the moment I am innocent of *all* amorous involvement, so please do not start to wonder who else I may be romping with."

She went a little pink. "I shall not say another word on the subject."

"Good. Now, then, we were talking about our two shadows. As soon as I detected mine this morning, I wondered if the same was being done to you, and that's why I went to the hotel. The doorman directed me to the art shop, where I noticed my fellow talking to his pugilist acquaintance. It's hardly a coincidence that they are both following us along Piccadilly. Our every move will be reported back to Exton."

"I-I almost wish I'd never become tangled in all this," Susannah murmured. Almost, but not quite. There was still the tiara. And there was this devastatingly exciting man, whom common sense told her she should not trust at all.

Gareth smiled at her. "I thought you were made of sterner stuff, Mrs. Leighton."

"I am," she said more firmly.

"Good, for I would hate to abandon our mission now."

"Mission?"

"To come to the duchess's rescue. Speaking of which, shall we give Exton's sneaks something to tell him?"

"I-I don't understand."

He smiled. "You soon will." He suddenly took her by the arms and pulled her close to kiss her on the lips.

Chapter 13

But the tender kiss was rather rudely interrupted by Chatterji's loud screech of protest, for just as Gareth's lips met Susannah's, the monkey found himself being squashed. Gareth dropped the package he was carrying for her and stepped back as if scalded. Passersby halted in astonishment as the monkey's high-pitched displeasure rang out over Piccadilly.

Cheeks aflame, Susannah turned quickly to the pastry cook's window, as if she found Chelsea buns of intense interest. Chatterji bared his teeth and leaned out of the muff to glower at Gareth, whom he saw not only as the wicked perpetrator of an indignity upon his monkey person but also as a sudden rival for Susannah's affections.

Gareth retrieved the package and came to stand beside her, taking no notice of the furious monkey "Dear God, Susannah, I thought it was *you* making that noise," he said.

"*Me?* Sir Gareth Carew, your gallant compliments continue to take me aback!" Now it was Susannah's turn to be indignant.

"Forgive me?"

The two words, said softly and with just a hint of teasing, were those of a man who knew exactly how to get around a woman—any woman, even Susannah Leighton. Or perhaps especially Susannah Leighton. She couldn't help smiling. "Consider yourself forgiven, by me, at least. I'm not so sure about Chatterji."

Gareth looked down at the monkey, who looked back at him. Gareth read the expression in the animal's eyes. "So you're more jealous than compressed, eh, my simian friend?"

Chatterji's expression could not have been more sour if he had consumed an unripe lemon.

Susannah smoothed the monkey's turban. "He's not used to you, that's all," she said.

"Then he better had, for I think we should resume what was so rudely interrupted."

"Resume . . . ? Oh, I—"

But already Gareth's arm was around her waist, pulling her sideways toward him. Susannah instinctively held Chatterji plus muff well away as she turned her head and raised her lips for the kiss. She was ashamed of her willingness, nay, eagerness. The touch of his mouth upon hers felt quite wonderful, and so did all the delicious sensations that spread richly through her entire body. Oh, Lord, she seemed incapable of any resistance at all!

She drew guiltily back. "I-I should imagine that was sufficient to convince the duke's men," she said.

"I think you're right, more's the pity. I was quite enjoying it."

Her eyes went swiftly to his in the window glass. "I'll warrant you have a great reputation for being a tease, Sir Gareth."

"I have a reputation, it's true, but certainly not for mere teasing."

"I suppose you keep a tally of your conquests."

"What a very uncomplimentary remark."

"I owe you a few," she replied, watching the other side of the street in the window. "What if we don't convince them?" she said then. "What if the duke remains suspicious about an affair between you and Jane? Come to that, what if this has nothing whatsoever to do with his preoccupation with horns?"

"Oh, it does, Susannah, it does. The more I think about it, the more I'm sure. I'd stake my entire fortune upon it. Come, let's walk on." Once again he drew her hand over his sleeve and rested his own hand lovingly over hers. Chatterji, who numbered among his less likable qualities a tendency to bear grudges, immediately stretched out of his muff to sink his teeth into the nearest male finger.

Gareth gave a yell and snatched his hand away with a Welsh oath that singed the air. As he took off his glove and rubbed his sore finger, Susannah felt father guilty for not warning him. "Chatterji does take umbrage, I'm afraid," she explained belatedly.

"So do I," Gareth replied, casting a dire look at the monkey, who had subsided smugly into the muff.

"He's harmless really."

"*Harmless*? That'a a matter of opinion! I trust the flea-bitten pest isn't accompanying us to Exton Park?"

"He isn't flea-bitten, and I'm afraid he is coming with us; indeed, he is the main reason I've been invited."

"Then I sincerely hope the ayah will have him for the journey."

"Oh, no. He always stays with me."

"This time he and the ayah will be outside with my man Hector."

"Even if I promise he won't misbehave again?"

"Am I supposed to believe you can deliver on such a promise?" Gareth saw the look in her eyes. "No, I thought not. So the odious little primate is going to travel *outside*. Is that clear?"

"Very." Susannah was resentful, but then she saw how badly bitten his finger was. "Oh, dear, does it hurt much? I'm really very sorry, but he does go very cross if he's squashed."

"And I get equally cross when I'm savaged."

"Savaged? Oh, come now, sir, he's only a tiny monkey."

"With very sharp teeth."

"Why do men always make such a fuss about things? You call yourselves the stronger sex, but when it comes to whingeing, you beat women into a cocked hat."

"We also get childish," Gareth replied and promptly reached into the muff to tug the turban down over Chatterji's nose. "There, let that be a lesson to you," he said.

The furious monkey wrenched the turban away again, then shook a clenched paw at Gareth, for if there was one thing Chatterji could not bear, it was to have his vanity dented.

Susannah soothed her pet and then looked coolly at Gareth. "You're right, for that was very childish indeed."

"Maybe, but it did wonders for my temper," he replied dryly.

Just then a sixth sense drew Susannah's attention to the traffic approaching along the street ahead. A bright-red landau drawn by cream horses was caught up in a slight jam of other vehicles, and because its hoods were lowered, she was able to see the lady occupant clearly. It was Fleur Fitzgerald. The actress wore yellow and white, and a parasol twirled prettily above her head as she graciously acknowledged the salutes of several admirers on the pavement. Then her gaze happened to light upon Susannah and Gareth, and the parasol became still as her smile was instantly extinguished.

It was too much for Susannah, who simply *had* to poke the actress on the nose—figuratively speaking, of course. Gareth, whose attention had temporarily been drawn to a particularly fine set of dueling pistols in a gunsmith's window, turned as Susannah's hand touched his sleeve again. "Gareth," she breathed conspiratorily, "there's something about our two shadows across the street that makes me fear they haven't been taken in after all."

"Oh? He glanced over the busy road. "Why do you think that? They seem no different to me."

"I-I don't know." Susannah bit her lip and then raised her eyes to his. "I'd feel happier if we gave them another demonstration of our affection."

He was surprised. "Well, if that is what you wish . . ."

"It is." She smiled up at him, knowing full well that Fleur was observing everything. Chatterji and the muff were again held well to one side as Gareth bent forward to give his co-conspirator another lingering counterfeit kiss.

The landau had emerged from the jam now and was coming ~ward them at a spanking trot, each yard allowing the actress ~ter view of events on the pavement. As the vehicle swept ~t, Susannah only just prevented herself from giving a cheeky wave.

Gareth saw the landau at the last moment and gave Susannah a reproving look. "So that was for the benefit of the duke's men, was it?"

"Of course."

"Don't bat your eyelids as well, or you will really over-egg the pudding."

"I don't know *what* you mean," Susannah declared airily.

"I'm sure," he murmured, and they walked on.

He escorted her back to Grillion's, followed every step of the way by the duke's men. At the hotel entrance he took his leave of her. "Will eight o'clock be too early tomorrow morning?"

"Eight will do very well."

"And we are agreed about who will travel where during the journey?"

She gave him a look. "Yes. Anjuli and Chatterji will travel outside."

The sound of Chatterji's grumbling emanated from the muff, as if the monkey knew what had been decided. Gareth felt no remorse as he leaned down slightly to speak directly to the animal. "Sir, if it were not for the servants, I would wish for rain all the way," he said, thinking of his landau's outside seats.

Susannah moved the muff away protectively. "You have no heart, Sir Gareth Carew."

"Oh, but I do, sweet lady, I do," Gareth replied and put a hand to her cheek to turn her lips to meet his. As he kissed her again, it really was as if they had known each other for a long, long time.

Susannah found her eyes closing with pleasure and pulled her head back guiltily. "This is becoming too easy, sir."

"Practice makes perfect," he whispered.

"And familiarity breeds contempt."

"I prefer the first one," he said, handing her the package he had carried since leaving the art shop. "À bientôt, cariad," he murmured, mixing his languages without a second thought. Then he turned to walk quickly away, and the duke's shadow immediately followed.

When Susannah looked out of her apartment window several hours later, the man the duke had assigned to follow her was standing in the alleyway opposite, where he had been since she and Gareth parted. She smiled to herself, for she had left the hotel in the meantime to purchase some cloth and buttons for a new coat for Chatterji. Grillion's had two entrances, and not even the Duke of Exton's man could keep watch on both!

Chapter 14

It was misty but quite warm the following morning as Gareth's postilion landau, its hoods lowered, drove out of London past Hyde Park. The park was far from deserted, for there were a number of riders out enjoying the early-morning air, including a very colorful cavalcade cantering in procession toward the gates into Park Lane. It was Abbas Ali and an entourage of about twenty attendants, all in turbans and bright robes, with scimitars thrust through their sashes. They were riding beautiful long-tailed Arabian horses, but none more beautiful than the white stallion rode by Abbas Ali himself. High-stepping and mettlesome, it drew the envious gaze of every gentleman who saw it. The emissary, although gray-bearded and rather stout, was a fine horseman, controlling the stallion with such effortless ease that it might as well have been a docile pony.

Susannah, who wore a wide-brimmed straw hat with cream ribbons fluttering loose and a lime-green silk pelisse and matching gown, turned to watch until she could see no more, then faced the front again. As long as she drew breath, the Holland tiara would *never* go to Constantinople! A few minutes later the landau passed through the Knightsbridge turnpike gates and headed west for the Cotswold Hills. There wasn't a great deal of traffic on the open road at such an early hour, and the team of four bays soon came up to a brisk trot, skillfully managed by the postilion in Carew livery.

Anjuli and Gareth's man, Hector, were side by side on the seat at the rear of the vehicle. The former "Human Monkey" of Astley's Amphitheatre had the wizened face of a man far older than his forty years, and his ears were very rounded and pronounced. He liked to keep himself to himself, and he did not know what to make of Anjuli. To him the ayah did not look like a lady's maid; indeed, she reminded him of an Indian pantomime that had once been put on at Astley's. But he had already seen the spices she had with her—curries were his great delight, the hotter the better. So he was more than prepared to like Anjuli, no matter *how* strange she looked!

Anjuli, who traveled in her best blue sari, did not know what to make of Hector at first. He looked so like Chatterji's elder brother that she was convinced he was one Englishman who *must* have a tail! She liked him, however, for he was kind and thoughtful, even to carrying her bag of spices for her. And when he spoke of curries, she knew he was a man after her own heart.

Between them on the seat was a black-and-white-striped hatbox containing Chatterji and his muff. The hatbox was open, and the monkey was standing on his hind legs to peer out. He wore his turban and the new yellow coat that Susannah had made for him the night before, but he was not a happy monkey; indeed, he was a downright furious one. He wasn't used to being separated from Susannah, and he knew that Gareth was to blame. The Welshman had already offended him with ordeal by squashing, and then insult by turban, so *this* wasn't going to be allowed to pass unchallenged. Oh, indeed, no! Chatterji bared his teeth and scowled at the back of Gareth's head.

Gareth was blissfully unaware of the monkey daggers being directed at him from the rear of the vehicle. He wore a sky-blue coat and gray breeches, and his top hat was at a rakish angle on his thick blond hair. There was no sign of the dreaded ennui; indeed, that had begun to fade from the moment he decided to take up the Duke of Exton's invitation to the theater. It had been dispelled completely when Susannah Leighton placed a kiss upon his cheek and declared herself his long-lost lover! He was enjoying all this immensely; he hadn't been so intrigued and entertained since a certain time in St. Petersburg. But that was another story, as was the fact that he was certain he and the delightful Mrs. Leighton had met before. If only he could remember where, and when. . . .

Susannah was thinking about him too. He had been the first thing on her mind when she awoke that morning, and he had seldom been out of her thoughts since. She had been aware of the thrill of anticipation before he arrived, the pleasure she felt on seeing him at last, the excitement aroused by his welcoming smile. She had not felt this way in a long, long time, and Sir

Gareth Carew was one of the very last men she had ever expected to be the cause.

The landau drove smartly on into the soft-green spring countryside, stopping briefly at the Golden Cross Inn, Hounslow, and then at several more stages before at last reaching the Huntsman, where they were to eat. The hostelry was so renowned for its fine food that the yard was filled with as many private carriages as stagecoaches, and it was so busy that it was well over an hour before there were free places for Susannah and Gareth in the low-beamed dining room. Hector and Anjuli, together with Chatterji and the hatbox, had been shown to a lesser dining room, where servants and similar persons were accommodated at long tables with benches. This was another insult as far as Chatterji was concerned, for he was accustomed to being fed tidbits by Susannah. As he was borne out of the yard, he glared over the top of the hatbox at Gareth, who would long since have expired if the monkey's visual daggers had been real.

When Anjuli and Hector took their places at the table, where the meal was a simple but hearty stew, the meat content of which was hard to identify, the ayah immediately produced her spices. She selected the ones that could be used without being cooked and made a friend for life of Hector by giving the stew the curry flavor he relished so much.

At last Susannah and Gareth were shown to a small side table by the window of the main dining room, where they were served some very tasty roast mutton with mint sauce and potatoes. They talked about this and that, but when the plates were removed, Gareth sat back and ran a finger around he rim of his wineglass. "Are we still agreed that this whole business is the result of the duke's obsession?" he asked suddenly.

"You seemed convinced enough yesterday. Have you changed your mind?"

"No, not really. I was just wondering if there might be something else we've missed."

"We can hardly miss what we don't know. Besides, I'm sure it will all become much more clear once we've reached Exton Park and are able to speak with Jane."

"Ah, yes, the duchess in distress," he murmured.

"Do you doubt that as well?"

He smiled. "No, of course not. We agreed to do what we could to help her situation, and I still stand by that. It's just . . ."

"Yes?"

"I can't help feeling . . ."

"Yes?" she pressed.

He spread his hands. "Damn it, I don't know! I just have this feeling, I can't describe it, but it's there."

"What sort of feeling is it?"

"A suspicion that the duke may not be entirely in the wrong."

"You think Jane is at fault?"

"Her fidelity is the subject of intense debate." He told her about all the wagers, then shrugged. "Maybe she has succumbed, and Exton knows it."

"He isn't exactly the soul of fidelity," Susannah said, thinking of the long liaison with Fleur Fitzgerald.

"That's different."

Susannah lowered her wineglass crossly. "Oh, yes, because it's perfectly all right for a man to be as unfaithful as he chooses!"

Gareth met her angry eyes across the table. "I didn't say that."

"No, but it's what you meant."

"*Cariad,* you're never going to change things."

"Don't call me that."

"It springs to mind when I see that splendid flash in your eyes."

She looked at him. "Don't change the subject."

He laughed. "Oh, Susannah, are you so determined to argue?"

"I happen to feel strongly about it. Why should there be one rule for men and another for women? And if you say it's because women are the weaker sex, so help me I'll break that wine bottle over your head!" All Richard's infidelities had come flooding back, bringing with them the feelings of worthlessness he had initially managed to instill in her.

"I wasn't going to say any such thing," he replied, quickly moving the bottle out of her reach. "As it happens, I agree with you. Fidelity should be expected of both or of neither. As far as I'm concerned, from the first time Exton broke his vows, he released his wife from hers."

"Two wrongs make a right?" She remembered the advances she had received from Richard's friends in Bengal. They had all been turned away, but there had been one she had regretted afterward. Gareth might tease her now, but would he ever make sincere advances? Would she turn him away if he did? Perhaps, perhaps not. . . .

He gave her a bemused look. "There is no satisfying you today, Mrs. Leighton."

"Perhaps, perhaps not," she murmured aloud, then straightened suddenly as she saw Anjuli hurrying anxiously toward their table. The ayah's exotic appearance attracted a great deal of interest from the other diners, for it wasn't every day that saris were seen at an English inn, but she hardly seemed to notice as she bent to speak urgently to Susannah. "Oh, memsahib, the most terrible thing has happened. Chatterji has escaped from his hatbox!"

Gareth groaned and tossed his napkin on to the table, thinking that spit-roasted monkey would be an excellent addition to any menu.

"Escaped? When?" Susannah asked in dismay.

"Only a minute or so ago, memsahib, but Hector saw him coming toward this room. And memsahib . . . ?"

"Yes?"

"He is a very *cross* monkey. He is not accustomed to being kept away from you, and he is intent upon mischief."

"Oh, no." Susannah's haunted gaze swept around the thronged room, for she knew only too well how badly Chatterji could behave when he chose.

"What shall we do, memsahib?" Anjuli pressed anxiously.

Do? What *could* they do, except keep their fingers crossed? thought Susannah. But Gareth had another suggestion.

"I'll tell you what the wisest thing would be. We should leave right now, *without* the obnoxious little pest."

Susannah flashed him a cross look. "I shall ignore that monstrous remark," she said, then looked at the ayah again. "We can't do anything, except trust that he won't get up to too many tricks. Just go back to Hector and finish your meal, Anjuli."

As the ayah returned to the other room, Gareth looked at Susannah. "That monkey is a pain in the posterior, and if he doesn't misbehave, I'll eat my hat."

"I look forward to watching you," she said defiantly, but almost immediately Chatterji dashed any hope she had of witnessing such an entertaining spectacle.

The monkey was under a table by the feet of an overrouged lady in a rose-pink gown with a fringed hem. The monkey tugged at the fringe, and with an outraged squeak the lady glared at the gentleman opposite her. "How *dare* you!" she cried in booming tones and stood up to deal him a sharp slap.

The unfortunate man was thunderstruck. "I say, madam, what on earth—!"

"You sirrah, are a blackguard!" the lady declared roundly, then caught up her skirts to stalk from the room, much to the amusement of the other diners.

Chatterji, meanwhile, had moved on to the next table, where he clambered up the tablecloth to slyly inspect the plates of two elderly clergymen engaged in a lively discussion on texts from the New Testament. The monkey began to secretly help himself to the choicest tidbits from both plates, and gradually the clergymen realized that their meals were diminishing suspiciously. Naturally, each thought the other was employing a thieving fork, and the lively discussion became an argument.

Susannah hardly dared imagine what the monkey might do next. She was soon to find out, for a flicker of movement on a window curtain revealed Chatterji making for the pelmet, always a favorite place from which to view proceedings. There he sat, his teeth bared in a delighted grin as he watched the clergymen's argument become more and more rancorous. Then he was distracted by something on the pelmet, a large, very dead spider. He picked it up to examine, and Susannah's heart sank. Oh, no, please no . . . But even as she thought, the monkey deliberately dropped the spider straight onto the plate of a rather stout lady, who immediately screamed fit to shatter the windowpanes. A passing waiter was so startled he dropped his fully laden tray of brown Windsor soup; soup and crockery went flying, splattering all the nearby diners, including Gareth, and in a moment there was pandemonium. Chatterji, alarmed by the noise, fled. The last Susannah saw was his tail disappearing through the door to the yard.

Gareth was too incensed to speak, and as he mopped the brown Windsor from his hitherto immaculate coat, Susannah didn't know what to say, "I-I really am terribly sorry," she managed at last. How inadequate she thought, glancing at the mess on his clothes and the shambles of the dining room.

"So you should be!" Gareth snapped, inspecting his ruined neckcloth. "By Gad, I wish I'd wagered you to eat *your* hat, for right now I'd insist you did just that!"

"It was hardly *my* fault!" she cried, needled.

"If you hadn't brought the cantankerous little demon with you, it wouldn't have happened!"

"Nor would it if *you* hadn't been so utterly fixed upon banishing him to the outside!"

His green eyes were bright with anger. "So all this is *my* fault?"

"Yes." Her jaw was set as she met his eyes.

"You are, without a doubt, the most irrational woman it has ever been my misfortune to meet," he breathed, and without another word he left the table.

Furious, Susannah remained where she was, but her anger faded into guilt as she observed the continuing chaos in the dining room. The gentleman who'd fallen foul of the booming lady was in a state of collapse, and the unfortunate waiter was trying to clear up the mess of soup and broken crockery. The plump woman was still having the vapors about the spider, the clergymen had now almost come to blows, and the diners who'd been splashed with soup were so vociferous about it that the landlord came running to see what on earth had befallen his usually smoothly run dining room. Susannah waited no longer but hurriedly followed Gareth outside.

He was waiting for her by the landau, his arms folded, his foot tapping. Anjuli and Hector were on their seat at the back, with the hatbox resting ominously between them, its lid tightly in place. Gareth nodded toward a stagecoach that was about to depart for London. "I suggest you dispatch your ayah and that cursed hatbox back to town," he said stiffly.

Susannah's indignation was rekindled. "I shall do no such thing!" she declared defiantly, then lowered her tone so that neither Anjuli nor Hector could hear. "Just who do you think you are, sirrah?"

"I am the owner of the vehicle in which you are traveling, madam, and be warned that I'm quite in the mood to dispatch you in the stagecoach as well."

"You presume, sir, *and* you forget that Chatterji is a necessary element for our stay at Exton Park. Jane wants him there."

For a moment they glared at each other, but then he climbed down. "Very well, we will continue, but I vow that if I catch that damned monkey in any further wrongdoing . . . !" Without finishing the threat, he went the rear of the landau, reached past Hector to open the hatbox, and gazed sternly inside at Chatterji.

"Be warned, you little tyke. Your tail would make an excellent noose, and I'd take great pleasure in stringing you up by it!" Chatterji squeaked and hid his face. "Yes, well you might do that, sir," Gareth muttered and slammed the hatbox lid down again.

Within moments the landau had maneuvered out of the yard and come up to a smart pace for the remainder of the journey to the beautiful Cotswold Hills of Gloucestershire. Susannah stared fixedly out of the vehicle. She would never be pleasant to Sir Gareth Carew again, ever!

But before they traveled more than a mile he had charmed her into smiling again.

Chapter 15

The May evening was drawing in fast as the landau left the highway that wound across the Cotswolds from Cirencester to Stroud and began to descend a wooded south-facing slope. Almost immediately the lodge and armorial gates of Exton Park appeared on the right, and the landau swept through into a drive that led high along the wooded flank of an isolated valley, where a chain of three lakes shone between the trees. The sky was turning to gold and crimson, the glades were carpeted with bluebells and wood anemones, and long shadows lay across the way. There was a freshness in the air that was almost exhilarating, and the evening chorus of birdsong rang out gloriously. Susannah's senses feasted upon the English springtime she had missed so very much while far away in Chinsura; would she now miss India in the same way? Perhaps, perhaps not . . . Her glance slid toward Gareth. *Would* she spurn his advances? Perhaps not.

Just as she was beginning to think Exton Park itself would never come into sight, the drive turned down the slope once more, and the woods splayed back to reveal the north front of what was acknowledged to be one of the finest country houses in England. Designed by the great Robert Adam, Exton Park was the embodiment of the grand tour, a blend of everything that was admired about ancient Rome, but Susannah immediately thought it intimidating. Or was it perhaps that she judged it by its master? She drew a long breath. It didn't matter what she thought of either Exton Park or the duke; it only mattered that she was now very close indeed to the Holland tiara.

Gareth eyed the house as well. Amused as he was by this jaunt, he wasn't about to take any chances with a man like Exton. A precaution or two might be sensible, indeed advisable. He had seen a very convenient barn up on the highway. . . . He glanced at his postilion, Billings, a sturdy, long-faced fellow who had occasionally accompanied Hector and him to St. Petersburg.

Susannah sensed nothing of his thoughts as she continued to gaze at the house. Vast, golden, and breathtakingly grand, it comprised a porticoed central block that was flanked on all four corners by mansion-size pavilions that were joined to it by curving external corridors. From the sky it must look like a huge, oblong beetle with bowlegs and square feet, Susannah thought irreverently. She was soon to learn that the central block held only state rooms, while the northeastern pavilion contained the private family apartments, the northwestern the kitchens, and the southwestern the chapel and conservatory. The final pavilion, to the southeast, was for guests, and that was where she and Gareth were to stay.

The landau drew up before the soaring portico, and almost immediately a little procession of footmen hurried from a discreet doorway below the double flight of stone steps that led up to the great main entrance. Anjuli and Hector were shepherded away to be taken directly to their master's and mistress's apartments, and Chatterji and the hatbox went with them. The monkey was now very tired and irritable, as could be heard by the cross noises emanating from the box.

Susannah sincerely hoped her pet's conduct would not be an embarrassment at a place like this, and she turned to say as much to Gareth, but he and his postilion were engrossed in examining the landau's front axle. They whispered together for a few moments, and the postilion nodded, then Gareth straightened and came over to her. "I'm a little concerned about the axle, so tomorrow Billings will take it to the best coach builder in Cirencester," he announced rather loudly.

His tone puzzled Susannah as much as what he said. "But what's wrong with the axle? I didn't notice anything as we were driving along," she replied, then whispered. "Why are you speaking so loud?"

"Oh, the problem was barely detectable," he answered without lowering his voice at all, then he bent his head close. "It's merely a small safeguard."

"Against what?"

"Nothing, hopefully. Ah, we are about to be conducted into the house." He turned as a footman bowed low to them both.

"If you will follow me, sir, madam."

As they were led ceremoniously up the steps, Susannah heard excited barking and a man's raised voice coming from an open window in the northeastern pavilion, which she would soon discover was where the private family apartments lay. She glanced at Gareth, but he didn't seem to have noticed anything. They were admitted into an opulent marble hall where the echo of their steps was picked up and flung from every cornice and corner. Gray alabaster columns rose the full height of the house to a domed ceiling where a star-shaped window provided the only daylight. All around there were pale-blue niches and alcoves containing statues of gods and heroes, and every door was topped by a richly sculpted entablature depicting a scene from the labors of Hercules. The only item of furniture was a marble table built against the wall close to the entrance, upon which stood the usual assembly of candlesticks for use after dark. Susannah shivered a little, for the air was very cold, perhaps from such a surfeit of marble, she thought as she gazed around. Which way did the tiara lie? North, south, east, or west?

The footman withdrew as a thin woman, aged somewhere in her middle fifties, crossed the inlaid floor to greet them. She wore a lace bonnet and a dark-blue gown, and her light steps were picked up by an extraordinarily sensitive echo, as was the jingling of the housekeeper's keys dangling from a chain at her waist. She had a closed face that gave nothing away and quick nondescript eyes that missed nothing. Her hair, once black but now graying, was parted over a wide forehead, and her full lips seemed too large for her small chin. Something about her aroused an instinctive unease in Susannah, who also thought she seemed peculiarly familiar. What was it? The eyes, perhaps? No, it was the lower part of her face, the line of the jaw, the slight pucker of the full lips.

"Good evening, Sir Gareth, Mrs. Leighton," the woman said as she bobbed the briefest of curtsies. "Welcome to Exton Park. My name is Mrs. Wilberforce, and I am the housekeeper." Her accent was vaguely north country, although which county it came from Susannah could not tell. It might have been anywhere. The echo had heard it too and missed not a word; a japer might have been peering secretly down through one of the skylights far above them.

"Good evening, Mrs. Wilberforce," Gareth replied, and Su-

sannah smiled as the intrusive echo kept hissing the last sylla-
ble of the woman's name.

"I trust you had a good journey?" Mrs. Wilberforce inquired
politely.

"Excellent," Gareth responded.

"If you will come with me, I will conduct you to the duke
and duchess." The woman inclined her head again and walked
away, her keys jingling. The echo jingled too and imitated her
slow steps.

As they followed, Susannah raised an eyebrow at Gareth. "A
homely place, is it not?" she whispered. The echo heard nothing because it was now far too busy with footsteps.

Gareth smiled. "Ideal for relaxation and contemplation," he
replied.

"And so cold!" Susannah shivered again.

"You should try Pengower Castle at this time of year. It's a
positive icehouse, but then it *is* a medieval stronghold with walls
four feet thick."

"I hope our rooms have fires lit," she said with feeling, then
glanced at him. "Did you hear the racket when we arrived? It
was coming from the pavilion to which I rather think we are
being taken."

"I didn't hear anything. What sort of racket?"

"A dog was barking and a man was shouting. Well, almost
shouting. I think it was the duke."

He smiled. "Would it be too much to hope that the former
has bitten the latter?"

"Far too much, I fear." Susannah moved closer to him. "What
do you think of Mrs. Wilberforce?" she asked after a moment.

"Think of her? In what way?"

"She seems familiar. No, that's not quite right. What I mean
is that she reminds me of someone, but I can't think who."

"She looks just like any other housekeeper to me," he replied.

Mrs. Wilberfore led them out of the hall into a music room
worthy of a king's palace. From there they entered the curved
external corridor that connected the main building to the northwestern pavilion. It seemed a very long walk, and the way was
alternately in dark shadow and vivid with bands of sunset stream-
ing through tall windows, but at last they reached double doors,
which the housekeeper flung open to reveal an inner vestibule
where a footman had just finished lighting a brilliant crystal

chandelier. He stood aside as Mrs. Wilberforce opened another
door, and they were shown into a blue-and-gold drawing room
where their hosts awaited.

The Duke and Duchess of Exton were seated on gold-and-
white-striped sofas on either side of a black marble fireplace,
where a very welcome fire crackled around a fresh log. They were
both dressed for dinner—Jane in a silver chenille tunic over a
peach satin slip, with long strands of evenly matched pearls around
her throat, the duke in mauve brocade, with his wig tied with
dark-blue ribbon. His nose seemed somehow more a snout than
ever, Susannah thought.

The housekeeper withdrew, but as the duke rose to receive his
guests, a fat white poodle suddenly erupted from the floor at
Jane's feet, dashed between his legs, and came to leap excitedly
all around the new arrivals. The duke, almost knocked over, uttered the sort of oath that should never be heard in the company of ladies, but then the excited poodle dashed back through
his legs again, and this time he really did go down, landing on
his back like a joint of beef on a butcher's slab. There was a
shocked silence, during which the delighted poodle dashed round
and around Jane's sofa like a thing demented. Jane pressed her
hands to her mouth, her eyes wide as she stared at her prostrate
husband.

Susannah was rooted, but Gareth quickly went to help the
fallen man to his feet. "Are you all right?"

"Yes, yes, I'm all right," the duke growled rather ungraciously,
then turned sharply on his wife like an angry boar. "This time
that damned dog really will have to go, madam!"

Jane jumped up in dismay. "Oh, no, Delavel! Minette is only
pleased to see our guests." She caught the poodle's jeweled collar to prevent another revolution of the sofa. Minette came up
with a choked sound, then sat meekly, tongue lolling. To Susannah it seemed a remarkably silly dog, and the prospect of its
getting together with the troublesome likes of Chatterji was too
awful to mention. What on earth had Jane been thinking of? Absolute bedlam lay ahead!

Jane shook the poodle's collar to make it look at her, then she
wagged a stern finger. "That was naughty, Minette. Now you
must say sorry." Minette grinned up at her, tongue still lolling,
but suddenly sat up, pawed the air, and whined appealingly. Jane

was delighted, as if all was now well again. "There, Delavel, see how contrite she is!"

"Contrite? The damned mongrel would as soon do it again as look at me," he replied accurately. "Maybe I'll let it pass this time, but if anything like this happens again, that dog will be helped from this house by the toe of my boot. Do you understand?"

"Perfectly, Delavel," Jane murmured demurely, then turned to smile at Susannah and Gareth. "Welcome to Exton Park. I promise we aren't always as chaotic as this, but I fear Minette has been a little unmanageable today." She hurried to take Susannah's hands. "I do hope you've brought Chatterji with you?"

Susannah smiled. "Yes, but he's in disgrace," she replied, stealing a glance at the stains on Gareth's coat.

Jane followed her gaze. "Oh, dear. Was that Chatterji's fault?"

Gareth's eyebrow twitched. "That monkey came within an inch of strangulation."

Jane pulled an understanding face. "Minette has not exactly covered herself in glory either, as you've just witnessed. Susannah, do tell me when I may see Chatterji?"

"He's a little grumpy after the journey, so I think tomorrow morning would be best." Grumpy? Downright peevish was the description that sprang to mind.

Jane was disappointed. "Well, never mind. I'm sure I can endure until then. Minette will be delighted with him, I just know she will."

The duke's face was a picture. "I can hardly wait," he declared dryly, then paused as the ormulu clock on the mantel began to chime. With a frown he took out his pocket watch, which immediately added its piping notes to the sound of the clock. Clearly the times matched, for he closed it with a snap. "Now, then, my dear," he said to Jane, "I'm sure our guests would prefer to refresh themselves in their apartments before dinner," he said pointedly.

For once Susannah was grateful to him. "I do feel rather travel-worn," she admitted.

"Then you must be shown to your accommodations without further delay." He reached for a small bell on a nearby table. "Dinner will be here in our private dining room in half an hour. A footman will escort you to your rooms and then back here in due course."

The door opened and the footman who'd attended to the vestibule chandelier came in and bowed. "You rang, Your Grace?"

"Show our guests to their apartments," the duke commanded.

"Your Grace."

Chapter 16

It seemed an inordinately long walk from the pavilion in the northeast to the guest apartments in the southeast, and it wasn't pleasant to leave the warmth of the private apartments behind. The footman led Susannah and Gareth back along the chilly external corridor, through the music room into the marble hall, the entire length of which they had to cross to another vast chamber, which formed the focus of the house's southern aspect. Called the saloon, this circular chamber was as warm to the eye as the marble hall was cold. Rose, crimson, gold, and leaf-green were the chosen tints, which blended with the woods and sunset as seen through an immense set of glass doors that gave onto a wide terrace. From the terrace the grounds swept down the valley slope toward the lakes, which now glistened like molten copper and gold as the sun sank ever lower in the west. There was no time to admire the view, however, as they were led swiftly from the saloon into the adjacent library, then out into another external corridor—or beetle leg, as Susannah preferred to think of it—and at last to the guest pavilion.

Gareth's apartment was on the ground floor, but Susannah had been allocated rooms on the floor above. She was shivering as she entered and to her relief found that there was a fire flickering in the hearth. Anjuli was busy unpacking in the principal bedroom, which like the rest of the apartment was decorated in dove-gray and gold, and Chatterji, his grumpiness temporarily forgotten, was helping himself to grapes and peaches from a dish on a table in the drawing room. The fruit had been grown at Exton Park conservatory and was so plump and ripe that juice was running down the monkey's beard and chin. As soon as he saw Susannah, he leapt eagerly into her arms. The flames of the fire danced pleasantly, sending shadows and light over everything as she carried the monkey to the window and gazed down toward the lakes. "Well, my little friend, the tiara is very close by now. All I have to do is find it," she murmured. *All* she had to do? In a house of this size?

She was about to turn away from the window when a slight movement down in the valley caught her attention. It was by the fringe of woodland edging the nearest and largest lake. Someone was down there, almost hidden by the low-hanging branches of an immense copper beech tree that seemed almost on fire in the sunset. A man, a gentleman by the look of his clothes, was gazing up at the house, but after a moment he drew back, and she realized he had a horse hidden among the trees. He mounted and vanished into the woods, with only the swaying of a copper-colored branch to mark his passing. Who was he? Susannah wondered as she left the window to go into the bedroom.

"Anjuli, dinner is in half an hour—well, I suppose in considerably less than that after the veritable route march from the private apartments. If I have to walk there and back very often, I vow I shall soon be very fit and healthy. Anyway, could you unpack my white taffeta?"

"All is in readiness, memsahib," replied the ayah, indicating the adjacent dressing room, where the requested gown was hanging on the wardrobe, together with the blue silk shawl Susannah always wore with it.

Susannah looked at her in amazement. "How did you know I'd choose that particular gown?"

"It is an ayah's duty to know these things," said Anjuli, coming to take Chatterji and place him on the bed. "Come, memsahib, a jug of hot water has already been brought, and I have scented it with your favorite perfume. You will be fresh again in a moment, and all will be accomplished in good time for dinner."

All was indeed accomplished in time, and soon Susannah was seated before the dressing table as Anjuli put the finishing touches to her hair. The ayah was much in awe of Exton Park, likening it to the finest palace of the Nawab of Bengal. "The duke is clearly as important a fellow as the nawab," she declared as she tweaked the curls around Susannah's forehead.

Susannah smiled. "He is an important fellow, Anjuli, but not *that* important. He just has a very large, very cold house. You will keep an eye on our monkey friend tonight, won't you? I'm just not in the mood for any more of his antics. Tomorrow will be soon enough to cope with him again. And with the dreaded Minette."

"Minette, memsahib?"

"The duchess's poodle."

Anjuli looked askance in the mirror. "*Poodle,* memsahib? What is a poodle?"

"A kind of dog."

"The duchess has a dog to be dreaded?" The ayah looked alarmed, clearly picturing an enormous, savage beast with slavering jaws and vicious teeth.

"I just mean that Minette is almost as troublesome as Chatterji, that's all. By the way, where *is* Chatterji? I haven't seen him for a while."

As she spoke, the monkey jumped up onto the dressing table and began to open her jewelry box. He selected a pair of aquamarine earrings and held them out to Susannah, who accepted them with a smile. "You think I should wear these tonight?"

The monkey bared his teeth in a grin, so she slipped the earrings into place. "There, how does that look?"

Chatterji jabbered and nodded approvingly.

Anjuli smiled. "He has good taste, that bad monkey," she said, dropping unused pins into a dish. "But if he is naughty tonight, I will put him in his hatbox, with something very heavy on top."

Chatterji recognized the word "hatbox," and his bright eyes went toward the item in question. Then he put his tongue out at the ayah and made a rude noise before darting up to the pelmet, out of reach.

Susannah felt a sudden breath of cold air, and at the same time the fire flared slightly as an evening breeze picked up outside. "Anjuli, do you feel a draft?" she asked.

"A draft, memsahib? Why, yes, now you say it, I do feel such a thing. I will look if a window was been left open." The ayah hastened from window to window, but found them all tightly closed; however, she found the main door of the apartment slightly ajar. Puzzled, she closed it and returned to Susannah. "Memsahib, that is very strange. I know the door was closed a few minutes ago, and yet now it is open." She paused. "And Chatterji has just reappeared," she added pointedly.

Susannah looked swiftly at the monkey. "You don't think he . . . ?"

"Well, he did get out somehow at the hotel, memsahib."

There was a knock at the outer door as the footman arrived with Gareth for the return to the northeastern pavilion. There was no more time to speculate about Chatterji's possible new skill. Susannah donned her blue shawl and left her rooms on Gareth's arm. The latter looked superb, or so she thought, trying not to steal too many glances at him. Formal black suited him so well and was so striking with his fair hair catching the light from the candelabrum carried by the footman. His green eyes were almost magical in such light, and his air of Welsh mystery exerted its influence so strongly that she had to take a deep breath. This wasn't fair—it wasn't fair at all. Why did she have to be so vulnerable to him? When she had been in exile in Bengal, it had almost been comforting to be able to loathe him along with the duke and Fleur Fitzgerald; but from the moment of meeting him again, loathing had been out of the question! Her cheeks flushed in the darkness as they passed through the cold, unlit marble hall, where once again their steps echoed uncannily.

Something made Susannah glance back, and she saw that Mrs. Wilberforce had emerged from the shadows by the entrance to the saloon. She carried no candle, but the white of her face was very clear as she stared after them. Susannah moved instinctively closer to Gareth, who thought she was nervous about the evening ahead. "Courage, *cariad.* I doubt very much that we are about to be poisoned," he said softly.

There was no sign of Minette when they were announced this time, nor was the duke in the same bad humor he had been in before. Indeed, he seemed disposed to be agreeable—well, as agreeable as was possible for a man like Delavel Harmon. It wasn't until they'd adjourned from the drawing room to the dining table that his true colors reemerged.

He beamed at his guests past an epergne that tumbled with fruit and flowers. "I trust you will enjoy the menu tonight, for I rather selfishly chose it myself. The main course is to be wood pigeon, which I know isn't rated very high on the usual lists, but it happens to be my favorite. They're from the estate, of course, and my liking for them gives my keepers an excellent incentive to shoot them." He paused deliberately, then went on. "Because of this, I'm afraid things could be rather hazardous for anyone foolish enough to wander from the signposted ride. Only my keepers are permitted the run of the entire park."

Jane, who had been reasonably at ease until that moment, now became quite flustered and almost knocked over her glass of wine. Neither Susannah nor Gareth quite knew what to say, for the undercurrents in the room were suddenly almost tangible. Susannah suddenly thought of the secretive horseman by the lake. Surely he was too well dressed by far to be one of the duke's gamekeepers? He certainly couldn't have been a poacher! But if he wasn't either, who was he? His furtiveness suggested that he had no right being where he was. She glanced at Jane, who was doing her best to appear unconcerned. Her best wasn't good enough, for it was clear that she was quite rattled by the turn the conversation had taken.

The duke continued to smile at his guests. "So if you wish to ride in the park during your stay, please be sure to follow the signposts. That way you will be safe."

Jane gave a brittle laugh. "Good heavens, Delavel, you make it sound quite frightening."

"I just wish to protect our guests, my dear," he replied smoothly. "One wouldn't wish anything untoward to happen to people who have every right to be here, would one?"

Jane gazed at him like a trapped animal, then with a huge effort turned to Susannah. "Now, then, you promised to tell me all about Chatterji's naughtiness," she prompted with embarrassingly false lightheartedness.

The duke was having none of it. "We were discussing the woods, my dear," he said levelly.

Jane fell awkwardly silent, and Susannah glanced at Gareth, to find his eyes already upon her. They were both wondering what the duke was really getting at, and why Jane was at such nervous pains to divert the conversation. Susannah again found herself thinking of the man by the lake.

The duke proceeded. "Apart from the danger of overzealous gamekeepers, I fear there is now an additional hazard of thieves."

"Thieves?" Gareth repeated. "What do you mean?"

"As you know, I was called urgently back from London. It seems there was an intruder in the house in the small hours of the night before last. The fellow had tied a kerchief over the lower part of his face and wore his top hat pulled very low on his forehead. He had ransacked the library in an unsuccessful search for the key to my wall safe and in desperation was about to employ a crowbar upon the safe itself, when he was interrupted by footmen. He outran them to the woods, where he managed to get clean away."

Jane toyed with her glass, at last seeming to have gotten control of herself. "Well, I'm sure that getting into such a close scrape will deter him from trying again," she said.

The duke grunted. "He left empty-handed, so it is my opinion that he will return."

Gareth looked at him. "What do you think he was after?"

"The safe contains the Exton collection."

The Exton collection? All Susannah could think of was the tiara. If this thief, whoever he was, should manage to steal the entire collection, he would steal the Holland heirloom along with it!

Gareth was a little concerned. "You keep the complete collection in one place? Isn't that rather, er . . . ?"

"Risky?" The duke sat back. "Possibly, but until now there has never been any problem, and the key is kept very securely. Too many people now know about the safe itself—in fact, I doubt if there's a servant who hasn't long been aware that it's in the marble frieze beside the fireplace, even more so since that dastard performed his vandalism with a crowbar. But the key is a very different matter; no one knows where that is, except me." He answered Gareth, but his eyes were upon his wife, who gazed fixedly at the epergne.

Gareth was intrigued. "Do I take it you carry it upon you at all times?"

"No, for pickpockets can be only too skillful. I keep it actually in the library. Would that the place in question were large enough to accommodate everything, but it will only hold the key."

Gareth smiled. "I feel challenged to search for it."

"Feel free to try, sir, for I am quite confident you will be as unsuccessful as the would-be thief."

Susannah's heart had been sinking by the moment. Where on earth could it be? The duke seemed so very confident that she feared she could not succeed either. And if the male intruder hadn't managed to force the safe with a crowbar, what chance did a woman have? Well, she certainly didn't want the intruder to stand any chance at all, so perhaps the duke should be informed about the man by the lake. "I-I believe you are right to think the intruder may return," she said to him, but as she related what she had observed from the window, she was aware of Jane's eyes upon her. Their expression made her wish she had remained silent.

The duke seemed unconcerned. "If it's him, which I suppose it must be, he's too late. Well, almost too late." He chuckled.

Susannah was curious. "What do you mean?"

"The application of a crowbar made it crystal clear to me that the Exton collection requires a new place of safety, one known only to me and one that I alone will prepare. Everything is under way. I expect to finish it tomorrow afternoon, after my usual rounds on the estate. By tomorrow evening, everything will have been moved."

Susannah strove not to show her dismay. A new secret place by this time tomorrow? That meant she would have to exchange the tiara for the fake tonight!

Jane spoke up. "A new place of safety? Don't you mean a new safe, Delavel?"

"No, I mean a new place of safety, and in the meantime I will have the house and grounds doubly guarded."

Jane gave him a puzzled smile. "But Delavel, am *I* not to know where the jewels will be kept from now on? After all, I am supposed to wear them."

"And wear them you shall, my dear. Things will not be so very different, for as it is you ask me for the key. In future you will have to tell me which necklace, ring, or bracelet you require, and I will see that you have it. With the exception of the Holland tiara, of course, but that will be going soon anyway."

Jane gave a sigh. "I wish you weren't selling it, Delavel, for I really rather like it."

His small eyes seemed to become even smaller. "You've only worn it once, my dear, and look what happened then."

Gareth sat forward. "What *did* happen then?" he asked, knowing the answer full well but feeling like stirring the mud a little to see what came to the surface.

There was a moment's heavy silence, during which Fleur Fitzgerald's name was in everyone's head, but then the duke smiled. "Why Abbas Ali saw it, of course, and now he is to buy it from me for a king's ransom."

Gareth raised an eyebrow. "Provided the light-fingered gentleman doesn't get to it tonight," he murmured.

And provided *I* don't get to it either, thought Susannah, sighing inwardly at the thought of trying to find something as tiny as a key in a room as large as the library! What if the duke kept it in one of the books? There were hundreds of them!

Chapter 17

The apartment curtains were undrawn, and the full moon bathed the room with silver as Susannah got out of bed to put on her slippers and frilled pink muslin wrap. Then she took the substitute tiara from the valise and carefully tucked it inside her wrap. She needed to be sure that Chatterji wouldn't impose himself upon her nocturnal activities, so she went to check on the monkey, who had removed his muff from the despised hat-box and was now ensconced in a comfortable chair by the fire-place. He was curled up asleep, with his long tail wrapped around him. His turban and new coat lay on the arm of the chair. In the other bedroom Anjuli's deep breathing signified that she hadn't been disturbed either, so Susannah tiptoed out of the apartment.

She closed the door very softly behind her, then stood there to try to quieten her pounding heart. The passage was cold, and from a window she could see the lake and valley. Everything was crystal clear, like daylight drained of color. At first nothing seemed to move, but then she saw two footmen walking slowly past toward the terrace. They turned and called out to some companions out of sight to her. The duke had warned that the house and grounds would be doubly guarded tonight, and he had meant it. She closed her eyes and took a long, steadying breath. This was it, the moment she had been planning, but suddenly she felt paralyzed with nerves. She pressed her lips frustratedly together. Now wasn't the moment for her resolve to weaken! She was a Holland, and it was her *duty* to take back that which had been taken from her family. Gradually she opened her eyes, and her heart slowed to a more bearable pace.

Clutching the tiara to her breast, she hurried down the stair-case, then past Gareth's apartment on the ground floor. All was still quiet as she reached the doors into the external corridor, and her slippers made no sound as she made her way to the library. She was convinced that the patrolling footmen would deter the other thief, so she concerned herself only with the whereabouts of the all-important key.

At the end of the corridor she paused in the doorway to gaze around the lofty moonlit library, where the outline of the safe was easy enough to make out in the marble frieze beside a caryatid supporting the mantel shelf. As the duke had said, the intruder had been guilty of considerable vandalism when he had applied a crowbar to the delicate sculpture. She continued to look around. Bookshelves stretched from floor to ceiling, and two large Roman sarcophagi were set in the alcoves on either side of the fireplace. The sarcophagi had no lids, and therefore resembled ornate horse troughs, or so she thought. Apart from two sofas, a reading stand, and a wheeled ladder for reaching the topmost bookshelves, the only other item of furniture was an imposing desk, leather-topped and slender-legged, that stood in the center of the room. The desk was the obvious place to start, she decided.

But as she reached for the first drawer, something suddenly landed with a thud on her shoulder. It felt like a hand, and she cried out with fright, thinking someone had caught her in the act, but then came an all too familiar gibbering, and to her huge relief she realized it was only Chatterji. "Oh, you little wretch!" she breathed. Her heart was thundering and she felt so shaken that she had to lean her hands on the desk for a moment to steady herself. Had her cry been heard? She listened carefully but heard nothing. Chatterji, once again dressed in his turban and coat, jumped down onto the desk to inspect the large silver gilt inkstand, which shone enticingly in the light from the windows, and she gave him a cross look. "There are times when I wish I'd left you in Bengal," she muttered, then paused as a thought occurred to her. He had been sound asleep, and she had closed the door behind her, so he couldn't be here now unless he had opened the door himself! It was a skill she wished he had left undiscovered.

She waited a few seconds more, still listening for any sound from the saloon or beyond, but everything was silent, except for Chatterji's little clucking noises as he examined his peculiarly distorted reflection in the inkstand. So she resumed her search, which was soon hampered by the monkey's assistance as he gleefully deserted the inkstand to riffle through everything in the drawers. He was in his element, tossing sheets of paper and letters everywhere until Susannah wagged a very stern finger at him. "No! You're not helping at all," she said firmly and removed his busy paws from a collection of seals he had found. Miffed, he shuffled to the far edge of the desk and sat with his arms crossed and his mouth turned down. It worked, for Susannah immediately felt remorseful. After all, he was only trying to help. She gave him some of the duke's best quills to play with instead and was soon forgiven as he amused himself by bending and chewing them until they were useless for writing. But at least he was quiet, she thought, determining to hide the evidence afterward!

After nearly half an hour of poking and prying, she gave up on the desk and picked up all the scattered papers. She couldn't leave them lying around—they would tell tales. Nor could she hope to replace them in the correct order, or even the correct drawer, so she crammed them all into one drawer and forced it closed. By now Chatterji was bored with the quills and began to grumble in his high-pitched monkey way. He opened the inkwell, and before she knew it he had jammed the quills in upside down. Ink splashed on the pristine leather surface, and Susannah hastily applied the blotter. Then she gathered Chatterji into her arms and stepped back from the desk before he could do any more damage.

It was then that the moon came to her rescue, revealing a faint horizontal line in one of the desk's classically fluted legs. Hardly daring to hope, she ran a fingertip over it. The slight pressure caused a tiny drawer to slide out; in it lay a key that shone in a beam of light from the window. She reached out to take it, but Chatterji was quicker. The gleam of the metal attracted him, and he bounded from her arms to seize the key, then raced away with it to the nearest sofa. There he perched on the scrolled arm, pretending to turn the key in an imaginary lock.

"Bring it back, Chatterji," Susannah commanded.

He put his nose in the air and inspected the key like a jeweler with a fine diamond. Susannah looked at him in despair, knowing that if she took one step toward him, he would leap elsewhere. Oh, plague take all monkeys! This time she couldn't blackmail him with threats to his clothes because he was wearing them. So, what else could she do? For a moment her mind remained blank, but then she decided that the best plan would be to make him think she didn't want the key after all. She went back to the desk and began to go through the biggest drawer again. It happened to be the one containing the seals, which she made a point of rattling. From the corner of her eye she could see Chatterji watching her, so she rattled them again. It was too much for him; he dropped the key and came over to jump right into the drawer in order to see what she was doing.

In a trice she had closed him in. "There, my laddo! You can stay where you are until I've finished."

Chatterji screeched with rage and scratched furiously in an effort to get out, but his noise was muffled by the thickness of the wood. Susannah ignored him as she retrieved the key from the sofa and went to the safe. The key turned sweetly in the lock, and the door opened as if by magic. There were four jewelry caskets inside, and she carried them one by one to the desk. Within each she found the most wonderful treasure trove she could ever have imagined. There was something for every conceivable occasion—necklaces, earrings, brooches, pendants, bracelets, pins, rings, lockets, diadems, and tiaras; then, in the very last box, *the* tiara. She recognized its blue leather case immediately, for she had known it from childhood. Holding her breath, she took out the tiara. Chatterji had fallen silent for a moment, and from the saloon she distinctly heard the opening and closing of the corridor doors to the southwestern pavilion, where lay the chapel and the conservatory. Then came the soft, measured tread of a man crossing the saloon toward the library!

Hastily she exchanged her replica tiara for the real one, then gathered all the jewelry boxes as swiftly and quietly as she could and pushed them into the safe. She fled back to the desk to return the key to its place, but as she tried to open Chatterji's drawer, it jammed tight! The monkey chattered from inside as she struggled with it, but then she dared not stay any longer, for the steps were almost at the entrance to the library. All she could think of was hiding, so she hissed a warning to Chatterji and scrambled into the nearest sarcophagus. Chatterji detected the urgency in her voice and fell silent and still as the man entered the room.

Clutching the tiara very tightly inside her wrap, Susannah raised her head cautiously and saw a tall, top-hatted figure pause just inside the doorway. He had a kerchief tied over the lower part of his face, and he carried a crowbar. It was the intruder. Clearly the duke's extra guards had not proved sufficient. She watched him, then glanced at the desk. To her horror she saw that the key drawer hadn't fully closed but was protruding very visibly in the moonlight. The intruder saw it too, and she heard his triumphant exhalation of breath as he carefully placed the crowbar on the desk, then bent to remove the key. She watched him go to the safe, and take out the caskets, just as she herself had done a few moments before. There was still no sound from Chatterji as the man began to sift through the Exton collection, ignoring everything until he too came to the blue case containing the Holland tiara.

Susannah stared as he removed her replica and took *another* from his pocket! She was shaken to the very core. The intruder was concerned with the tiara and only the tiara? But why? Was it because of its imminent and much vaunted sale to Abbas Ali? Did he think the tiara really was worth the hugely inflated sum the Turk was prepared to pay?

The man pushed her replica into his pocket, then began to replace everything in the safe. He had almost finished when the impossible happened: *more* footsteps approached, a woman's this time, coming swiftly from the marble hall into the saloon. The man closed the safe, and ran back to replace the key, then Susannah ducked hastily out of sight again as he looked desperately around for somewhere to hide. Please don't jump in here with me! she pleaded silently. To her immeasurable relief, he decided a window embrasure offered the better option because although the velvet curtains were not drawn, they were so heavily draped as to provide an ideal hiding place. She heard the slight sound of the folded shutter as he pressed back against it, then there was nothing except the swiftly approaching female footsteps. Susannah raised her head cautiously as the woman entered the library. The latest player on the stage wore a hooded cloak, and Susannah's first suspicion—Jane—was dashed, for this person was much shorter. The actress Fleur Fitzgerald was the second possibility to flash into Susannah's mind, but the woman was too short to be Fleur either.

Over the next minute or so, history repeated itself quite uncannily, for not only had the key drawer failed to close a second time but the woman quickly noticed it and hurried to the safe. She removed the caskets and went through them until she found the blue leather case. Once again, the tiara inside was exchanged for another, then everything was put away. Now there were *four* tiaras! Three fakes and the original. She glanced toward the window and saw the man peering around the curtains as he, too, watched the proceedings. She sensed his confidence that the woman was wasting her time because *he* had the original. But then an awful possibility began to insinuate itself in her mind. What if her own confidence was equally misplaced? Given the astonishing procession of thieves in the Duke of Exton's library tonight—all, no doubt, as intent as she herself was upon taking the tiara before it was sold to the emissary—what if someone *else* had gotten to the bonbon dish before her?

The woman bent to replace the key in the drawer, but at that moment Chatterji became impatient. He rapped hard with one of the seals, and the woman leapt backward with a startled cry. Chatterji responded in no uncertain terms, screeching at the top of his little monkey lungs. The terrified woman fled, and in a trice the man made his getaway back toward the southwestern pavilion, after first casting an alarmed glance at the drawer, from which truly horrible noises were now emanating. The moment the library was empty, Susannah clambered out of the sarcophagus and dashed to release Chatterji. He erupted from imprisonment and bounded away into the guest pavilion corridor. As Susannah ran after him, she heard shouts from outside. Someone had seen the man fleeing from the house and the alarm had been raised.

She reached her apartment and, once inside, leaned thankfully against the door. Only then did she realize that Chatterji hadn't returned ahead of her. So where had he gone? She moved wearily away from the door. So much had happened in the last hour that she felt quite muddle-headed. But she had succeeded in her mission; at least, she hoped she had. She went quickly to the fire to light a candle in order to examine the tiara she had purloined. If it was the genuine article, there would be a tiny scratch, left when her mother had dropped it on her wedding day. Slowly she turned the tiara over in the candlelight. Her heart plummeted as she saw only a flawless surface. Someone else *had* been at the bonbon dish before her! At least *five* tiaras altogether.

Suddenly there came a tap at the door, startling her so that she almost dropped the tiara. "Who is it?" she called quietly, trying not to awaken Anjuli, who thankfully always slept heavily.

"It's me, and I have your wretched monkey," said Gareth's voice.

Chapter 18

In a trice Susannah pushed the tiara behind a cushion on the sofa. Then she straightened her wrap and went to open the door.

Gareth stood there in the moonlight. He wore a sage-green brocade dressing gown, his blond hair was disheveled from sleep, and he held a wriggling Chatterji aloft by the scruff of the neck.

Susannah was dismayed. "Oh, you mustn't do that!" she cried, taking the insulted monkey from him.

"It was the only way to save myself from being bitten," Gareth replied.

Chatterji clenched both fists and jabbered in outrage, but Susannah was more concerned about the voices that she suddenly heard at the foot of the nearby staircase. Gareth watched the expressions cross her face in the silvery light. "Now who on earth could that be?" he murmured.

"I have no idea," she replied, giving him a wide-eyed look. "Well, thank you for bringing Chatterji," she said, taking the wriggling monkey from him and making as if to close the door.

He immediately put a foot in the way. "Oh, no. I have questions to ask you, Susannah."

She was dismayed. "Questions? In the middle of the night?"

"I fear so."

Their eyes met, and as if on cue the voices became louder. If Susannah wasn't mistaken, one of them belonged to Mrs. Wilberforce. "Please return to your apartment, Gareth, for it is hardly seemly for us to be—" she began.

"For us to be what, Susannah?" he interrupted, folding his arms and giving every sign of remaining precisely where he was until she gave in.

"You know perfectly well, sir!"

"Then invite me in and we can discuss how Hector and I found Chatterji," he said reasonably.

She felt like telling him to take himself to perdition, but with Mrs. Wilberforce and the duke's footmen advancing by the second, she knew she had to bow to him. "You leave me no choice," she said and stood aside just as footsteps began to ascend the staircase.

Gareth entered and she closed the door quickly. Within seconds there was a polite knock. "Begging your pardon, Mrs. Leighton?" came Mrs. Wilberforce's low voice.

Susannah waited until Gareth had stepped out of sight just inside her bedroom, then she opened the door, still clutching Chatterji, who squirmed and complained for all he was worth until she tapped a peremptory finger on his nose, at which he subsided into low grumbling. The housekeeper stood outside with a tall, well-built footman who held a lighted candle. Susannah tried not to give a start on seeing him, for it was the pugilist who had followed her in London.

Mrs. Wilberforce's hair hung in two neat plaits, and she wore a warm blue woolen robe over her nightgown. She addressed Susannah respectfully. "I do beg your pardon for disturbing you, madam, but there has been another unfortunate incident with the intruder. The miscreant is still at large, and the duke wishes me to advise you to stay in your apartment."

Susannah managed to look suitably alarmed. "The intruder again? Oh, dear, I-I hope he was not successful this time?"

"He took nothing, madam. We believe he was disturbed in time. You will be safe if you stay inside."

"I will be sure to do that," Susannah said.

Mrs. Wilberforce gave a faint smile. "Well, I won't keep you from your bed, madam," she murmured, then inclined her head and turned to walk away, accompanied by the footman, who shielded his candle with his hand.

Again Susannah closed the door "You can come out now, sir," she said, glancing uneasily toward the other bedroom door. Please let Anjuli sleep on, she thought desperately. The last thing she needed now was to have to cope with the ayah's outraged disapproval because there was a man in the room.

Gareth came back into the drawing room. "Right. I don't think we will be disturbed again, so the time has come for you to answer some questions."

"Oh, has it indeed?" she replied in annoyance. Just who did he think he was?

He paid no heed to her resentment. "Why was Chatterji out and about tonight, Susannah? He let himself into my apartment and jumped all over poor Hector, frightening him half to death."

"Well, I'm very sorry about Hector, but if Chatterji let himself into your apartment, he clearly let himself out of this one." She drew a long breath and went to put the monkey down on his fireside chair, where he immediately hurled off his turban and coat and retreated into his muff in a very surly manner. Susannah turned back to face Gareth. "Chatterji's comings and goings aren't important, Gareth, but I do think you should know that the footman who accompanied Mrs. Wilberforce just now was the man who followed me in London."

"I've already noticed him around and about, and the man who followed me. The Duke of Exton has some very strange servants. While most footmen are chosen for their grace and fine calves, those at Exton Park seem clearly selected for their ability to deal bruises." He rested his hands on the back of the sofa where she had hidden the tiara! Too late she wondered if she had concealed it sufficiently. Please don't let him glance down, for he was by the very cushion . . . !

He studied her for a long time in the flickering light from the candle and the fire. "Oh, Susannah," he murmured, "you are an excellent actress and could probably challenge the great Fleur Fitzgerald, but I can still see through you. Chatterji was out and about tonight because *you* were out and about. Now, are you going to tell me what you've been up to, or am I going to have to guess? And before you answer, you may as well know that I will not budge from here until you tell me what's going on."

"I haven't been up to anything, sir. Chatterji knows how to open and close doors, it's as simple as that." She looked squarely into his eyes across the room.

He smiled. "I suspect you would be excellent at playing cards, too, so perhaps it's as well that establishments like the Union Club do not admit ladies."

"Gareth, there is nothing to tell, so I do wish you would just return to your own apartment."

To her astonishment he left the sofa as if to comply, but then strode swiftly over to seize her by the arms. "There is a long way to go before you have my full trust, Susannah, but I suggest you begin to earn it by being honest with me about tonight! What have you to do with the intruder?"

"Nothing! Nothing at all, I *swear* it! Now please let me go!" she gasped, glancing at Anjuli's door again.

He could feel her warmth through her flimsy wrap and he could smell the faint fragrance of flowers that seemed to cling to her hair. Both were affecting him more than he wished. "I wish I could believe you, Susannah," he breathed, conscious of arousal stirring through his body.

She was so aware of him that it was as if a current of electricity were passing through her. "Please let me go, Gareth," she whispered, but her entire being ached to say the opposite. *Hold me close, make love to me, stay with me until dawn. . . .*

He saw the paradox in her eyes, felt it flood through him from the fingers that touched her. She was trapped by her own sensuality; they both were. Slowly he put a hand to the nape of her neck and forced her lips to his. She tried to struggle, tried to push him away, tried everything she could to pretend she didn't want the kiss. But she did want it, she wanted it so much that she knew she would surrender completely if he wished it. There was no perhaps, perhaps not, just a wonderful elation that swept her toward complete abandonment. Gareth felt her soften in his arms as their shared desire kindled into a burning flame. His body molded to hers, and as she responded he felt control ebbing. No counterfeit kiss this. . . .

The sensuous spell was shattered by Anjuli's outraged voice. "Unhand my memsahib this instant, Sir Gareth sahib, or—or I will strike you upon your wicked head!"

Gareth whirled about to see the furious ayah advancing upon him with a poker. Chatterji, deciding to add his contribution, bounded to the table in the middle of the room and began to hurl grapes at Gareth. Each one found its target, and when he ran out of grapes, he resorted to a large and very squashy peach. Luckily for Gareth, it fell short.

Susannah, covered with confusion and dismay, hid her face in her hands. This was not happening, it *could* not be happening.

Anjuli waved the poker threateningly. "Out you go, Sir Gareth sahib!" she cried.

He looked at Susannah, then left without another word. Chatterji was ecstatic. Revenge had never been more sweet, and as the door closed upon his enemy, he tossed another soft peach as hard as he could. It burst very messily against the gleaming woodwork, and Susannah rounded on him. "For heaven's sake, Chatterji, you've caused enough trouble tonight! Go to your muff this instant!" she cried.

The monkey's face fell, and he sullenly did as she commanded. Susannah then faced the ayah, trying to find words to explain away what had happened. "Anjuli . . ." Her voice trailed into silence.

Anjuli looked anxiously at her. "Sir Gareth sahib is a bad fellow, memsahib. I thought better of him than to force himself upon you in such a terrible way."

Susannah knew she had to be truthful. "He wasn't forcing himself, Anjuli."

The ayah's lips parted, but instead of delivering the expected lecture, she spoke very gently. "Memsahib, you were a good and faithful wife who patiently endured Leighton sahib's thoughtlessness and neglect, so maybe it is now time for you to flower again. But please be certain that Sir Gareth sahib is the right bee." With that she replaced the poker in the hearth and went back to her bed.

Susannah stood there for a long moment, struggling to regain her woefully lost composure, then she made herself put the second fake tiara safely away. What a dreadful, dreadful night! Nothing had gone right. First she exchanged one replica tiara for another, and now this. Tears pricked her eyes. For the first time in her life she was falling in love. Until Sir Gareth Carew she had never known what true desire could be, but she knew it now. Oh, yes, how she knew it now.

Chapter 19

Susannah felt far from refreshed when she was awakened the following morning by the sound of a carriage departing from the stableyard. The morning sun was warm, and because Anjuli had crept in a little earlier to open the window, sounds from outside were carried on the light breeze. Susannah opened her eyes. It hadn't been the sound of the carriage itself that had disturbed her, but the shout of Gareth's postilion, Billings, as he brought the fresh, impatient team into hand for the journey to the coach builder in Cirencester. She lay there remembering what had happened as they arrived the evening before. Something had been wrong with the landau axle. Her brows drew together. What had Gareth said? A safeguard? She had meant to ask him more but had forgotten all about it until now.

Anjuli came in with the tray of morning tea, Susannah's favorite Assam. "Good morning, memsahib," Anjuli said, placing the tray beside the bed and then going to fling back the curtains.

Susannah made herself sit up. "Good morning, Anjuli," she answered, pushing her disheveled hair back from her face and blinking as the morning sunlight streamed into the room. Memories of the night were only too sharp, and she knew her cheeks were still tinged with a guilty flush.

"Breakfast will be served in exactly one hour, memsahib."

"I-I think I will dispense with breakfast," Susannah replied, giving in to a weasel urge to avoid facing Gareth.

The ayah was aghast. "Go without breakfast, memsahib? Oh, no, that will not do at all! Breakfast is the most important meal of the day."

"I don't feel at all hungry."

"Only because you were very foolish in the night," the ayah pointed out.

Susannah gave her a look. "Anjuli, there are times when I wish you had remained at Chinsura."

"Maybe, but I am here, and it is my duty to see that you eat properly."

Susannah knew when the ayah meant what she said, and so she didn't argue anymore, but the prospect of breakfast was far from pleasant. It wasn't the business of the tiaras that upset her so this morning but the certainty that she had made a grave mistake with Gareth. She had behaved like a wanton, and he was bound to judge her for it. She was wrapped in her dismal thoughts as Anjuli handed her a cup of tea.

"Come now, memsahib, there is no need to be so doleful."

"I made an utter idiot of myself last night," Susannah replied unhappily, not even able to raise a smile when the ayah brought a tiny porcelain dish from the dressing room and poured Chatterji a cup of tea as well. The monkey had ventured out of his muff the moment the tea arrived, and now sat neatly at the foot of the bed, the dish held in both paws as he drank. He wore his turban and yellow coat and was on his best behavior. Anjuli had cleaned away the sticky mess of peach from the door and had wagged a stern finger at him afterward. He knew when he was in everyone's bad books, and he had evidently decided to be at his angelic best in an effort to redeem himself.

Anjuli came to rest a gentle hand on her mistress's shoulder. "I am sure Sir Gareth sahib did not think you were an idiot, memsahib. I saw how he held you, how he wanted you. And I saw how you wanted him."

"Yes, I did," Susannah admitted.

"Just remember what I say about flowers and bees, memsahib. Bees are needed by the flower, but bees can also sting. Just be sure of this bee before you let him sip the nectar."

Susannah had to smile. "I'll try, Anjuli, truly I will, but when he kisses me . . ."

Anjuli raised her hands. "Oh, I know, memsahib, indeed I do!"

"You do?"

"Did you think there were no bees in Chinsura?"

"But did they sting you?"

"One or two, maybe, but there were others . . ." Anjuli raised her eyebrows and pursed her lips smilingly.

"Do you miss any of these . . . others?"

"Oh, no, memsahib, not now that—" The ayah broke off, and

Susannah looked up swiftly to see an unexpectedly coy look on the ayah's face.

"Not now that what, Anjuli?"

"Nothing, memsahib."

"Come on, Anjuli, tell me."

"Well, it is Hector, memsahib."

Susannah stared up at her. "You and *Hector*?"

"He is a very kind man, memsahib, and I like him very much. I think too that he likes me. At least, he likes it that I can cook curry. He is very fond of curry, very fond indeed." The ayah smiled. "There, now we both have a secret, memsahib."

Susannah didn't know what to say, for Anjuli and Hector Ambleforth were the very last people she would have expected to become a pair.

The ayah went toward the dressing room. "Which gown shall I put ready, memsahib?"

"The yellow-and-white lawn, I think."

"As you wish, memsahib." There was a pause, and then Anjuli looked back into the bedroom. "You will not have to take breakfast with the duke sahib, for he has gone out on his horse. He is going down toward the lake at this very moment."

"Is he?" Susannah stretched up in the bed to look out of the window. Sure enough, the duke was riding swiftly down the slope from the house. He wore the same bright-red coat she had seen at Grillion's, and there was something very purposeful about the way he rode. The usual estate rounds, he had said, she recalled. A herd of deer scattered before him, and as he reached the lakeside, a flock of started waterfowl rose from the water.

Susannah's gaze went to the scene in general. The valley basked in the May sunshine, and beyond it the rich and beautiful Cotswold Hills rolled toward an indistinct horizon. The woods were hazy with bluebells, and here and there the spring foliage was dotted with a tree in full blossom. Down by the lake, where the flat rock jutted beneath the copper beech, all was very still and quiet. There was no one hiding there today, she thought.

At that moment there came a light knock at the door. "Susannah, are you awake?" It was Jane.

Anjuli hastened to admit her, but the instant the door was opened, Minette hurtled excitedly in, tail wagging. The poodle ran around and around the apartment, barking occasionally, and

Chatterji lowered his dish of tea in horror, for all the world as if he were a maiden aunt instead of a very wayward monkey.

Jane entered, looking very fresh and almost pretty in an apricot silk robe that became her very well indeed. "Oh, I do apologize for Minette! I'm afraid she gets quite carried away. Minette! Behave this instant!" she cried, unable to keep from laughing as the foolish poodle jumped up at her and almost knocked her over.

Chatterji told the poodle off, and Minette whirled about at the strange sound. Never having seen a monkey before, she immediately came over to investigate, standing up with her front paws on the bed. Chatterji set his almost empty dish aside and advanced cautiously until he could touch the poodle's springy coat. Both animals eyed each other curiously, and then Chatterji decided he liked the peculiar curly dog and jumped onto her back. Minette leapt away in shock, then turned around and around as she tried to look at him.

Jane gave a squeal of delighted laughter. "Oh, look! I *knew* they would be amazing together!"

Minette suddenly gave up her pointless revolutions and trotted to the open door. Chatterji's face bore an uncertain expression, but he didn't leap off. The duo departed, like a small horse with a diminutive rider, and Susannah turned anxiously at Anjuli. "Don't let Chatterji go! We don't know what he'll get up to!"

"Certainly, memsahib," the ayah replied and began to hurry away, but Jane called her back.

"Don't worry, they will be quite all right. If Exton Park can cope with Minette, it can cope with a monkey." She sat on the edge of the bed. "Chatterji is as enchanting as I remembered, and I'm absolutely delighted you've brought him. He and Minette will be fast friends within minutes, I promise you."

Susannah smiled, then changed the subject. "I see the duke will not be joining us for breakfast?" She nodded toward the window. "I saw him leave," she explained.

"He said he has much to do this morning, and so he has set out early. He makes his apologies, of course."

"I almost envy him riding out on a day like this."

"Would you like to ride this morning as well? It can easily be arranged. We could go together, Sir Gareth as well."

"Well, I did say *almost* envy. You see, I'm a rather indiffer-

ent horsewoman. No, that's not true. I'm a dreadful horsewoman!" Oh, the humiliation she had always endured because
of her equestrian incompetence. She must have been the only
gentlewoman in Lincolnshire who could not ride to hounds like
a Valkyrie!

Jane brushed her protests aside. "Then a horse will be provided that is as comfortable and steady as an armchair. No argument—a ride it is."

Susannah managed a reluctant smile, for she did not know
which was worse, the thought of having to ride or of having to
confront Gareth. "Very well, but on your head be it if I make
a spectacle of myself."

"I'm sure you won't do any such thing."

"I hope not."

"We'll follow the five-mile circuit. It's really rather good, leading past a succession of follies and so on; I especially like the
ruined abbey, for it has such atmosphere!" Her face became serious. "But you must promise to remain on the track as Delavel
warned."

"I wouldn't dream of doing otherwise." Susannah looked at
her. "Will we *really* be in danger from the keepers if we don't?"

"Well, I-I could not really say, but it's best not to find out the
hard way, don't you think?" Jane gave a quick smile, suggesting that in spite of her words, she definitely *did* think they would
be in danger.

Susannah cleared her throat uncomfortably. "At least a ride
will give us the opportunity to discuss everything we need to.
Unless, of course, you'd like to talk now?"

"I-I think I'd rather wait," Jane said, her glance wandering
toward Anjuli, who was busying herself at the dressing table,
putting out pins, comb, brush, and ribbons in readiness.

Susannah would have sent the ayah on an errand, but Jane
prevented her. "No, it's all right. We can talk properly when we
are out riding. It's probably better that way."

"As you wish." So the long-awaited explanation was to be delayed again. Susannah sipped her tea, beginning to think that the
cancellation of the drive in Hyde Park was no coincidence either. Jane was postponing the moment for as long as she could.
Susannah would have liked to be forthright about her thoughts
but couldn't bring herself to it, and so she changed the subject.
Well, diverted it slightly. "I gather the house had an unwanted

visitor last night? I know because Mrs. Wilberforce came to the door to advise me not to leave these rooms."

Jane looked quickly away. "It was the same man as before, but something scared him off and he was seen running from the house. Nothing was taken from the safe."

That's what you think, thought Susannah, recalling the succession of thieves in the library.

Jane fiddled with a fringe on the bed coverlet. "Well, he has been thwarted now, because by tonight Delavel's new hidey-hole will be ready and the old safe quite empty."

"Yes." Susannah's thoughts wandered to the puzzle of the real tiara. She felt further away from her goal than ever before. Why hadn't it been in the safe along with everything else? The duke had distinctly said that it was here at Exton Park and that the entire Exton collection was in the safe. Yet when she had opened that blue leather case, the tiara inside had been a replica. Who else had had their fingers in the bonbon dish? Another party intent upon gaining the tiara before it was sold? Or had the duke himself performed the exchange, for reasons that might be anyone's guess? All she knew for certain was that after all that creeping around in the middle of the night, she still did not have what she had come here for. And by tonight the old safe would be empty and everything moved elsewhere. Not that finding the new hiding place would avail her of anything, for she knew that the tiara now reposing in the blue leather case had been placed there by the mysterious cloaked woman, who was hardly likely to have come to conveniently remove a copy and leave the real thing. Oh, how truly *vexing* it all was!

Anjuli finished at the dressing table and went to straighten one of the bedroom curtains, which did not hang just as she liked. Something outside caught her attention. "Memsahib, may I speak?"

"Of course. What is it, Anjuli?" Susannah answered.

"I could not help overhearing what you have just said, and now I wonder if the intruder is watching the house at this very moment?"

"What makes you say that?"

"Well, a fellow has just appeared by the edge of the lake, and he is behaving in a manner most suspicious."

Susannah got quickly out of bed, and she and Jane went to

the window. Anjuli pointed. "There, by that big red tree. Do you
see him?"

Sure enough, the man was beneath the copper beech again,
his face turned toward the house. "Who is he, I wonder?" Susannah murmured.

"I-I have no idea," Jane answered.

"He's certainly taking a risk, given what the duke said last
night about his keepers firing willy-nilly at pigeons."

"Yes, I know." Jane's voice was barely above a whisper, and
Susannah looked quickly at her. The Duchess of Exton knew
more than she was admitting!

At that moment a shotgun went off in the woods. The man
jerked back out of sight, and the reverberation of the shot was
lost amid the alarm cries of waterfowl startled from the lake.
The herd of deer bolted, fleeing from the open into the trees,
and a dog began to bark excitedly somewhere close to the house;
Susannah thought it was Minette.

Anjuli opened the window, and the barking became much more
loud as she leaned out to peer down where the man had been.
All was now still. "Well, memsahib, either the unfortunate fellow has managed to escape or he is lying wounded, maybe even
dead," she declared bluntly.

Chapter 20

It was when Jane cried off the ride that Susannah knew for certain the duchess was deliberately avoiding the issue of explaining. First Hyde Park, then in the bedroom this morning, and now this. At first glance Jane's reason for not accompanying her two guests on the ride seemed genuine enough—there was a crisis in the kitchens that required the presence of the mistress of the house—but Susannah sensed that the crisis was fictitious.

But if Jane didn't join the ride, Minette and Chatterji certainly did. As the poodle dashed ahead of the horses with the monkey clinging to his back, Chatterji's turban and coat looked like the racing silks of a miniature jockey. The two had already become inseparable, just as Jane had predicted.

Susannah's emerald-green riding habit was very bright in the morning sunshine, and its cut and style were so classic that its Calcutta origins were virtually impossible to detect. With it she wore a jaunty brown top hat with a little net veil that concealed most of her face. She had been provided with a sedate roan mare whose high-stepping action betrayed some hackney blood, but high-stepping or not, the animal was indeed as steady and comfortable as the promised armchair, especially at the easy trot with which the excursion commenced.

Confronting Gareth again had been more difficult than she had feared, since he behaved as if nothing whatsoever had happened between them! Contrary to making her feel easier, this upset her all the more. With all the contrariness of her sex, what she had *really* wanted was for him to sweep her into his arms again the moment he saw her. Instead he had been the epitome of gallantry and manners, and the only kiss she had received had been upon her hand! She saw things very much in black and white; she was sure that he regretted last night and wished to pretend it hadn't happened! Her humiliation complete, she wished she had emulated Jane and avoided the ride.

If Gareth sensed her feelings, he gave no outward sign; the previous night had not happened, and that was that. Unlike the duke, he wore the pine-green coat that was de rigueur for gentlemen riders, and his horse was certainly not an armchair. The head groom had selected for him a large black thoroughbred with bright, determined eyes and a fiery temperament, but there was nothing indifferent about Gareth's horsemanship, and he kept the animal very much in check, even when Minette and Chatterji dashed right in front of it.

Susannah grappled with her complex emotions. It took a superhuman effort, but somehow she triumphed, and when they were well clear of the house, she appeared quite calm and collected as she told him her suspicions regarding Jane. "Our hostess is doing all she can to postpone, if not actually prevent, the moment of truth. I'm also sure she knows who the gentleman watcher is."

He reined in swiftly at this, and she told him about the conversation in her bedroom before breakfast. "And when Anjuli said that the man must be lying wounded or dead, I thought Jane would faint away. She went quite white, and it was all she could do not to burst into tears. She made an excuse to hurry away, but I heard her sob as she went downstairs."

"How very intriguing," he murmured, glancing back up toward the house.

"What can be going on here?" Susannah wondered aloud. "We have a duke who seems to have an ulterior motive for every word he utters, a duchess who behaves very peculiarly, a strange gentleman who spies from the trees, and a persistent nighttime intruder." A thicket of thieves, a tangle of tiaras; old Uncle Tom Cobbley and all . . .

"And a lady guest with secrets," Gareth added.

She glanced at him. "The gentleman guest being as pure as the driven snow, I suppose."

"Oh, I confess there are footprints in the snow—quite a few, actually," he replied, then kicked his heels to urge his horse into a gallop down the slope toward the first lake. Minette hurtled after him, with Chatterji gibbering at the top of his lungs.

Susannah hesitated, and then gingerly persuaded the mare to follow, although when the animal broke into a swift canter, she panicked and tried to slow down again. Oh, the shame of it! The shame of *everything!*

Gareth waited for her at the water's edge, by a signpost indicating that the circuit of the park was formed by a track that wound past the lake and disappeared into the trees some three hundred yards away in the direction of the second lake, which could not be seen from down here in the valley. Across the water, directly opposite where he waited, was the copper beech where the gentleman had been. Chatterji and Minette were with him, the poodle lying on the grass with her tongue lolling foolishly, the monkey standing on his hind legs, the better to watch the brilliance of the sunlight upon the gently washing water.

When Susannah reined in, Gareth gave her a wry smile. "Well, you told me you weren't an equestrienne, and you did not lie."

"I can hardly keep it a secret," she replied, hauling upon the reins to halt her mount before it continued into the lake.

Gareth leaned across to steady the animal by the bridle. "No doubt you'll have greatly improved by the time we return to the house. Five miles is quite a long ride." He released the now quiet mare.

"Right now five miles seems endless."

"Come now, I'm sure you'll enjoy it if you try."

The words struck a chord. "That's what my brother used to say."

He was surprised. "I didn't know you had a brother."

"We, er, we fell out, and I haven't seen him in ages." She looked deliberately away, signifying that the subject was closed, and he took the hint, but she felt she had been abrupt and so sought something else to say. The morning departure of the landau sprang to mind. "I heard Billings leaving with the landau this morning. You said something yesterday about a safeguard. What did you mean?" she asked.

"It's too long a story to tell you now, and besides, it isn't important." He turned in the saddle to look across the lake. "Where exactly did you see the man?"

Clearly two could close a subject, she thought, and she took the hint as well. "The man? I'll show you," she said, but as she began to maneuver her horse toward the quickest way around the lake, which meant leaving the signposted route, Gareth grasped the bridle again to stop her.

"*I'm* going to look, Susannah. You're going to stay here."

"Why?"

"The duke warned us not to leave the track, and I intend to see to it that you at least do exactly that."

"But it's all right if *you* go?"

"Danger and I are old friends."

She thought she detected male condescension and so responded with female tartness. "Ah, yes, the so-called 'business' you mentioned in Piccadilly. No doubt you seek to impress with such bragging, but it certainly doesn't impress me."

For once he had no sense of humor. "I'm not bragging, madam. I go abroad as a secret government agent for Lord Hawkesbury—although not so secret now, thanks to chitter-chatter at his lordship's dinner table—and I have been in many a corner far tighter than the Duke of Exton's woods. So please oblige me by staying here!"

"A secret government agent?" she repeated incredulously.

"That's what I said. Now, I repeat—where did you see the man?"

Not knowing quite whether to believe him or not, she pretended to give in to him. "Very well. He was beneath that copper beech opposite." She pointed with her riding crop.

"You wait here while I take a look. I'll rejoin you in a few minutes." Before she could say anything more, he urged his horse away around the lake. Minette and Chatterji needed no second bidding. The monkey remounted his woolly racehorse, and they charged noisily after Gareth, Minette barking, Chatterji gibbering.

Susannah waited a while, and then she followed as well. If Sir Gareth Carew thought he could order *her* around, he would have to think again! Gareth had reached the copper beech by the time he realized what she was doing. He faced her angrily as she rode toward him. "Madam, I told you to stay where you were!"

"I don't like being *told,* sir."

"I had your safety in mind," he said coldly.

"Well, I am not a servant whom you may order at will." She was in a defiant mood, and to emphasize her point she slipped lightly down from the saddle and walked beneath the tree to look at the rock where the man had been. She passed Minette and Chatterji, who were sprawled together in the cool grass. The poodle was out of breath, but the monkey, who after all had done very little, was playing with something he had found. Susannah hardly glanced at it, for she was more concerned with the mysterious watching man—and with putting Sir Gareth Carew well and truly in his place!

Gareth pressed his lips together in annoyance, but as he watched her walk away, her figure shown off so well by her riding habit, his irritation began to fade into something else. Now just how well would she look *without* the riding habit? Without anything at all, preferably. Too good, he decided philosophically. Too damned good by far. "Oh, plague take it!" he muttered and dismounted. If it hadn't been for Anjuli's untimely interruption. . . . Today he simply hadn't known how to approach Susannah. For the first time in his life—his *experienced* life!—he had felt like a naïve boy. He had wanted to crush his lips to hers again, but all he had done was kiss her hand. Her hand! Damn it all above, what good was that? And now they were strangers again; no, not strangers exactly, more accomplices. It wasn't what he wanted, it wasn't what he wanted at all.

He went to join her by the rock, and together they looked across the shimmering sheet of water toward the house. The view was perfect, and Exton Park looked quite magnificent on the slope opposite. What a shame, Susannah thought, that such an estate should belong to the likes of Delavel Harmon. Gareth glanced around at the ground. There were hoofprints leading out of the woods and then back into them again, but that was all.

Susannah watched him. "I wonder who the man is?" she mused.

"Jane's lover?" Gareth replied lightly.

Susannah stared at him. "Do you think so?"

"It's as likely an explanation as any. We are agreed that the duke may suspect me of being her lover, but I know I'm not. However, he may still have good reason to doubt her fidelity. Her behavior is hardly that of a relaxed, contented wife, and on your own admission she reacted rather oddly when that shot was fired earlier. I'm sure that's what is behind all this. The duke rightly suspects his wife but wrongly concludes that I am the cause."

"Even so, he has no business playing the outraged husband." Susannah was again thinking of Fleur Fitzgerald.

Gareth smiled a little. "We've been over *that* too, and we are in agreement."

Chatterji came over to her and held up the thing he had been playing with. It was a little silk label, brightly stitched with gold, such as might be found inside a hat. Indeed, that was exactly what it was, for when she took it from the monkey and looked more closely, she saw the words "McArthur's, Hatters, Boston" woven into it. "Look at what Chatterji has found," she said, handing it to Gareth.

He examined it. "Our man must have connections in Lincolnshire," he murmured.

"I suppose so." Her home county. How very odd a coincidence, she thought, bending to pick up the monkey, who was stretching up his arms like a child wanting a cuddle. The monkey chattered delightedly and was about to nestle down in her embrace when something made him stiffen and stand up to look over her shoulder. She could feel him quivering as his gaze fixed on a point where the woods peeled back from the shore. Then Minette got up as well, growling low in her throat as she, too, stared toward the same place. Susannah turned to look. At first she saw only a dense carpet of bluebells and young ferns uncurling prettily beneath the trees, but she soon sensed what the animals already knew.

Quickly she put a hand on Gareth's arm. "We're being spied upon!" she breathed.

"Who? Where?" he demanded, his gaze raking the surrounding trees.

She nodded at the point in question, trying hard not to be obvious about it. "Over there. Chatterji and Minette can see someone, but I can't. Let's go away from here, Gareth. I don't like it."

He lifted Chatterji down. "Go to Minette," he ordered, and the monkey seemed to know what was expected, for he ran straight to the waiting poodle and scrambled onto her back. Then Gareth took Susannah by the hand. "Don't be afraid, *cariad,* it's probably only a Peeping Tom gamekeeper," he said reassuringly as he led her quickly back to the waiting horses.

But as they made their way back around the lake toward the track, Susannah could still feel the watching eyes upon them, and she did not think they belonged to a gamekeeper.

Chapter 21

Drift upon drift of bluebells spread gloriously on either side of the signposted track as Susannah and Gareth left the first lake and rode into the woods. The prying eyes near the copper beech were virtually forgotten, and Susannah laughed as Minette bounced ecstatically through the flowers with Chatterji tightly gripping the scruff of her neck.

As Jane had said, the circuit was designed to encompass a succession of follies, each one standing in a glade or clearing. First there was a temple of Flora, graceful and perfect in its classical symmetry, then a rustic cottage where picnics could be enjoyed beside a stream. Next came a subterranean grotto that was built into a gentle rise in the shore of the second lake. The track emerged from the trees within yards of the grotto, then swung away from the lake again almost immediately, plunging back into the woods in the direction of the third lake, and eventually the house.

The second lake was on the boundary of the park, and a high perimeter wall was just visible beyond a tall stand of conifers that shielded the grotto from public view. The conifers were thick, but through them there was a glimpse of the rusting gates and crumbling lodge of an access to the park that had been abandoned to ensure the seclusion of the grotto.

As Susannah and Gareth paused to rest the horses, they heard the trickle of water coming from the grotto and saw that a spring had been channeled out of the bank into a little raised pool, where a reclining statue of Venus trailed a graceful stone hand. Minette showed scant respect for the goddess, placing front paws on her thigh in order to lap from the pool. Chatterji drank too, his tail curling up like a question mark as he balanced precariously on the pool's narrow, mossy edge. Forget-me-nots bloomed around the spring, and dragonflies whirred on the air, their bright blue-green bodies and wings flashing brilliantly in the sunlight. Wild honeysuckle climbed around the grotto entrance, where shell-studded steps led underground, and the young green blades of yellow flags sprang up out of the damp ground where water from the pool overflowed.

Gareth stood up in his stirrups to look at the lodge and gates through the conifers. His eyes narrowed, and then he smiled. "I believe this is the way our man comes and goes."

"Why do you say that?"

"Because the gates have been forced open recently and overgrown shrubs damaged in the process."

She stretched up in the saddle to look as well and saw that he was right. The view wasn't good, but she could see how the foliage had been thrust aside when the gates had been used again after a long interval.

"Well, now, that's interesting," Gareth murmured.

"What is?"

"There's a chain and padlock, so whoever opened the gates must have had a key. Stay here while I take a look." He urged his horse around the conifers toward the lodge. She heard the metallic rattle of the gates as he tested them, then he rode back. "Whoever it is not only has a key but also has a liking for oddly feminine cloth." He showed her a torn fragment of sapphire-blue silk.

Susannah stared at it. "That doesn't look like anything a man would wear."

"It certainly doesn't, but there are men and men." Gareth smiled and tucked the cloth into his pocket.

"If he's *that* sort of man, I cannot imagine he's also Jane's lover," Susannah pointed out.

Gareth laughed. "You must have led a very sheltered life in India, Susannah Leighton! Come on, let's continue the ride."

They continued along the track, and soon the grotto was far behind. After about five minutes, however, they came upon a great oak tree newly felled right across the way. It could only have lain there a day or so, for the leaves had yet to wither and the splintered wood was very fresh and white. A makeshift sign post had been erected, little more than a rudely carved arrow nailed to a post, indicating a path that wended its way through the trees to the left.

Gareth reined in curiously. "It would seem a change of route has been decreed," he observed.

"I wonder why we can't ride on?" Susannah asked.

"It could be anything—and this time I don't intend to deviate. If the path is where the arrow points, then the path is where we'll go."

But at that moment Minette bounded past the tree and away down the closed track with Chatterji bumping on her back. "Minette! Come back!" Susannah called in dismay, but to no avail, for the poodle went merrily on.

Gareth muttered something very rude in Welsh, then looked at Susannah. "You stay here. I'll go after them, for heaven knows why the track has been closed."

"I'm not staying here," she answered quickly, suddenly remembering the watching eyes by the copper beech.

"Susannah—"

"No!" She looked mulishly at him, and he gave in.

"Oh, very well, but be damned careful."

They rode around the tree and then on along the track. Of Minette and Chatterji there was now no sign, nor was there any response when the two delinquents were called. Susannah began to feel anxious, for until now the animals had always been audible, if not visible. Suddenly another clearing opened before them, in the center of which stood an eastern temple built on the flat top of a low, stepped pyramid. Its stonework was richly carved with monkeys and other exotic animals, and the entire structure, which could not have been more than forty years old, had been given a romantically decayed appearance. Vines and other creeping plants had been deliberately trained all over it, and extraneous pieces of masonry lay in the grass at the foot of the pyramid, as if the entire edifice was awaiting discovery in the heart of an unexplored jungle.

All was quiet, but then both Susannah and Gareth heard a muffled bark from inside the temple. Susannah called. "Minette? Minette, come on out! And you, Chatterji!"

Almost immediately Chatterji came bounding out into the sunshine, his turban and coat bright specks of color against the gray stonework. He dashed down the steps to the grass, then jumped up and down, jabbering and waving a paw toward the temple. Susannah understood. "Something's happened to Minette."

Gareth groaned. "I don't know who's more stupid, the poodle for going in there in the first place or me for following," he grumbled, dismounting and making his horse fast to one of the pieces of masonry.

"I'll come with you," Susannah said, slipping down from the saddle before he could argue.

He gave her a weary look. "Is there *any* point in asking you to stay out here?"

"None whatsoever."

"Then stay close to me," he instructed, taking her hand and leading her up the pyramid steps toward the temple doorway. Chatterji loped up ahead of them and disappeared into the darkness within.

Minette barked again, and this time the sound ended on a mournful howl that made Susannah shiver. "I can't say I exactly like this place," she said.

"It's hardly Grillion's," Gareth murmured, assisting her up the final step to the entrance, where a slight draft fluttered the encroaching vines and creepers. Slowly they both went inside, and as Susannah's eyes became accustomed to the dark, she realized to her surprise that there was absolutely nothing there. It was quite empty! So where was Minette? And Chatterji, come to that?

"Minette?" called Gareth, and from somewhere apparently in the depths of the earth came the poodle's relieved response. Then Chatterji reappeared, apparently out of the solid floor! Gareth produced a little bottle of lucifers from his pocket, extracted one, and held it up until it ignited. The swaying flame revealed a rectangular opening in the floor, with steps leading down into the heart of the pyramid. Minette seemed able to see the light, for her barks became positively ecstatic.

"All right, all right, I'll get you out somehow," Gareth promised, then eyed Susannah in the flickering light. "This time you *will* stay here. Is that clear?"

"But—"

"Susannah!"

"Yes, I'll stay here," she promised quickly.

The first lucifer went out, so he lit another, then thrust his top hat into her hands before descending the steps. He was watched closely by Chatterji, who peered down after him, and after a moment Susannah advanced curiously to the edge as well. The light of the flame flickered faintly far below. "Can you see her?" she called.

"Yes. The steps have crumbled, and she's slipped behind some loose stonework. Oh, damn!" There was a thud as if a piece of masonry had fallen, and Minette yelped as there came the sound of spilling water. The lucifer went out, and the Welsh oaths that then drifted up to Susannah did not bear translation.

After a moment, she called down anxiously. "Are you all right?"

"Yes, just plaguey soaked through! There was rainwater trapped behind a stone. I moved the stone to get at this idiotic dog, and I got a drenching for my pains! Anyway, I'll have her out in a moment." There followed some grunts and more Welsh mutterings, then some happy whining. Paws pattered up the steps, and a very wet Minette appeared. She dashed for the doorway and disappeared into the sunshine, and Chatterji bounded eagerly after her.

After a moment Gareth ascended from the depths. He was very wet, and Susannah's eyes were now so accustomed to the shadows that she could clearly see the dirty marks on his hitherto pristine riding breeches. He took his top hat from her and rammed it down on his disheveled hair. "That's *more* costly apparel successfully ruined by other people's animals!" he muttered.

"Well, I'll gladly apologize again for Chatterji's misconduct at the inn, but I can't be held to account for Minette too."

He gave a wry smile. "True, but you were unscathed then as well. Is there some secret? Why is it that *I* am always on the firing line, while you remain spotlessly, exquisitely elegant?"

"In my out-of-date Calcutta clothes?"

Their eyes met in the gloom. "Being à la mode does not necessarily make the woman. You, my lovely Susannah, will always be exquisitely elegant to your very fingertips, and the latest fashionable rage will not change that."

"That is a very flattering compliment, sir."

"It is merely the truth. Now, let's get out of here," he said, taking her by the arm and leading her toward the entrance. But as they emerged into the daylight again, they found that the clearing was no longer empty, for the duke and two of his gamekeepers were riding toward the pyramid, having just seen the two tethered horses. Of Minette and Chatterji there was once again no sign.

Chapter 22

The duke reined in, his face dark with displeasure as he looked up the steps at Susannah and Gareth. "Didn't you see the sign at the fallen oak?" he demanded, his small eyes moving swiftly from one to the other.

Gareth was provoked. "Yes, we saw, but the duchess's poodle didn't!" he snapped.

Fearing a clash, Susannah stepped hastily forward. "Minette went missing, and Chatterji with her. You could hardly expect us not to look for them." As she spoke she saw the two animals concerned peeping from behind one of the larger pieces of masonry scattered on the grass.

"It would have been better if you had not, Mrs. Leighton, for by ignoring both the signs and my warning, you placed yourselves at hazard. Besides, all animals eventually find their way home," the duke replied.

"Minette wouldn't have been able to. She was trapped inside this pyramid," Gareth answered.

"The unsafe condition of the pyramid is the very reason my men diverted your route."

Gareth was amazed. "A mature oak in perfectly healthy condition was felled simply to persuade two riders to go another way? That's a little extreme, isn't it?"

"I've decided to make another clearing at that point. Jane has a fancy for a Chinese pagoda, and I am always ready to grant her wishes. But none of this alters the fact that you ignored my warnings. The temple is not the only hazard in these woods." The duke indicated his armed companions, who on closer inspection weren't keepers at all but the two footmen who'd followed Susannah and Gareth in London.

Gareth felt himself bridling still more. He and Susannah weren't naughty children to be admonished in such a way! "We went against your advice out of necessity, sir, and if your damned keepers were worth their wages, they would know the difference between your guests and unwanted intruders!"

The duke's eyes narrowed. "No doubt it was also necessity when at the commencement of your outing you rode well away from the marked track in order to go to the copper beech?"

Susannah's lips parted. "*You* were watching us from the trees?" she gasped.

"Hardly, madam! It isn't my habit to spy upon people! It was reported to me."

Gareth was incensed. "By God, sir, this is intolerable! What manner of estate do you run here? It smacks of Robespierre's Paris!"

Susannah's hand tightened anxiously over his. "It's of no real consequence," she said quickly, for the animosity that had sprung up between the two men was so fierce it could almost be felt.

The duke heard her remark and smiled. "Mrs. Leighton is right, Sir Gareth. We quarrel over nothing. If I spoke sharply it was due to my alarm on finding your horses here and no sign of you. As you have discovered, the temple is no longer safe; indeed, it is soon to be pulled down and replaced by a replica of Stonehenge. Another of the duchess's whims," he added. "Please feel free to finish your ride. There is no point in returning to the oak now. You may as well carry on along the track."

Gareth felt like telling him what he could do with every inch of the felled tree, but he said nothing as he took Susannah by the arm to assist her down the steps to the waiting horses. He lifted her onto her mare and then turned toward his own mount. For a split second his eyes again met the duke's, and a sharp stab of warning pierced through him. It had been very ill-advised indeed to tangle with Delavel Harmon a second time. Nothing more was said as Susannah and Gareth rode away from the temple, followed by Minette and Chatterji. The poodle ran belly low until she was out of the duke's sight. Gareth remained silent, and Susannah put it down to anger over the duke's preposterous attitude.

After a while they rounded the shores of the third and smallest lake and then came upon the next folly, the ruined monastery arch that Jane had said was her favorite. After that, almost at the end of the five miles, where the valley was narrow and par-

ticularly steep-sided, was the final folly, a Grecian grove surrounded by statues of gods and goddesses. In the middle was
a fountain fed by a stream diverted from the hillside above.
The fountain was another stone Venus, not reclining this time
but standing up with an urn held gracefully above her lovely
head. Stream water spilled from the urn onto mossy rocks at
the goddess's feet, splashed on the surrounding ground, which
was soft and muddy beneath its cloak of lush grass and marsh
marigolds, then disappeared into a shallow underground chan-
nel that carried it away to the lake.

Minette had paused to lap water from the fountain, but Chatterji was staring up at the Venus, almost as if he recognized her.
Gareth roused himself from his thoughts and reined in as he realized what the monkey had seen. He gave Susannah a wry grin.
"Why, Mrs. Leighton, Chatterji has perceived your twin! Were
you the sculptor's model, perchance?"

Since the Venus was beautiful, but hadn't so much as a stitch
on, Susannah did not know whether to be flattered again or em-
barrassed. She tossed him a haughty glance. "Sirrah, I shall over-
look the unwarranted attack upon my modesty, but from the
amount of moss and discoloration on the lady's form, I perceive
an even greater attack upon my age."

He smiled again. "I crave your forgiveness," he murmured,
sweeping off his hat and bowing his head.

She smiled too, but then became serious. "Are you still angry
about the duke?"

"Angry, and wary." He leaned forward on the pommel.
"Today's events have convinced me that Exton's obsessions go
beyond acceptable bounds, so I think it best if we leave Exton
Park as soon as possible."

Hardly had the words left his lips than a shotgun report close
by split the peace of the woods. Birds rose in a noisy clamor,
and the horses jerked away uneasily, tossing their heads. Chatterji fled in terror toward the nearest shelter of trees, followed
by Minette, whose tail was between her legs. Susannah froze
with shock as she heard the shot whine past, but Gareth's reaction was immediate. He leapt from his mount, losing his top hat
in the process, and hauled her down as well, flinging them both
to the ground at the foot of the fountain just as a second report
resounded between the steep sides of the valley.

The horses reared and would have bolted had not Gareth had

the presence of mind to snatch the trailing reins. Susannah's riding hat had been torn from its pins, her habit was plastered with mud from the wet ground, and her face and hair were covered with marsh marigold petals as she tried to make herself as low as possible against the ground. The second shot struck Venus's urn, sending splinters of marble flying in all directions, and Susannah managed to crane her neck to look up at the damage. Her eyes widened immediately, for the fountain could only have been hit at that particular point because Gareth had flung himself from his horse when he did. If he had delayed a split second longer, he would surely have been shot!

Her heart missed a beat. Had someone deliberately trained sights on him? She instinctively began to raise her head to look in the direction from which the shots must have come, but Gareth put out a strong hand and forced her down again.

"Keep down! Have you no sense?"

"But—"

"For God's own sake, do as you're told!"

She lay very still, except for her hand, which crept fearfully to his. Her fingers trembled as his folded tightly around them, and she closed her eyes. She was afraid, but not for herself. Somehow she knew she wasn't in danger—but he certainly was.

Gradually all went quiet. The fountain continued to splash gently, and the birds settled and began to sing again. But then she heard a rustling sound and raised her head slightly just in time to see a man peering through the leaves where the track entered the clearing. She saw him for only a moment before he drew back, but she was sure it was the prizefighter footman. Then there came the sound of hooves as someone rode swiftly back along the track.

Only then did Gareth scramble to his feet. "It's safe now," he said, holding a hand down to help her up as well.

She was still trembling as she tried to shake out her damp, mud-stained skirts. "I-I saw him," she whispered. "It-it was—"

"The duke's footman? I know," he broke in gently, brushing the petals from her cheeks and then bending to retrieve her hat. "I would guess that Delavel Harmon is still persuaded that I am Jane's lover."

"To the extent of trying to *kill* you?" she whispered incredulously. Tears began to fill her eyes as the closeness of the scrape finally began to sink in.

He pulled her into his arms, sliding comforting fingers into her hair. "If that is the case, he failed," he murmured.

Their hearts beat close together as she pressed her forehead against his shoulder. Her fingers dug into his back like little claws. "If you'd still been on your horse when the gun was fired again . . ."

"But I wasn't, *cariad*."

She drew her head back, her eyes shimmering with tears. "That's not the point!" she cried, wrenching herself from his arms. "Just before it happened, you said that we should leave here, and now I could not agree more! I know we wanted to help Jane, but she isn't exactly being helpful in return, is she?"

"I agree. She's using us, and leaving us in the dark as well. That will not do."

"No, it won't." Susannah knew a pang of conscience, for wasn't she doing something very similar? It wasn't friendship that had brought her to Exton Park, but an ulterior motive! She had used Jane.

Chatterji and Minette emerged from the undergrowth and came warily back to the fountain. The monkey made nervous little sounds, and the poodle was very subdued, but that changed when Gareth turned to retrieve his top hat from the grass and accidentally trod on Chatterji's tail. The monkey howled with outrage, and before Gareth could say or do anything to indicate it had not been intentional, Chatterji snatched the top hat and made off with it toward the open park and the house, which were just visible about two hundred yards further on, where the track finally emerged from the woods. Minette dashed after her friend, barking loudly.

Gareth gazed wearily after them. "By God," he muttered, "if ever there were two of God's creatures I'll be glad never to see again . . ."

Susannah went up to him. "Forget them, Gareth. We were talking about leaving here. I want to go back to the house right now, pack, and be gone from Exton Park before another hour has passed." *I no longer care about the tiara, I only care about you.*

He took her hand again. "That is my instinct too, but I don't relish letting Exton know that we intend to go. What I saw in his eyes back at the temple does not lead me to conclude that common sense has much to do with his actions. Therefore I do not wish to, er, encourage any precipitate ducal reaction, shall we say?"

Susannah swallowed. "How shall we do it, then?"

"You asked me earlier what I meant by safeguard. Well, my landau isn't in Cirencester at all, but is concealed in an empty barn not far from the main gates. Call it a sixth sense if you like, but when we arrived I felt it would be wise to make provision for a hasty and secret retreat if that proved necessary. Discreet withdrawals aren't really possible if one has to harness a team, then drive a carriage out of an echoing cobbled stableyard. Such a racket is apt to draw unwelcome attention, but a sly slipping away from a nearby hideout? That's different."

She stared at him. "Once a secret agent . . . ?"

"Always a secret agent," he finished for her. "I've learned a great deal in the years I've acted for Hawkesbury, and one thing is very clear: Having an escape route in readiness is *always* a comfort."

She glanced around the clearing, which was so tranquil now that if it were not for the damage to Venus's urn, she could almost think she had imagined the shots. "All right, if we don't wish to alert the duke, when are we going to leave?"

"After dark tonight. No luggage, just you, me, Hector, and Anjuli. And that dratted monkey, I suppose. The servants can go one at a time, pretending to want a breath of fresh air, and then you and I will go for a romantic walk in the moonlight, although how romantic one can be with Chatterji along, I really don't know. We'll just keep walking until we reach the barn, then we'll show Exton Park some very clean heels."

She nodded. "All right."

"We'll soon be safely away. I promise."

"I-I hope you're right."

"In the meantime I don't intend to mention the shotgun incident to anyone."

"Not mention it? But the duke's man tried to murder you!" she cried.

"Precisely—the duke's man. To say anything would be to risk a denouement of some sort, and I've already pointed out the hazards of that. So let's keep things calm. Then we can slip away with ease tonight."

She nodded. "I will do whatever you say."

"Oh, don't tempt me, *cariad,* don't tempt me," he muttered, lifting her up onto her mare.

Chapter 23

Chatterji had decided to leave Gareth's top hat perched on top of a statue of Hercules that stood where the track emerged from the woods. The statue was tall, and Gareth had to clamber up to retrieve it, which Susannah did not doubt had been fully in the monkey's mind when he chose the spot. Chatterji had also taken great care to tilt the hat at just the angle Gareth so often wore it, a fact that made Susannah smile in spite of all that had just happened.

At the stableyard Susannah and Gareth parted company, he to examine the other fine horses in the stalls, she to return to her apartment to tell Anjuli they would be leaving that night. As she entered the house by way of the front steps, she happened to glance toward the private apartments, and a furtive movement at an upper window immediately caught her eye. It was Jane, who moved quickly out of sight on realizing she had been observed.

Susannah was suddenly incensed. How *dare* Jane continue to avoid the issue when Gareth might just have been killed! The Duchess of Exton had much explaining to do, and now seemed as good a time as any to demand a proper accounting. Forgetting how wet, muddy, and disheveled she was, she snatched up the skirts of her cumbersome riding habit and swept furiously into the house.

Jane must have guessed a confrontation was in the offing, for she sent her maid to fob Susannah off at the double doors of the private apartments. Susannah was startled to recognize her as the girl she had collided with outside the Bond Street jeweler, although the girl did not recognize her. "Begging your pardon, madam, but my mistress sends her regrets. She is indisposed and—"

"And nothing," Susannah snapped and walked on past, pon-

ering this latest strange coincidence. How odd to have bumped
ito Jane's maid before actually meeting Jane herself. And out-
de a jeweler's shop, at that. . . .

The maid hastened after her. "But, madam, the duchess is un-
ell!"

"Then I shall offer her my sympathy and concern," Susannah
plied shortly and hurried upstairs to open door after door until
t last she found the one to Jane's suite.

The maid hurried in as well. "I couldn't stop her, Your Grace!"

"It's quite all right, Sanders. That will be all, you may go,"
ane replied quietly, straightening from fussing with Minette.
he relieved maid withdrew and closed the door behind her.

Susannah and Jane faced each other in the lavishly furnished
ream-and-gold apartment, then Jane saw the state of Susannah's
iding habit. "What on earth happened? Did you have a fall?"

"Something of the sort," Susannah replied coldly, taking off
er hat and placing it with her gloves on a table. Marsh marigold
etals fluttered down from her hair. "One of the duke's footmen
ied to shoot Gareth in the woods, and I want—no, I *demand*—
hat you tell me what is going on here."

Jane went pale. "Tried to *shoot* him?"

"Yes."

"You must be mistaken—"

"I know what happened, Jane, and it wasn't an accident."

Jane lowered her eyes. "No, it probably wasn't," she admit-
ed.

Susannah exhaled slowly. "Why does the duke wish Gareth
uch ill? Is it because he returned your glove to you in Hyde
ark?"

Jane's eyes widened. "You—you know about that?"

"Gareth told me."

Jane turned away, her hands pressed nervously to her mouth.
he took a moment or so to recover. "So Delavel *did* see," she
whispered then.

"He cannot fail to have done, for Gareth saw him watching
rom the window of Abbas Ali's house in Park Lane."

"I-I was afraid that might have been the case, but I hoped
gainst hope that I was wrong."

"Is that why you wrote to Gareth in the bookshop?"

"You know about that too?"

"The name and address were clear on the letter."

"I couldn't be sure, you see. I was afraid that Delavel had seen what happened and that he would misinterpret, so when realized that Gareth had been invited to join us at Sadler's Wells I was terrified. I wrote the letter, begging him to stay away. Then you came in, and I began to realize that through you I might be able to calm Delavel's suspicions."

"That you and Gareth are lovers?"

"Yes. Delavel is a very jealous man, Susannah, not because he wants me himself—not *that* way, at least—but because he i afraid of-of . . ."

"Being cuckolded? Yes, I know." Susannah searched her face "You intended from the outset to press me into pretending I wa Gareth's former lover, didn't you?"

"Yes, I'm afraid I did, but I hoped right up to the last mo ment that Gareth wouldn't come. When he did, I had to enlis your help. After that, when you both went along with it so con vincingly, I was so relieved I almost bubbled over."

"You certainly have a surprising capacity for chameleor changes, Jane. One moment you can be all of a dither, the nex you are all concentration and single-mindedness, then before any one knows it, you've wildly dispensed with all caution."

"I'm afraid I've always been like that. I know it's discon certing, and sometimes it gets everyone into a frightful muddle but I really cannot help it. It's how I'm made."

"Yes, I'm beginning to realize that. But Jane, why was it nec essary to go so far as to invite Gareth *here*? We could all four have shared the box for that one night, and that would have been that, but instead you had to go further, and as a result you've placed him in very real danger."

"I meant every word about wanting your company here, Su sannah—and you have certainly never been at risk from Delavel—but I'm truly ashamed of having dragged Gareth fur ther into it. I panicked, you see. You saw how Delavel was that night. I was frightened, and I acted on impulse."

May the Lord spare everyone from the Duchess of Exton's impulsiveness, thought Susannah. "All right, Jane, I accept every thing you've said so far, but why would the simple business of returning a dropped glove arouse the duke to such an over whelming extent that he has tried to kill Gareth? Could it pos sibly be that his suspicions regarding your fidelity are well founded?"

Jane stared at her.

"Tell me, Jane!"

The other flinched. "Yes," she whispered. "Yes, his suspicions are well founded, although I have not yet . . ."

"Actually lain with your lover?" Susannah supplied for her.

Jane nodded. Blinking back tears, she went to the window seat, and after a moment Susannah went to join her. "Who is he?" she asked more gently.

"Don't ask me to divulge his name, for if Delavel should discover who he is . . ." Jane bit her lip.

"How long has it been going on?"

"Six months."

"Is he the man watching the house from down by the lake?"

"Yes."

"And is he also the intruder?"

Jane nodded reluctantly. "Yes, but he isn't a thief!"

Oh, yes, he is, thought Susannah, for he's after the Holland tiara before it's sold, and so far has had as much luck as I have. Suddenly the Bond Street incident with Jane's maid flashed into her mind. The package that had been dropped outside the jeweler's was the right size to contain a tiara case! Had Jane commissioned the copy that her lover had left last night after taking what he believed to be the real tiara?

Jane spoke again. "I-I know he was almost caught while going through Delavel's safe, but he wasn't trying to steal anything." She sighed. "Oh, how I wish things were different, that I'd never met Delavel, never become Duchess of Exton!"

"But you *are* Duchess of Exton, Jane, and if the duke's suspicions are so very strong and dangerous, wouldn't it be far wiser to refrain from your affair for the time being?"

"Since when did wisdom enter into matters of the heart?" Jane said quietly. "Besides, we intend to run away together soon."

Susannah was startled. "Run away? Jane, have you any idea what a scandal that would cause? To have an affair is one thing, but to actually leave your husband . . ."

"I don't care about the scandal because we aren't going to stay here in England. We had planned to leave tonight but—"

"*Tonight?*" The exclamation slipped out more loudly than Susannah intended, and Jane became flustered.

"Oh, please keep your voice down, for you never know who may be listening." She glanced uneasily toward the door of the apartment. "Mrs. Wilberforce is always creeping around the house, and if I encounter her she addresses me in that odd accent of hers. I know it is from somewhere in the north, but where? Sometimes I feel certain it is Yorkshire, then other times Lancashire. When I asked her, she said she came from Cambridgeshire. Well, that is definitely not a Cambridgeshire accent! Oh, I know I'm being silly, but she makes me shiver, and she *does* listen at doors."

"I know what you mean, but all that apart, if she or anyone else has been eavesdropping, they will have heard more than sufficient minutes ago," Susannah pointed out practically. "Look, can I ask why you aren't leaving tonight?"

"Because of a problem that seems insurmountable right now. Oh, just when it all seemed to have been accomplished, too." Jane sighed forlornly.

Susannah couldn't help wondering if the delay was on account of the lover's having realized he hadn't got the real tiara after all. "What can possibly be so important?" she asked.

"It's a matter of honor."

"Yours, or your lover's?"

"His, of course." Jane got up and paced the room restlessly. "Delavel struck him a terrible blow some years ago, and now he seeks restitution."

Susannah had to look quickly out of the window. Wasn't that why she, too, had entered this lion's den? Who could this man be?

Chapter 24

Jane stopped pacing. "Whatever you may think right now, Susannah, my lover is a very honorable man."

"Is it honorable to place you in jeopardy? To say nothing of what so nearly befell Gareth! Jane, forgive me for this, but could your seduction be part of your lover's revenge upon the duke?"

"No! I agreed to help him before there was any hint of love between us, so please don't think that."

"All right, but it would have been nice to have been taken into your confidence before things got to this point." You charlatan, Susannah Leighton, she thought guiltily. What right have you, of all women, to lecture upon such things?

"I know I've behaved shabbily toward you and Gareth, and I did intend to join you for the ride today, truly I did. I knew you both deserved a proper explanation, but after I'd spoken to you in your room, a secret message from my lover informed me that everything had gone wrong. It upset me, so I made an excuse and stayed here in my rooms." Jane drew a quick breath. "I-I really didn't think Delavel would go as far as he did today, not on the flimsy evidence of a returned glove! But I don't know of any other reason why he would wish Gareth harm. I'm certain they've never had dealings before."

"But I thought they were once allies."

"*Allies?*" Jane laughed. "Nothing could be further from the truth. They would not cross the road to assist each other."

Susannah was guiltily silent. She had said some dreadful things to Gareth that New Year's Eve, and she had thought some even worse things while far away in Chinsura. How glad she was that she had so swiftly changed her mind on meeting "Sir Lackey" again.

"What are you thinking?" Jane asked.

"Mm? Oh, just about Gareth and the duke. There was a contretemps between them at that eastern temple folly. I think their long-standing dislike for each other simply came to a head. It was shortly afterward that the shots were fired."

Jane exhaled slowly. "But Gareth is all right?"

"Thanks to his own quick reactions, yes. But it was a close thing, Jane."

"Oh, how I wish I had never listened to Lord Faringdon! Delavel was almost bearable when Fleur Fitzgerald was his mistress, but ever since the creature dismissed him, he has been vile!"

Susannah was puzzled. "What has your listening to Lord Faringdon to do with it?"

Jane resumed her seat. "Well, normally I don't care who Delavel takes to his bed, so long as it isn't me, and until just over a year ago I hadn't given a fig about Fleur Fitzgerald, provided I wasn't expected to have anything to do with her. But then the trollop had the temerity to speak to me in front of everyone at the Ascot races. She did it not once but three times, and I was grossly humiliated because Delavel obliged me to endure it. That I could not forgive. Lord Faringdon, who subsequently turned out to be a mischief-making rival for her affections, told me that if I wished to cause real trouble between Delavel and her, all I had to do was to appear in public in the Holland tiara. Delavel had won the tiara at cards some years earlier, and I had always been expressively forbidden to wear it—with hindsight, I realize that the ban was to placate her. Anyway, within days of Lord Faringdon's urging me thus, I attended the St. James's Palace reception for Abbas Ali on my own, and I was still so angry that I positively *flaunted* the tiara. The newspapers reported the clothes and jewels of every lady of rank, and within days Delavel and the Fitzgerald woman had a much-recounted argument in the green room at Drury Lane, during which he was heard to inform her that she wasn't worth a single ruby, let alone the twenty-five in the tiara. She sent him packing and hasn't spoken to him since. She's Lord Faringdon's *belle de nuit* now. At the time I didn't know the significance of the tiara to her, but I've since learned that her family has always considered it to be theirs."

As false a claim as ever existed, Susannah thought. "What did the duke say to you for wearing the tiara?"

"Not as much as I expected. It was about that time that his gal affairs got in a precarious way."

"Precarious?"

"Oh, yes. Delavel became too devious for his own good, and some of the resultant pigeons came home to roost. There was a great deal of panicked to-ing and fro-ing to the premises of his lawyer, Mr. Godber, and after a while things quietened. It gave Delavel quite a jolt and certainly diverted his attention from my son. On top of that, I believe the parting from La Fitzgerald was so vitriolic that he had had enough of her. That was then, of course. I think he would take her back now, except that she hates the sight of him and he knows it. Now he takes his anger out on me. That's why I wish I had ignored Lord Faringdon. If I had never worn the tiara to St. James's Palace, Delavel would still be enjoying La Fitzgerald's favors and would hardly be giving me a second thought. As it is . . ." Jane blinked back tears. "I would have been a faithful wife, Susannah, truly I would, for I did not take my vows lightly. My family were in financial straits, and Delavel rescued them when I agreed to marry him. I know he chose me because I am the original plain Jane, but for my family's sake I was prepared to be the sort of bride he demanded. I was unspeakably wretched from the moment I accepted his ring, but now I've met—" She broke off, her eyes darting anxiously toward the door.

Susannah got up swiftly to investigate, but there was no one there.

Jane breathed out. "I know that Mrs. Wilberforce is always watching and listening. Susannah, there's something about the way she glides silently around the house with her keys chinking. And she has a habit of appearing when one least expects her."

"I know what you mean." Susannah's brows drew together. "Actually, I thought she seemed familiar when Gareth and I first arrived," she recalled. "I think she just reminds me of someone."

"Medusa, probably," Jane replied. "I wish Mrs. Armstrong were still here."

"Mrs. Armstrong?"

"The previous housekeeper. She had been at Exton Park for simply ages, but had to retire a few months ago due to poor health. That was when Mrs. W. came here. It wasn't long after

Abbas Ali returned on his second diplomatic mission and approached Delavel for the tiara. Oh, how I wish I knew what the fascination is with that wretched piece of jewelry! *Everyone* seems to desire it."

Including your lover, Susannah thought.

Jane glanced out of the window. "I suppose you will not stay now that this has happened," she said sadly.

"It would be rather foolhardy to remain, don't you think?"

"When will you go?"

"Tonight."

Jane swallowed. "I see."

"But you will not mention it in front of anyone, will you? Gareth doesn't want the duke to know. Nor must you mention the shots that were fired."

"Of course I won't speak of it." Jane got up and moved restlessly around the room. "Oh, how I wish my lover and I were going with you. You cannot imagine how caged I feel in this odious marriage! I look at Delavel and see an ogre of the very worst kind. I look at my love, and see a sweet, charming, handsome, adorable, loving, tender . . . A veritable paragon of every virtue there ever was."

"He has clearly won your heart."

"Oh, yes. I have never loved anyone as I love him." Jane smiled a little. "I wish I could tell you who he is, but I must keep his name a secret. You understand, don't you?"

"Yes, of course." Susannah hid her disappointment, for the man's identity might give some indication of why he was so interested in her family's tiara.

Jane continued to pace around the room, touching an ornament here, a drapery there. "We met while Delavel was in London, and I was alone back here. I went out riding almost every day and encountered him one misty morning. He just rode out of the haze toward me. He gave me quite a fright and stopped to reassure me that he wasn't a highwayman or some such villain. We fell to talking and hit it off immediately. He was a stranger to these parts, staying at an inn, so it seemed quite natural that we should ride together. I soon learned his story, and since it merely confirmed all the mean things I already knew about Delavel, I decided to help him. Help led to love." Jane smiled suddenly. "And the same thing can be said of you and

Gareth, can it not? You have been flung together through helping me, and now you have fallen in love."

Susannah lowered her eyes. "Well, *I* have," she admitted.

"He has too—you may count upon it."

"I would like to think you are right."

"I am," Jane insisted. "You and he will be as happy as my
lover and I will be."

Susannah suddenly knew that when Gareth learned all that
Jane had confessed, he would not leave Exton Park, no matter
what the danger to himself. The only satisfactory outcome to
this whole horrid business would be for two pairs of lovers to
flee this house. Three, if one counted Anjuli and Hector, but that
match still seemed so unlikely that Susannah found it hard to
believe, curries or not.

She put her hand over Jane's "We won't leave you," she said
quietly.

Chapter 25

Susannah had much to dwell upon as she at last made her way back to the guest pavilion, where she intended to order an immediate hot bath. The mud had now dried upon her riding habit, which she doubted would ever be the same again, and she knew she looked quite terrible. Her hat was grass-stained and its veil ripped, and her gloves were surely past all redemption. Still, it was all hardly surprising, given what had occurred in the Grecian glade.

She had just reached the marble hall when a thorn pricked her foot inside her riding boot. After taking the boot off to remove the offending article, she decided to take off the second boot as well, rather than hobble the rest of the way. Thus there was no warning of her approach as she crossed the saloon to the library.

There she halted in the doorway with a gasp, for Gareth was quite blatantly rummaging through the duke's safe. He whirled about, and they stared at each other. She found her tongue first. "What on earth are you doing?" she cried, thinking that to do such a thing in broad daylight was the height of lunacy.

Gareth smiled. "Well, if you recall, at dinner last night His Grace of Exton told me to feel free to search for the key."

"Yes, but he didn't mean you to also feel free to go through the contents of the safe."

"True, but he isn't going to know, is he?"

"He might have walked in just now, instead of me."

"I'd have heard him; in fact, I'd have heard anyone else," Gareth replied, glancing down at her stockinged feet and the riding boots in her hand. His gaze moved over her. "Well, it has to be said that right now you do not look like an illustration from a fashion journal," he said dryly.

"Nor do I feel like one, so I'm about to order a hot bath."

he looked at the marks on his clothes. "A bath would seem in
rder for you as well, Sir Gareth Carew."

His green eyes were wicked. "Shall we share?"

"Certainly not. Order your own."

"What a killjoy you are, to be sure."

She moved a little closer. "Where did you find the key?" she
sked, forcing herself not to look anywhere near the desk.

"In the leg of the desk. It was a fluke really, for there is a
esk by the same cabinetmaker in the czar's Winter Palace. It
ook Hector and me four days to find the key there, but here we
new the maker's methods and found it immediately."

"We?" There was no sign of Hector.

He pointed at the wall above the doorway behind her, and she
whirled about to see the little man clinging there like Chatterji,
with one foot on the entablature above the door, the other upon
he nearest bookcase. He had been engaged in moving aside a
portrait of one of the duke's forebears but had paused the moment she entered. "Good morning, madam," he said, for all the
world as if it were the most natural thing in the world to climb
up a wall instead of using the library ladder provided.

"Er, good morning," she replied, so taken aback that she
didn't know what else to say.

Gareth read her thoughts. "Ladders are cumbersome and take
time. Hector can swarm up a wall in seconds," he explained,
then nodded at the little man. "It's all right, Hector, you may
continue."

"Very well, sir." Hector touched his forehead to her and resumed his work.

As he went on trying to shift the portrait, her bemused glance
returned to Gareth, who was now removing the jewelry caskets
from the safe.

"What do you expect to find?" she asked.

"I don't know, exactly, I just wanted to take a peek before
His Grace had everything moved to that new place he mentioned," he murmured. "Any joy, Hector?"

"No, sir, it's not here."

"What's not there?" Susannah asked.

Gareth answered. "The new safe, or whatever it is. Paintings
make excellent fronts, and Hector has been making sure of everything in this room." He waved an arm at the other portraits and
landscapes adorning the walls above the bookcases. "Well, Su-

sannah, now that you're here you may as well be of some use. It would be helpful to have as much warning as possible of anyone coming, so if you could listen by the door, I'd be much obliged."

She did as he asked, but everything seemed very quiet. After a moment Hector jumped lightly down from the wall. "Where shall I look now, sir?" he asked.

"Well, to be truthful, I don't think we'll find the new place here. You may go now."

"Very well, sir." After a quick bow to both of them, Hector hurried away, intending to enjoy a cup of tea in the kitchen.

Susannah watched Gareth from the doorway as he began to go through the jewelry caskets. "I'm still surprised you should take such a chance in broad daylight," she said.

"Well, if last night is anything to go by, the hours of darkness are a little busy in this house," he replied drolly. "But then you already know that, don't you?"

She felt her cheeks going pink. "I've already said that I didn't leave my apartment last night."

He smiled as he continued examining the contents of the caskets. "Yes, that is indeed what you have said," he murmured.

"Chatterji *can* open and close doors," she repeated.

Gareth hardly heard, for he had come to the blue leather case. He opened it, and then exhaled slowly as he held the tiara up so that the rubies caught the light from the windows. "And here we have the object of Abbas Ali's desire," he murmured, then paused. "Or do we? This isn't the Holland tiara, it's a fake!"

The swiftness of his pronouncement took her aback. "What—what makes you say that?"

He looked sharply at her for a moment, then continued to concentrate on the tiara. "I recognize paste when I see it, and to be honest, this isn't even particularly good paste."

Susannah had to see for herself, so she hurried over. He was right—it wasn't very good. The false diamonds weren't brilliant, and the rubies were really quite dull. It was no match for the copy that she herself had brought from Calcutta, nor for the replica she had removed in mistake for the real one. The light-fingered woman hadn't gone to great expense!

Gareth had been watching her face. "Have you something on your mind, Susannah?" he asked quietly.

"No, of course not. I-I'm just astonished that this isn't what

purports to be." At that moment she heard footsteps. "Some-
ne's coming!" she gasped.

In a trice they had replaced everything in the safe and locked
, and he had returned the key to the desk leg. Then, before Su-
annah knew it, he had pulled her into his arms and brought his
ps down upon hers in a kiss so passionate that it took her breath
way. She hardly had time to return the embrace before Mrs.
Vilberforce entered.

"Oh, a thousand pardons, sir, madam," the housekeeper cried
n confusion, then hastened away again, her keys chinking.

Susannah expected Gareth to release her immediately, but he
idn't. His mouth continued to move sensuously over hers, and
is hands explored her back, sliding down to press her hips to
is. Pleasure mounted through her, and she felt warm and weak
vhen at last he drew away. "You are very good to kiss, Susan-
ah Leighton," he breathed.

"And you are very good to be kissed by, Sir Gareth," she
eplied.

He touched a stray lock of her rich dark-red hair. "Base male
hat I am, I have to confess that kisses begin to be insufficient,"
e said softly. "I want to bed you, madam, in fact, I want to
ed you more every time we meet."

She looked up into his eyes. "Is it base to feel like that?"

"I fear so."

"Then I am base too," she confessed.

He smiled, and brushed his lips to hers again. "Oh, *cariad,*
'm glad you said that. When we are out of this place and safely
ack in London . . ." he whispered, gathering her close once
nore.

Her love for him twisted through her like a knife, and she
pulled away, knowing she had to tell him about her long conversation with Jane. "Gareth, there's something you should know.
t-it concerns Jane."

"Jane? I thought it would concern you more than her. Well,
no matter. So what about Jane?"

"I-I've told her we'll stay."

He paused. "You've what?"

"I know I should not have said such a thing without consult-
ing you, but—"

"Well, it *is* my life that is at risk!" he pointed out, turning
away and running his hand through his hair.

"Please don't be angry with me, Gareth, for I think that when you know what she told me, you will wish to stay as well." But even as she spoke she knew there was more to his anger than just this.

He wheeled around to face her again. "This had best be a good tale, Susannah. In fact, it had better be very good indeed, because all the Duchess of Exton has done so far is arouse my impatience, not my willingness to expire on her behalf!"

Susannah glanced back at the doorway into the saloon. "Look, we must not talk here. Let's go to my apartment."

Chapter 26

Anjuli wasn't in the apartment when Susannah and Gareth arrived. The ayah had gone to the kitchens to beg some tidbits for Chatterji and had become embroiled in a lengthy and not very amicable disagreement with the cook. It was Anjuli's contention that British cuisine would benefit greatly from the addition of the many spices she had brought with her from Bengal, but the cook, Mrs. Webster, was not amused—indeed, she was most offended. Anjuli took no notice. She was of the opinion that the mutton stew simmering on the great kitchen fire both appeared and smelled anemic, and she was tactless enough to say so. Battle lines were drawn as it was agreed that the stew should be divided, one half to be served in the English fashion, the other in the Indian. The results would be judged by the many servants who had been drawn by the loud argument. Hector arrived just in time to be dragged in as umpire should there be an indecisive outcome—not that he was impartial, for curries were his weakness.

But all that was incidental as Susannah faced Gareth in her apartment. Chatterji took a very dim view of his foe's presence and claimed a position on the drawing room pelmet, from which he could make the occasional rude noise, to say nothing of poking his tongue out. The monkey's rude noises reminded Gareth of Bull Barker's bulldog, Hercules, and the night at the Union Club when the Holland tiara had changed hands. And thinking of that particular night brought other memories too, memories that were suddenly very hurtful indeed. . . .

Susannah sat on the sofa, looking nervously at Gareth as he stood by the fireplace. "If I have offended you . . ." she began.

"Oh, yes, you've offended me, madam, but what does it matter? I have just given you two opportunities to confide in me, but you chose not to. That tells me precisely where I stand in your estimation."

She stared at him. "I-I don't understand. If you don't wish to stay on here, then we will leave . . ."

"*We* will not be doing anything, Mrs. Leighton. You have suited yourself, and that is clearly what counts."

She felt quite numb at the change in him. Only a minute or so ago they had shared a rapturous kiss that had almost turned her heart over; now he was so bitter that he seemed a different man. If only she knew what she had done. . . .

He looked coldly at her. "Now, then, what exactly is Jane supposed to have said that was so momentous?"

She dragged her wretchedness around her like a cloak and related all that had been said in Jane's apartment. When she had finished he was silent for a long moment, then he nodded. "If all this is true, then of course we must stay."

She gave him a tentative smile. "I knew that was how you would feel."

But he didn't smile back. "I only said *if* it is true."

"Why would I lie about such things?" she cried, stung by the implication.

"Because you've lied about so much. No, I correct that, you haven't lied so much as misled by omission. And it's all because of the Holland tiara, isn't it, Susannah?"

"What makes you say that?" She was caught off guard, for she hadn't mentioned the tiara.

"Well, apart from other things that are now glaringly obvious, when I examined the contents of the safe, everything was in order except for that one item. I believe that the imminent sale to Abbas Ali has galvanized certain persons into action, one of those persons being Jane's lover, the mysterious intruder. When he was almost caught the first time, he failed to substitute a replica tiara for the original, so he returned again last night. He was almost caught again, but this time he successfully executed the exchange."

If he did but know it, there was a trio of thieves last night, Susannah thought, blinking back tears, and not one of them laid hands upon the real tiara. She was crushed by his coldness and did not know what to say to make things right again.

He spoke again. "But *why* are Jane and her unnamed lover so concerned with the Holland tiara? Jane says he seeks retribution

'or a wrong that was done him by the duke." He paused. "I believe I know who that lover is, Susannah."

"You do?" She stared at him.

"Oh, yes, in fact I'm sure I do. This man fits the bill exactly,
right down to a connection with the tiara."

Susannah held her breath. "Who is he?"

"Stephen Holland, from whom Exton won the tiara in the first
place. Or rather, from whom Exton *stole* it in the first place."

Susannah's heart stopped. "Stephen Holland?" she repeated
stupidly. "But isn't he in America?" The words slipped out without thinking.

Gareth held her gaze. " 'Begnal,' he called it, but that was because he was drunk. What he really meant to say was Bengal.
Two letters transposed, that is all, but a world of difference. And
McArthur's the hatters are of Boston, Massachusetts, not the
Boston in this country. Another world of difference." He smiled
coolly at her stunned expression. "It's taken me an uncon-
scionable length of time to fit together the pieces of the jigsaw,
Susannah, but fit them I have. I knew that night at the theater
that you and I had met before, because there was something
about your voice, if not your face. My suspicions have never
died away, and things clarified considerably when I saw the way
you looked at the tiara a few minutes ago; now you've given
yourself away fully. You are the former Miss Holland, who was
so monstrously rude and ungrateful when, after trying to save
him from himself all night, I brought her drunken fool of a
brother home. 'Sir Lackey' was the phrase, I believe."

Susannah continued to stare at him, shaken to the core by the
calmness with which he had peeled back the layers to reveal the
truth beneath.

He gave a mirthless laugh. "The lady is lost for words! Madam,
you have clearly known all along that your brother is not only
back in England, but that he is Jane's lover."

Her voice worked at last. "I haven't known anything of the
sort! I admit that I'm Stephen's sister, but *you* have concluded
that he is not only back in England but Jane's lover as well. She
certainly hasn't said so, and I certainly haven't been informed.
As far as I am aware, Stephen is still in America."

"Liar. You and Stephen have involved Jane in your crusade
to retrieve the tiara before it goes beyond reach in Constan-

tinople, and now Sir Lackey has been dragged in as well. Overdue revenge, no doubt."

"Gareth, I bitterly regret what I said to you that New Year's Eve. Believe me, if I could take back those words, I would do so."

"Believe *you*? Madam, I'm finding it damned difficult to fathom where the truth ends and the falsehoods begin, so don't expect me to take anything you say on trust."

"I-I suppose I deserve that."

"Yes, you most certainly do."

She took a steadying breath. "I'm alone in my crusade, as you are pleased to call it. I haven't seen Stephen in three years or more, and I repeat, as far as I am aware, he is still in America. And of *course* I don't want the tiara to leave England—it belongs to Stephen, and in his absence, it belongs to me!" Her tongue passed regretfully over her lower lip. "Everything I told you about how I met Jane was the truth, and so was what I told you at the theater. All I've omitted has been my own personal purpose."

"*All?* Forgive me, madam, but it's quite a lot!"

She faltered. "Please, Gareth, let me explain . . ."

He waved an impatient arm. "Oh, say your piece, but I doubt it will make any difference to the hurt and disillusionment I feel right now."

"Hurt and disillusionment?"

"Your kisses were calculated, Susannah, and that I cannot forgive. I thought you shared my feelings, and in the library, when I realized who you were, I gave you *two* chances to tell me the full truth. You ignored them both."

"Gareth, I—"

"Just get on with your fairy tale, madam!" he snapped.

Somehow she mastered herself sufficiently to continue. "I did leave this apartment last night, and it was to do exactly what I caught you doing a short while ago—go through the duke's safe in search of the tiara. Chatterji opened the door to follow me." She described all that had happened to the moment the intruder exchanged the tiaras. "If it was Stephen, I did not know it, for his face was hidden throughout. Anyway, then someone else was heard coming and—"

"You amaze me, Mrs. Leighton! Don't tell me we now have *three* thieves?" Gareth gave a sardonic laugh.

"Yes, that's exactly what I'm telling you. A woman came in this time. I have no idea who she was, nor would I know her again because her hood was raised. All I can say is that she was too short to be either Jane or Fleur Fitzgerald. Whoever she was, she left the tiara that is in the safe now."

He looked coolly at her. "Do you really expect me to believe such a Grimaldi pantomime was performed in this house last night?"

"It's true, I swear it!"

"Balderdash, madam!"

"I can prove at least part of it!" She ran to fetch the tiara she had stolen. "This is the one I took. It wasn't until I got back here afterward that I realized I too had acquired a fake, because there should be a scratch just here." She pointed to the place. "So to my knowledge there are no less than *four* copies of the Holland tiara, the three that were brought to the library last night and the one that was already there. As to the real one, I cannot begin to guess where it might be. I imagine it must be in the house somewhere, because Abbas Ali is coming here for it. Unless—"

"Unless what?"

"Well, Jane said that the duke was in temporary difficulties about the time she wore the tiara to St. James's Palace. She said his legal affairs were precarious, but maybe that meant financial affairs as well. The usual reason a copy is made is that the original must be sold to meet pressing debts. Maybe the duke sold the real tiara."

"That would be a likely explanation if Exton's finances were a problem, but they are not and never have been. My uncle happens to be his banker, and I can assure you that Delavel Harmon's fortune has always waxed, never waned. If he was responsible for the first copy of the tiara, you may count upon it that financial desperation was not his motive."

"What, then?"

"I have no idea, and frankly, right now I do not care. I wish you and your family heirloom in perdition, Susannah Holland, so pray do not attempt to embroil me further in your escapades."

Tears sprang to her eyes. "I've told you the truth, Gareth. I *swear* that I have."

"You and the truth are strangers, madam, but invention is your bedfellow." With that he strode from the apartment, and slammed the door behind him.

Chatterji, delighted that his enemy had gone, leapt down from the pelmet and danced a little jig in front of Susannah. But she did not think it funny—indeed, she burst into tears. The monkey's joy was extinguished, his tail drooped, and he stopped dancing. Why would *anyone* be sad that Sir Gareth Carew had left the room? he wondered.

Susannah was still sobbing heartbrokenly on her bed when Anjuli eventually returned triumphant from the kitchens, the curried stew having won by a mile.

Chapter 27

Susannah didn't know what to expect when next she saw
Gareth; indeed, at first she couldn't even be sure that he
would stay on at Exton Park. After all, he had told her he didn't
believe anything she said, and for all she knew that might now
include what she claimed Jane had said too. But he didn't leave.
Anjuli went secretly to see Hector and learned that no orders
had been issued for a surreptitious departure; indeed, Gareth had
indicated to Hector which clothes he wished to wear at dinner
that night.

So for the rest of that day Susannah remained in her apartment—no, to be strictly honest, she *hid* in her apartment, because she didn't have the courage to face Gareth. There could
be no avoiding dinner that evening, however, so somehow she
had to screw herself up to a bold pitch by then. Would she be
able to look him in the eye? Would he speak civilly to her if
she did? Was he even angry enough to expose her? The moment
this disloyal thought entered her head, Susannah was deeply
ashamed of herself. Gareth would never do such a shabby thing,
and it ill became her to think it even for a second.

Wearing her pink muslin wrap, with her hair loose about her
shoulders, she sat unhappily on the window seat, gazing down
toward the lake. At Chinsura she had dreamed endlessly of her
noble cause, of purloining the tiara from right under the nose
of the wicked duke and of getting her own back on Gareth—
maybe even on Fleur Fitzgerald as well. Now she was actually
here at Exton Park, but instead of sweeping to a glorious vic-
tory, she was completely adrift. All she had achieved was the exchange of one fake tiara for another, without being any the wiser
as to the whereabouts of the original. And she had discovered
that at least two other people were after the tiara, one of them
possibly being her own brother! On top of that, she had fallen

victim to love. If only she had read the signs properly and confessed when Gareth gave her the opportunity, but she hadn't realized, and now she had alienated the man she cared for with all her stupid heart.

Anjuli came to her. "Memsahib, which gown will you wear for dinner?"

"The orange silk, I think. With my diamonds." The combination was the first that came into Susannah's head.

"Very well, memsahib." The ayah hesitated. "Memsahib, I am afraid that Chatterji has gone out again."

"Oh, no. He's been so quiet I presumed he was asleep."

"I have looked everywhere, memsahib, but he is not here."

"Perhaps we should look for him. The last thing I need right now is for Chatterji to cause trouble of any kind." Susannah began to get up from the window seat.

Anjuli shook her head doubtfully. "But, memsahib, how will we find him in such a very large house?"

Susannah sat back resignedly. "I suppose you're right. Anyway, maybe he will behave himself this time."

"Chatterji cannot behave himself, memsahib. It is not in his nature. All monkeys are naughty, and he is more naughty than most."

The ayah went away, and Susannah leaned her head back against the shutter. Down by the lake, the copper beech was bright as the sun began to take on its evening hue, but the colors of the sky and the gradual cooling of the air gave warning of rain to come. A draft suddenly passed through the apartment, and with a shiver she turned her head in time to see the door swing as Chatterji returned. The monkey's coat and turban were very bright and colorful as he dropped down from the doorknob on the outside, came in, then pushed the door to again. When it didn't close properly, he scrambled up to the inner knob and held on to it with his feet while at the same time pulling with his paws upon the carved architrave until the catch clicked. It was neatly and efficiently done; proof positive that doors were something he now dealt with very deftly. Without realizing that he had been observed, he bounded away to find Anjuli, who always gave him something to eat at this time of day. There was a smug expression on his face, Susannah thought with a sinking heart. She was sure he had been up to no good. But what? And where?

The answer came all too swiftly with a sudden angry knock at the door. Anjuli answered and found Gareth there, in no mood to be particularly polite. "I demand to speak to Mrs. Leighton," he said without preamble.

"But my memsahib is not dressed to receive gentlemen, sahib," the ayah said, standing firmly in the doorway.

"Then tell her to get dressed, for I do not intend to go away until I have spoken to her!"

Susannah got up hastily from the window seat. "It's all right, Anjuli. I'll speak to Sir Gareth."

"But you are in your robe, memsahib!" protested the ayah.

"Nevertheless, I will receive him," Susannah replied.

The ayah stepped reluctantly aside, and Gareth strode in. "Where is it?" he demanded, his glance moving swiftly over Susannah, encompassing the way her red-gold hair shone about her shoulders and how the delicate pink muslin clung to her figure.

"Where is what, sir?"

"My box of neckcloth pins."

Susannah stared at him. "I don't know what you're talking about."

Chatterji appeared in the doorway of Anjuli's room, and Gareth pointed a furiously quivering finger. "That damned monkey stole it a minute or so ago, and I demand that you return it immediately!"

"I have no idea where it is, Gareth." Would addressing him by his first name make him realize she didn't wish to quarrel further?

Clearly not. "Then, *Mrs.* Leighton, I suggest that without further ado you persuade your damned pet to reveal its whereabouts."

"Sir Gareth, I'm very sorry if Chatterji has done something, and if I can find your box of pins, believe me, I will."

"I wish you to commence now, madam, not in your own good time. Those pins are valuable, and I wish them to be returned instantly."

Susannah bridled. How ridiculously overbearing! "Are you certain Chatterji took them?" she asked, beginning to think there was something rather comical about a gentleman of the *ton* becoming positively incandescent with rage over a mere monkey.

"I saw him!"

"There's no need to shout, sir." In spite of everything, a perverse desire to laugh started to bubble through her.

"There's every need, for you seem quite incapable of keeping the cursed creature under control."

Chatterji knew what the fuss was about, for he bared his teeth and grinned in a way calculated to annoy Gareth all the more. Susannah had to press her fingernails into her palms to stop herself from laughing. For some strange reason she could only see the funny side of the situation.

Gareth, already incensed, looked fit to tear the monkey limb from limb, and his green eyes were steel-bright as he addressed Susannah again. "I have just endured half an hour of that creature's antics, madam. My apartment is in chaos, and Hector has sprained his ankle while attempting to apprehend your thieving ape. I expect you not only to apologize most profusely but to return my stolen property!"

Susannah swallowed. "I am sorry, sir, truly I am."

Anjuli, who had been listening to everything, turned on her heel and hurried into her room. She emerged with her little box of herbs, spices, salves, and other medicines. "I will attend to Hector sahib," she declared, "and I will make right the wrong that had been done to your apartment, Sir Gareth sahib." Without waiting for permission from either of them, she hastened out into the corridor.

Susannah gazed after her in some astonishment. It must indeed be love, she thought, if Hector Ambleforth's sprained ankle was of more importance than a memsahib's state of dishabille!

Chatterji began to slyly follow Anjuli from the room, but Gareth's foot descended firmly on his tail. "Oh, no, you don't!" he cried and grabbed the tail, by which he then held up the wriggling, gibbering monkey. "Now, then," Gareth breathed, looking the simian transgressor in the eye, "where have you put my box of pins, hmm?"

Chatterji fell silent and stared mutinously back at him. By now Susannah was almost overcome with suppressed mirth; at least, more honestly, she didn't really know whether she was on the verge of giggles or more tears. She could see by the monkey's face that he knew exactly why he was in such trouble, so she spoke sharply to him. "Chatterji! Where is Sir Gareth's box?"

The monkey's jaw jutted, and he maintained a stony silence,

o she snatched off his turban, and held it in front of his nose.
Sir Gareth's pins, or I will fetch the scissors!" she warned.
Chatterji knew that dreaded word and screeched in dismay, but
t was not until she took a threatening step toward her workbox
hat he fell submissively silent. Susannah nodded at Gareth. "You
an put him down now."

"Are you sure?"

"Quite sure, for I still have his turban," she replied. "He'll
ead us to your box now."

He lowered the monkey to the floor, and with very ill grace
Chatterji went to the door, which Susannah hastily opened for
im. He shuffled reluctantly into the corridor and then to the
earest window, behind the curtains of which he had concealed
is ill-gotten gains, a little tortoiseshell box that had Gareth's
monogram set into it in diamonds. The diamonds had clearly
een too much of a temptation.

"Give it back to Sir Gareth," Susannah instructed, aware of
he quiver in her voice.

Chatterji scowled, but he did as he was told, taking the box
n both paws and holding it up to Gareth, who took it quickly
rom him.

Susannah had to dig her fingernails into her palms again.
There, Sir Gareth, you have your pins back, and—and I'm sure
Anjuli's salves will soon help Hector's ankle." Her voice shook
vith every word, and she didn't dare meet his eyes.

There was a long silence, and then he said. "If you laugh out
oud, Susannah Leighton, so help me I'll drown you in the lake!"

She saw that he was smiling, and together they exploded into
eals of laughter. Then suddenly—somehow—she was in his
arms, and their lips came together again. She feared she would
uddenly awaken and find it was a dream, but he was real. His
reath was sweet, his lips passionate, his arms tight, oh, so tight
round her. He thrust his fingers deep into her hair, and his
mouth moved intensely against hers. He forgave her everything,
ecause nothing, *nothing* was worth the agony of the past few
lesolate hours. He had not known her long, but in that time he
ad come to realize that she was the only woman for him. His
eloved, adored, wonderful Susannah. . . .

At last she looked up at him. "Forgive me for failing you,"
he whispered.

"Only if you forgive me."

"Forgive *you*? But you haven't—"

"My pride got in the way, Susannah, and I said things I di‹ not mean."

"I deserved them."

"No, you didn't." He cupped her face in his hands. "But ‹ wish you had trusted me enough to take me into your confi dence."

"I would have, truly I would, but after what happened in th‹ woods . . ." She drew away from him. "After that, the tiara sim‹ ply didn't seem to matter anymore. Not in the same way, at least Without realizing it, I think I had decided I would no longer tr‹ to take it back. Then, after I spoke with Jane, all I wanted wa for us *all* to be safe, you and me, Jane and her lover—Stephen if that is indeed who it is—and even Anjuli and Hector."

He raised an eyebrow. "Anjuli and Hector?"

"So it seems. A union based upon curry."

"Good God."

"That's what I thought, but it's true, as witness the haste wit‹ which she rushed off just now to attend to him."

Gareth smiled. "It would be good if we could achieve all tha‹ and get the tiara as well."

"Yes, it would indeed."

"Then somehow we will do it. I will help you in your cru sade, Susannah Leighton."

He gathered her close once more, and she raised her lips t‹ meet his. Chatterji's precious turban slipped out of her fingers and the monkey seized his stolen property with alacrity. Then the tortoiseshell box fell to the floor as well, scattering its costly contents everywhere, and Chatterji stared bemusedly at the jew‹ eled pins. He would never understand humans. Why had they made such a fuss about the box if they were only going to throw‹ everything on the floor anyway? He began to collect the pins examining each one approvingly, crooning as he polished a par‹ ticularly fine emerald on his fur. Then he admired its glitter. Oh how he loved bright things; *how* he loved them. . . .

Chapter 28

Susannah knew she glowed that evening at the dinner table. The orange silk became her particularly well, and her diamonds matched the sparkle in her eyes.

It was twilight, and a four-branched candlestick illuminated the table, while a little bowl of lilies of the valley filled the air with scent. The meal—brown Windsor soup, red mullet, roast venison, and lemon sorbet—was excellent, and was served from an immense sideboard that shone with polished silver-gilt plate. There were three liveried footmen to attend the diners, including the pugilist, who naturally gave no hint at all of the murderous act he had carried out for his master earlier in the day. As for the duke, he was the personification of charm and attentiveness. Not a word had been said about the morning's ride; indeed, it might as well not have taken place at all.

Jane wore oyster satin stitched with pearls, and her blond hair was fixed with a high ivory comb that was studded with pearls and turquoises. She was bright and seemingly lighthearted, although she could not conceal the truth in her eyes. Susannah glanced at her from time to time, wondering if it really were possible that Stephen was the secret lover. Jane was not the type he had once been drawn to, but time had passed since then, and he might have grown some wisdom, his critical sister thought, calling to mind a certain Fleur Fitzgerald.

The dinner passed with so little awkwardness that by the time the lemon sorbets were brought to the table, the duke's wife and two guests imagined all was going to be well. But it was then that the duke announced his displeasure with his wife's appearance, although as usual, his own left much to be desired. An electric-blue coat and yellow ribbon for his snowy wig were his choice tonight, and a very garish mixture it was, even in candlelight. "Jane, I mislike that comb in your hair. The Holland tiara would look far better," he declared suddenly.

Susannah and Gareth glanced at each other, and Jane almost dropped her sorbet spoon. "I-I beg your pardon?"

"You should have worn the Holland tiara tonight."

Jane's glance caught Susannah's for a split second, then she looked at her husband. "But, I-I thought you didn't like me to wear it. As I recall, you were rather annoyed when I wore it to St. James's Palace."

"All that is in the past, my dear, and right now I'm of a mind to see you wear it."

Jane's eyes widened, and she pushed her sorbet away as if it were suddenly unpalatable. "I-I would prefer not to, Delavel. I'm quite happy as I am," she said quickly, and Susannah suddenly knew something was very wrong. What could it be? Oh, no, surely Jane's lover wasn't in the house at that very moment attempting to find the real tiara?

The same possibility occurred to Gareth, and he gave a commendably relaxed laugh. "Wouldn't a tiara be a little too grand for such a small, informal gathering?" he said to the duke.

"I'd prefer her to wear the tiara while she still can. After all, it will soon be sold. In fact, I will bring it here to the table, so she may wear it for the rest of the evening." The duke got up and left the room.

Conscious of the three footmen waiting by the sideboard, Susannah immediately leaned across to whisper to Jane, who looked close to the vapors. "Jane, is your lover in the house right now?"

The other's eyes were as haunted as they had been at Sadler's Wells. "I-I believe he may be," she whispered back.

Gareth pushed his empty sorbet dish away and tossed his napkin onto the table. "Isn't that just the slightest bit stupid?" he breathed with masterful understatement.

"Don't you think I know that?" Jane's eyes filled with tears, which she strove to hide from the footmen, who weren't close enough to overhear what was being said but could certainly see the candlelit faces of the three people at the table. Gareth turned to them. "That will be all for the moment. You may withdraw," he said firmly.

The men looked at each other, then to everyone's relief, they bowed and left the room. As soon as the door had closed, Susannah spoke urgently to Jane. "Your lover is trying to steal the

Holland tiara, isn't he? Because he is Stephen Holland, my brother."

"Your *brother*?" Jane gasped aloud. She leaned closer to Susannah. "Stephen is your brother? But he told me his only sister was in . . ." Her voice died away as she realized. "Bengal," she finished lamely.

"Exactly. And I thought he was in America," Susannah replied. "But it seems that both Holland siblings are here, and with the same thing in mind."

Jane's lips parted. "*You* are after the tiara as well?" Then reproach entered her eyes. "How foolish I am to have thought our meeting at the bookshop was accidental."

"It *was* accidental, and if you are about to accuse me of using you, let me say that you used me too, remember? And you used Gareth, come to that."

Jane was contrite. "You're right, of course." She smiled apologetically. "Forgive me, I'm afraid I am a little overwrought. You—you say that you are trying to retrieve the tiara as well?"

"Yes." Susannah related all that had happened since her arrival, and Jane's astonishment grew.

"The cloaked woman was the *third* thief last night?"

"Yes, and the tiara that was last in the library safe was the one she left."

Jane smiled again. "Stephen left one I had ordered from a jeweler in Bond Street. The first time he broke into the house here he didn't have the copy to exchange and was only searching for the key. Yesterday morning I left the replica in a prearranged place in the stables, and he collected it last night."

Gareth looked at her. "Will you satisfy my curiosity about something? I already know why Susannah went to the trouble of acquiring a copy of the tiara, but why have you and Stephen bothered? Why didn't you simply decide to take the original and run away together?"

"Stephen *would* have just taken it, but then he met me and we fell in love, and he wanted us to be safely out of the country before Delavel realized it was missing and could set the law upon us for theft. So he provided me with the funds to order a copy when I was in London. Such copies are not cheap, not in England anyway. I don't know about Bengal." she smiled at Susannah. "Stephen has done very well in America, and he has a large estate near Boston. He is now far more wealthy than he ever was in this country."

"I'm truly pleased to hear it," Susannah replied.

Gareth cleared his throat. "We have wandered somewhat from the important fact of Stephen's possible presence in this house right now. Jane, what on earth possessed him to come here to the house so early in the evening? Damn it, it's still twilight outside!"

"It seemed an excellent time. Dinner takes an age, and while it's in progress all the servants are in the kitchen pavilion, either assisting with preparations or enjoying a well-earned break. The rest of the house is deserted."

"No house of this size is ever deserted before midnight," Gareth replied bluntly.

Jane fell silent, and Susannah didn't know what to say either, for Gareth was right. In the momentary pause, they all faintly heard Minette barking in the distance. Jane looked anxiously toward the door. "Minette sounds too far away. She should be in my apartment. I must see." She began to get up, but Gareth shot out a hand to restrain her.

"Which is more important to you? Stephen or your wretched poodle?"

Jane flushed and sat down again, and Gareth repented his tone. "Forgive my brusqueness, but I think you will concede that the situation is a little extraordinary. Now, what is the likelihood that he has come here?"

"Well, I-I cannot say for certain. He just told me he hoped to try again this evening, in case . . ." Jane bit her lip and lowered her eyes.

Susannah finished the sentence for her. "In case the real tiara had somehow found its way into the safe?"

Jane looked at her and nodded. "It was all we could hope."

Susannah nodded. "I can understand *that*, for I almost hoped the same."

Jane thought for a moment. "I know I wore the real one to St. James's Palace, because I noticed the little scratch you have described, Susannah. For some reason Delavel had brought it with him to the Mayfair house, and I knew it was in his room. I think he may have been about to give in to the demands of that odious Fitzgerald adventuress, but they fell out because I wore it."

"So where is it now? And why was there a fake instead?" Susannah murmured.

Gareth shrugged. "Well, *everything* has gone from the old safe now, I took a sly peek before dinner. But then, the duke said he would move it all as soon as he had personally completed this pesky new place. It would be interesting to know exactly when he had the replica made. If it was more than six months ago, I am mystified, but if it was within the last six months, then we have a reason."

Jane's eyes widened. "You—you mean he knows about Stephen?"

Gareth put a quick hand over hers. "It's possible. Don't forget, they are known to each other, and Stephen *has* entered Exton Park and its land more than once."

Tears filled her eyes. "Oh, how I pray he has stayed away tonight," she whispered.

"So do I," Gareth replied with feeling. "Now, look, on the assumption that he either stays away or at least escapes again tonight, I think we should meet with him as soon as possible." He looked at Susannah. "You said earlier that the tiara no longer matters to you in the same way. Do you still mean that?"

"Of course."

He smiled into her eyes. "Well, we decided we would leave as soon as we *all* could, and that moment cannot come too soon for me. Jane, how do you get in touch with Stephen?"

"I leave a note in one of the stables."

"Then leave one tonight. Tell Stephen to go to the barn up on the road from Cirencester to Stroud and wait there."

"The *barn*?"

"He'll find my landau there, together with my postilion, Billings."

"But—"

"Just tell him to do it," Gareth broke in.

Jane nodded.

Gareth looked at his fob watch. "The duke has been a long time, hasn't he? Just how far away is this new hiding place of his?"

They fell to discussing the situation generally, until at last the duke's footsteps could be heard returning. Jane sat forward hastily, her eyes suddenly suspiciously bright and determined in the candlelight. "Susannah, I know it's right to forget the tiara, but I also know how much it means to you and Stephen, so I'm going to do what I can to find out where it's hidden."

"What do you mean?" Susannah asked apprehensively, for she had seen Jane's lightning changes of mood before.

"The mouse duchess has become all lionheart," Jane declared, just as the door opened and her husband entered with the tiara's blue leather case in his hand.

His rather disheveled appearance startled the three at the table, for the folds of his neckcloth were no longer as pristine as before and there was a button missing from his electric-blue coat. His wig was slightly awry, and its yellow ribbon missing altogether. He also appeared to have a sore elbow, which he rubbed a great deal as he resumed his seat.

He looked, they all decided silently, as if he had been involved in a scuffle of some sort—which he had, for a great deal had happened since he had left the room. A very great deal.

Chapter 29

About the time the duke left the dining room to fetch the tiara, Hector hobbled back from the kitchens on his own. The ankle he had twisted when trying to catch Chatterji was very sore, but not as sore as it would have been if Anjuli had not ministered to it. He had been able to get only one of his boots on, and so had dispensed with both, knowing that way he would be safe enough from discovery while the "above stairs" dinner was in progress. After spending a little time drinking tea and chatting with the other servants, he was now returning to the guest pavilion to see Anjuli.

Hector smiled. She was a strange one, and no mistake, but when she smiled at him, he was done for! After all this time, Hector Ambleforth had been snared, not by a chit of an English maid—which was what he had always expected—but by a dark-eyed Eastern woman in a sari and bangles whose spicy cooking was a taste of heaven itself! It was on account of the spicy cooking that Anjuli wasn't with him now. Mrs. Webster had taken umbrage over the business of the stew and let it be known that the ayah's presence was definitely not required.

His progress was both slow and silent as he entered the marble hall, where all was in virtual darkness, except for a single lighted candle on the candlestick table. To his dismay, he heard the duke's heavy footsteps approaching from the private pavilion. The echo playfully magnified the sound until it seemed as if an army were on the march. Knowing he must not be caught in only his socks, Hector prudently limped out of sight behind one of the marble columns.

The duke carried a lighted candle, and shadows rose and shrank as he entered the hall. Shielding the flame with his hand, he passed close by Hector's column on his way toward the saloon. Suddenly a dark little shape dashed out of the music room behind him. It was Chatterji, who was playing a kind of tag with Minette. The monkey was so intent upon glancing back to see how close the poodle was that he didn't realize the duke was there. He ran right into the duke's legs, became momentarily tangled, then disappeared toward the saloon with shrieks of alarm made almost deafening by the echo. The duke teetered, lost his balance, and sat down with a thud that made Hector wince. Somehow the candle remained alight, although its flame flickered fiercely, as did the duke's temper, for he uttered a curse so shocking that Hector blushed.

Hardly had the duke hauled himself to his feet again, when Minette erupted out of the music room. The poodle should indeed have been safely in the private apartments, but Chatterji had opened the door to let his new friend out to play! Paws slithering on the marble floor, Minette was going too fast to stop. She hurtled into the duke, knocking him over again, and this time the candle went out. The poodle ran on after the monkey and began to bark frantically as she passed out of sight into the saloon. That was what Jane heard in the dining room.

The duke's expletives were blistering as he struggled painfully to his feet—and so was the response of the echo as it flung his words back at him. He kicked his dropped candlestick furiously away, and Hector could see by the light from the candle table that his wig was awry and his coat quite rumpled.

After procuring another candle, the duke continued his rudely interrupted passage to the saloon, and as soon as he had gone, Hector started to emerge from behind the column. But then the stealthy opening of the main doors of the house made him jerk hastily back out of sight again. He watched as a cloaked man in a top hat slipped into the hall. The lower half of the man's face was hidden behind a kerchief, and he moved as silently as he could, but the echo betrayed every step of his progress down the hall, until he, too, disappeared into the saloon.

Hector followed, expecting the man to have gone into the library, but there was no sign of him, and all likely hiding places were empty. As he searched, he heard Chatterji returning along the corridor. The monkey gibbered excitedly as Minette followed hot on his heels, and Hector stood swiftly aside for the two animals to pound past, so engrossed and delighted with their game that they didn't even notice him. They dashed through the saloon and then back into the marble hall, where Chatterji's noise was the echo's delight.

Hector glanced toward the corridor. The infallible instinct he shared with Gareth, born of their many adventures in St. Petersburg, told him that neither the duke nor the intruder had gone to the guest apartments, which left two possibilities—the southwestern pavilion or the doors from the saloon onto the south terrace. Retracing his steps, Hector examined the terrace doors and saw that they were locked with the key on the inside. Nevertheless, he limped briefly outside. It was a cool night, and clouds had covered the moon. A damp breeze swept over the terrace, and it began to rain as he surveyed the scene. There was no sign of either the duke or the intruder. He saw a lantern bobbing on the grounds as two patrolling footmen dashed back to get out of the rain, and at first that seemed the only light, but then he noticed the flicker of light against the stained-glass window in the southwestern pavilion. Someone was crossing the chapel toward the adjacent conservatory. The duke, Hector thought, his curiosity now well and truly aroused.

He went back into the house as quickly as he could and made his way to the chapel. The moon slid out from behind the clouds, shining fleetingly upon the dark oak pews, the richly draped altar, and the polished-brass eagle lectern in the pulpit, then everything was plunged into darkness again. A sound broke the silence. It was the grating of flagstones, and came from the conservatory, where there was just the faintest glow of candlelight.

Warm, moist air touched Hector's face as he silently crossed the chapel, and he could smell earth and hothouse plants. He peeked cautiously around the doorway, and his heart almost stopped, for the man in the cloak was barely two feet away, peering through the luxuriant fronds of tropical greenery to watch something beyond. The candlelight came from the floor, and the duke's shadow was monstrous as he hauled a flagstone slowly aside. The rain fell more heavily, and the drops tamped upon the surrounding glass of the conservatory.

More light swayed behind Hector, and he hobbled hastily to the shadows by the lectern just as the duke's two most trusted footmen—or rather, henchmen—entered the chapel carrying a lantern. They were the men Hector had seen running to the house to escape the rain, who were now slyly completing their patrol in the dry. The intruder wasn't as attuned to danger as Hector, and he didn't realize the footmen were there until it was too late. In a trice they were upon him, and his game was up. His top hat was dislodged as he struggled violently enough to drag his assailants back into the chapel, but he stood no real chance. He was thrust roughly against the wall, and his kerchief was tugged down beneath his chin. The lantern was held closer to his face, and Hector saw that he was a young man, pleasant-looking, with freckles, vivid blue eyes, and thick chestnut hair.

The duke emerged hastily from the conservatory, his snoutish face pinched with anger as at first he saw only the footmen, who had no business being inside, whether it was raining or not. "What in God's own name are you two doing in here?" he demanded, rubbing his still sore elbow, but then he saw their captive, and his anger dissolved into gloating triumph. "So, I have you at last, Holland!"

Hector's lips parted. Holland? Could the name have anything to do with the tiara? He had not learned of Susannah's connection with the tiara because Gareth had not mentioned it, and Anjuli did not know because Susannah never spoke of her past.

Stephen's face set defiantly. "May the devil take you, Exton!" he breathed.

The duke moved closer. "Did you really think I'd let you get away with this? You surely don't imagine I'm unaware that you and my wife are trying to steal the tiara? That much-disputed piece of jewelry is mine, Holland, and soon it will be rightfully the property of the Ottoman emissary to the Court of St. James's, who is going to pay me a vast sum for the privilege. It's funny the way things turn out, hmm? I purloin the tiara from you, ruining you in the process, then I sell it for a figure that will swell my already bursting coffers. There's no justice, is there?"

Stephen's blue eyes were bright in the lantern light. "I'll admit to anything you like regarding the tiara, but I will not utter a single word to sully the name of an innocent lady! The duchess is of impeccable character!"

"*Impeccable?*" The duke found this highly amusing. "Since when has it been impeccable for a wife to steal from her husband and take a lover?"

Stephen held his gaze steadily. "You wrong her greatly, sir. She is not a thief and I am not her lover," he said quietly, his only thought being to shield the woman he adored.

The duke gave a savage bark of laughter. "*You?* I didn't for a moment imagine you were! From the evidence of my own eyes in Hyde Park I know it's *Carew* who enjoys my wife's favors!" he cried. "His fake embraces with Mrs. Leighton don't fool me!" Wild fury was written large across his face, and his fists clenched convulsively.

Stephen did not respond. He had learned from Jane about the two guests at Exton Park, so he knew that the duke was referring to Gareth, but he still didn't realize that Mrs. Leighton was his own sister.

The duke managed to control himself, and when he spoke again his voice was level, except for the slight tremor that gave away his towering obsession. "I will deal with Carew presently. No man makes a cuckold of me and lives to tell the tale."

Hector felt a cold finger run down his spine. Had he understood correctly? Had the Duke of Exton just spoken of killing Sir Gareth?

The duke now rounded on the footman who had failed to eliminate Gareth in the woods that morning. "You'll pay for your imcompetence, Jones!"

Even in the lantern light, Hector could see how pale the man's face waxed. "I did my best, Your Grace! I swear it! But he flung himself to the ground, and I knew he wouldn't move until he was sure I'd gone. Then I panicked—"

"I have no time for those who fail," the duke interrupted.

"Give me another chance, Your Grace! I will not let you down again!" the man begged.

The duke hesitated. "Trust you with the same task again? I think not. But maybe you still have your uses."

"I will do anything you say, Your Grace."

"Yes, I'm sure you will," the duke murmured. "As to Carew, it's clear I can trust no hand but my own. Tonight does not feel right, but I will dispose of him first thing in the morning."

Hector swallowed. The duke was quite mad! Too many bells in his belfry, and no mistake! Well, he wouldn't find Sir Gareth easy prey. Forewarned was forearmed.

The duke turned back to Stephen, whose expression told clearly that he, too, thought Delavel Harmon was mad. "As for you, my dear fellow, well, one corpse on my land can be explained away, two might be awkward, and since you are not the one who has assisted my dear wife in cuckolding me, I will spare your miserable neck. But do not think you are going to get away scot-free. I intend to hold you prisoner until I can arrange your removal to the tender care of a press-gang."

Stephen stared incredulously at him. "They don't press *gentlemen* into service!"

"His Majesty's ships are full of fellows claiming they were wrongfully pressed. No one takes any notice."

"Go to hell, Exton!" Stephen cried and without warning made a desperate bid to escape. He took the footmen by surprise and dashed toward the corridor with them in hot pursuit. He might have gotten away if he hadn't stumbled in the chapel doorway, but in that second they were upon him. Again he put up such a fight that the two men were hard-pushed to contain him. The duke felt obliged to add the strength of his uninjured arm to the lists, but as he leaned over to help force the captive to the floor, Stephen wrenched a hand free and tried to pull him down as well, popping off a button of the electric-blue coat.

Gradually the footman reasserted themselves, and the duke used the ribbon from his wig to tie Stephen's wrists and ankles together. Then he stuffed an immaculate monogrammed handkerchief into Stephen's mouth and nodded at the footmen: "You know where to take him. Use the pony cart and make certain he's secure at all times, d'you hear? If he escapes into the woods on the way we'll never find him, and I'll have your hides."

"We'll make sure of him, Your Grace," the one promised, eager to atone for his previous inefficiency. Then he and his companion bent to pick Stephen up.

The duke put a hand on the second man's arm. "Ride to Bristol tomorrow. You know the tavern to go to and whom to ask for. Tell them I want Holland removed from here as quickly as possible. Is that clear?"

"Yes, Your Grace."

"Take him out through the conservatory. I'll open the doors. And don't draw attention to yourselves with *this*!" The duke seized the lantern, extinguished it, then led the way out of the chapel toward the faintly lit conservatory, where his candle still glowed on the floor.

Darkness swooped over the chapel, and Hector went to watch through the foliage as the duke opened the conservatory's outer doors. Cold night air and the sound of torrential rain swept briefly in, then the doors were closed once more and the duke returned to his candle, then lowered himself gingerly to the floor.

The sound of the rain on the glass drowned out everything except the familiar grating of the flagstone being dragged back into place, then the candlestick was picked up. Hector pressed back out of sight in the chapel as the duke emerged with a blue leather jewelry case in his hand.

As the dancing candlelight died away along the corridor, Hector hurried into the conservatory to try to see what the duke had been doing. It was very dark, but he could make out the paved central area where the duke had knelt. There was a scattering of earth where one of the flagstones had been moved, and on the ground beneath a pineapple plant he saw the crowbar that had been required for the task. Using it, Hector managed to lever the flagstone aside again and see what lay beneath it, a hole filled with the jewelry caskets from the library. One of the caskets was open, its contents scattered about, where the duke had searched for something. Hector noticed a leather tiara case lying open, the tiara inside askew as if it had been taken out and then tossed back. Treated like cheap paste, Hector thought, lowering the flagstone into place again.

He put the crowbar back where he had found it, but as he turned to leave the conservatory, he sensed someone at the entrance from the chapel. Then came the soft rustle of a woman's skirts and the chink of keys as Mrs. Wilberforce walked away. She *must* have realized he was there, he decided, so why hadn't she said anything? And exactly how long had she been present? Long enough to have witnessed what happened to Stephen Holland and to know the fate intended for Sir Gareth?

There was no sign of anyone as he limped as swiftly as he could along the corridor and then to Susannah's apartment to see Anjuli. Chatterji and Minette were asleep together on the armchair where the monkey's muff was kept. They had exhausted themselves in play and didn't even stir as he regaled Anjuli with his shocking tale.

The two servants then waited anxiously for Susannah and Gareth to return from dinner.

Chapter 30

Earlier, when the duke gingerly resumed his seat at the dining room table, he rubbed his sore elbow again. "Damned scurvy animals," he muttered under his breath.

Everyone had gazed at him in astonishment since the moment he returned, because he was now so very disheveled. Jane made no bones about it. "Whatever has happened to you, Delavel? You look as if you have been in a prize ring!"

His eyes met hers, their expression venomous for a second before he managed to dissemble. "No prize ring, my dear, although the effect is clearly the same. I have indeed suffered the indignity of being knocked down, first by that wretched simian, and then again by your flea-bitten poodle."

In spite of the pressing circumstances the other three at the table had been discussing only moments before, they were now reduced to hidden smiles. Susannah had to lower her eyes quickly because of the comic scene that began to form in her head. Jane swallowed, and Gareth cleared his throat. The duke's gaze slid toward the latter, and this time the malevolence in his eyes was harder to overcome.

Jane was dismayed about her pet. "*Minette* knocked you down?"

"She and that pesky monkey are on the loose, and they ran into me in the marble hall. I am fortunate to have suffered only a bruised elbow."

Susannah was forced to bite her lip in order not to laugh out loud. In her mind's eye she could see the two animals racing through the hall. Chatterji must have let himself out and then let Minette out as well.

Gareth's glance moved thoughtfully over the duke. The bruised elbow he could accept, but a missing button and wig ribbon as well? It was a little too much to result from the two tumbles described. Jane's remark about a prizefight seemed rather closer to the mark.

Susannah managed to address the duke. "I-I'm so very sorry that Chatterji has been a nuisance again."

"Sorry? So you should be, madam, so you should be."

"If your elbow has been hurt, I'm sure Anjuli will have an appropriate balm. She has done wonders for the ankle of Gareth's man, Hector."

"There is no need." The duke paused, tracing the edge of the tiara's leather case with a seemingly idle fingertip. Then he spoke to Gareth. "By the way, Carew, my keepers have all now been instructed as to your presence here. You will be perfectly safe if you ride again tomorrow. I will send word to my head groom that you and Mrs. Leighton wish to ride after breakfast."

Susannah felt horridly cold. There was no inquiry as to whether or not they wished to ride, just the fait accompli. There would be no mistake made the second time.

The duke smiled a little. "There's just one thing. I still cannot guarantee your safety if you venture into the temple, but you are, after all, fully aware of its dangerous state of disrepair." At last he opened the leather case and pushed it across the table to Jane so that the rubies and other precious stones of the Holland tiara twinkled brilliantly in the candlelight. "Here you are, my dear, your crowning glory."

Jane picked it up with reluctance, then gave a surprised gasp. "Why, Delavel, I am all confusion. Are there *two* tiaras?"

A pin could have been heard to drop as the duke watched his wife. "Whatever do you mean, my dear?"

Jane exuded an astonishingly believable calm. "Do you remember when we returned from London a few days ago, and I said I wished to wear my opal earrings?"

"Yes." The word was uttered slowly.

"Well, you went to open the safe as usual, and I followed after a few minutes."

"Yes, yes, do get on with it!"

"I looked through all the caskets for the earrings, and I glanced at the tiara when I came to it. This is the one I wore to St. James's Palace. Do you see this scratch on it? Well, there was no scratch on the tiara I saw that day."

Susannah was thunderstruck. The real tiara! So near, and yet so very far. Her eyes fled to Gareth, who gave her a swift smile.

The duke's brows had drawn together. "My dear, I didn't see you look at the tiara on that occasion."

Beneath the table Jane had her fingers crossed that the fake tiara had indeed been in the safe that day, for in truth she hadn't examined the contents of the blue leather case at all. She smiled, her eyes all innocence. "It was only fleeting. When you were looking in the desk drawer for your small seal. Now, lo and behold, here is the scratch again, so I *know* there are two tiaras. Do tell me what is going on, for I vow I am most intrigued."

Her audacity was quite splendid, thought Susannah. The mouse duchess was indeed a lionheart!

The duke reached for his glass of wine. "You are right, of course, my dear, there are indeed two tiaras. You clearly enjoyed wearing it to St. James's Palace, so I thought its sale should not come between you and any future enjoyment. I had the copy made during our recent stay in London, and it now reposes in my new place of concealment; what you hold in your hands is the real tiara."

Gareth swirled his wine. Something told him the duke was lying about the age of the replica. It hadn't been made in the past few weeks, or indeed at any time since the commencement of Jane's affair with Stephen, but well before then. Well before. Perchance as long ago as the commencement of his liaison with Fleur Fitzgerald? Now there was a thought. Had the noble duke wormed his way into the actress's bed by means of a *fake* tiara? If so, it would certainly explain Fleur's fury when Jane appeared at the palace. The realization that there were two tiaras would have sent the belle of the boards scuttling to the nearest jeweler, where she would have learned that she had only paste! Hence the unseemly fracas in the green room at Drury Lane when Exton had been given his congé. Gareth was amused, recalling Jane's mention of the duke having "for some reason" taken the tiara to Mayfair. She had surmised that it could have been because he had been about to give it to his mistress; maybe the closer truth was that he had regretted his deception to the point of seeing that Fleur received the real tiara. Jerry Faringdon reckoned the duke had come to feel more and more for Fleur as the liaison proceeded, even to the point of falling in love, whereas her attitude was always more mercenary. Dear me, how disagreeable for the poor fellow when his wife—and jealous erry Faringdon—upset everything, and he was left with egg on his snout.

Meanwhile, Jane tinkled with laughter. "Oh, Delavel, you had a copy made just for me? How thoughtful you are!"

The duke's smile was thin. "Tell me, my dear, if you realized the other day that there were two tiaras, why didn't you say something to me? After all, there had been an intruder who may have managed to switch the original for a substitute."

Susannah closed her eyes, but Jane wasn't fazed. "I was sure you must have switched them. After all, if the intruder had been successful, he would have removed the entire Exton collection. What point is there in taking one small tiara?"

"What point, indeed," the duke murmured, raising his glass to his lips.

"Unless, of course, he is a she," Jane added, then seemed covered with girlish confusion. "Forgive me, I should not have said that."

The duke lowered his glass. "What are you suggesting, my dear?"

"A wife is not supposed to mention her husband's lady friends."

Pins could have dropped again in the ensuing silence.

The duke was very still. "How indelicate of you, my dear."

"Maybe, but it has to be admitted that Fleur Fitzgerald has an interest in just the tiara. I'm right, am I not?"

"I have no idea," the duke replied barefacedly. "But it is no consequence either way, for the person who has been breaking into this house is most definitely a man. Whoever he is, he is doomed to disappointment, for he will never discover where the jewels are kept now."

"Please tell us, Delavel. We have been guessing in your absence. Susannah thinks it is in the music room, I say the stables, and Gareth said you had been so long bringing it that it must be in one of the follies in the park!" Jane giggled.

"You are all wrong, and I do not intend to satisfy your curiosity."

"Don't you trust us, Delavel?" Jane pressed.

"Remember the old adage, my dear. Foolish is the man who trusts his wife."

Awkwardness fell over the table, and since it was clear that Jane's lionheartedness was not going to pay the hoped-for dividend, Susannah brushed the moment aside by asking the duke a question. "May I be truly impudent, sir?"

"Impudent, Mrs. Leighton?"

"May I try the tiara on?"

Jane quickly held it toward her. "I'm sure you may, Susannah," she said, giving her husband an inquiring look. "You don't mind, do you, Delavel?"

"Why should I mind?" the duke replied.

Susannah's hands trembled as she raised it to her hair. It not only fitted snugly, it felt perfect.

Chapter 31

Minette and Chatterji were still asleep in the armchair when Susannah and Gareth returned at last to the guest pavilion, where Hector's news immediately reduced Susannah to tears for her brother; but she wept more urgently for Gareth, whose life she now knew for certain was in grave danger.

Gareth put tender fingers to her cheek. "Don't cry, sweetheart. We'll find Stephen before they take him away, and anyway, I have an admiral for an uncle, so even if your brother is press-ganged, we'll soon have him out again."

She gazed at him through a sea of tears. "That is easy to say."

"It can be done, *cariad*," he replied.

"I-I'm more frightened for you than for Stephen. You heard what Hector said—the duke intends to do away with you to-morrow. It is going to be done in the woods again. No wonder he left us no choice about going for another ride! Oh, I shudder when I think how he returned to that table and sat there toying with us like a monstrous cat with three silly mice. He is chillingly calculating, Gareth, and I am afraid to stay here. We *must* leave tonight!"

"We have Stephen and Jane to think of," he reminded her gently. "If at all possible, Stephen must be rescued before the press-gang gets to him. It's far easier to do that if we are still here. As for Jane—well, do you imagine she will be safe from the duke's vengeance once we have gone? We agreed to stay until we can *all* go, and nothing has changed my mind." He put an arm around her waist and ushered her to the sofa, then nodded at Anjuli. "Have you a draft of something calming?"

"Oh, yes, Sir Gareth sahib."

But Susannah stopped her. "No, I-I don't want anything. I need to be alert." She bowed her head, trying to hide the tears that now coursed down her cheeks. Her distress had already awakened the two animals, which now left the chair to come to her. Minette pawed worriedly at her skirt, and Chatterji climbed up to her shoulder to put his little brown arms around her neck and make sympathetic crooning sounds.

Gareth smiled and straightened the monkey's turban. "Perhaps you're not so bad after all, little chap," he murmured.

Chatterji caught the new note in his voice and looked uncertainly at him, but then he remembered that Gareth was his rival for Susannah's affections, so he scowled and clacked his teeth together in warning before resuming his cuddling and crooning.

After stroking the monkey for a few moments, Susannah found her courage revived a little. "I know what you say is right, but I put you before all else."

"To come first in your thoughts is an honor indeed," he said softly.

She looked bravely up into his eyes. "I love you," she said simply.

"As I love you."

The ghost of a smile played upon her lips. "How many hearts have you broken, Sir Gareth Carew? Is St. Petersburg strewn with ladies who have loved you and lost?"

"With one or two. No doubt Bengal is equally strewn with disconsolate men."

"With one or two."

"The past does not matter, just the now and the future. Susannah, we are going to succeed in everything we wish. Before tomorrow afternoon arrives, not only will we have rescued Stephen and Jane, but we will have dealt with the execrable Exton and appropriated the tiara."

"Will we?" Oh, how she wished that could be so.

"Trust me, my darling. As soon as it's light, I intend to find your brother. I will search every yard of the park if I have to. I will do so alone, just in case there is any awkwardness with the keepers." He put a finger to her lips to stop her protests. "No arguments. Exton won't be here, because he'll be on his way to London."

She stared. "London? But—"

"He's going to be called away urgently in a few hours' time by a hastily scribbled note delivered in the pouring rain by a nighttime messenger who immediately rides away again. I've done it before. The note will be a trumped-up message from his lawyer, Godber."

"Godber, Stanridge, and Cowper are my lawyers too. I have dealt with Mr. Cowper."

"Cowper is an honest square peg in a deviously round hole. Godber is the slyest legal tomcat in London. He and Exton are two of a kind and between them will have a number of sensitive matters they wish to hide at all costs. We know Exton had legal difficulties before, so we will resurrect them, and the message will be so alarming that he'll depart from here like a streak of lightning." He glanced at Hector. "Just as Prince Andrei did in St. Petersburg, but without the inconvenience of the frozen River Neva."

Hector grinned. "Yes, sir."

Susannah was concerned. "Gareth, it's all so risky . . ."

He took his handkerchief and gently dabbed her eyes. "It isn't risky at all, because Exton has no idea we're wise to him. He'll accept the message at face value, believe me," he said gently.

Chatterji, ever jealous, snatched the handkerchief to minister to her himself, and Gareth let him get on with it, but then his glance fell upon Minette. "Damn, we'll have to get this silly poodle back to Jane."

"We can tell her what's happened."

"Susannah, we cannot tell Jane any of this just yet."

She was dismayed. "But we must!"

"She may have been lionhearted at the dinner table, but if we tell her that Stephen has been captured and imprisoned somewhere in readiness to be dispatched to a press-gang, do you really think she'll cope? I believe not."

"I-I suppose you're right."

"I *am* right. Believe me, she's best left in ignorance until we have no choice but to tell her." He turned to Anjuli, who now stood with Hector at a discreet distance across the room. They were holding hands, but moved swiftly apart. "Anjuli, may I ask you to take Minette back to the duchess? Hector's ankle isn't exactly up to another long walk."

The ayah nodded quickly. "Of course I will take her, Sir Gareth sahib."

"And say nothing about all this."

"Of course not, sahib." Anjuli came to take Minette's collar then coaxed the poodle to the door. Hector decided it would be better to leave Susannah and Gareth alone together, so he made an excuse about having things to attend to in the other apartment, and he too went out. Chatterji considered joining the exodus, just to see what they were all doing, but that would be to leave Susannah in Gareth's clutches, so he stayed where he was.

As the door closed behind Hector, Gareth spoke to Susannah again. "Hopefully I'll find Stephen quickly, and we'll all be en route for Pengower before Exton knows what's happened."

"Pengower?"

"Where better? My castle is on a secluded shore of the Gower peninsula, and from there Stephen and Jane will be able to slip out of the country without anyone knowing, least of all the duke." Gareth smiled. "I confess that when I decided to hide my landau in the barn, I did not imagine I would be escaping with you, your rediscovered brother, a stolen tiara, two servants, luggage, a poodle, a monkey, and the giddy Duchess of Exton as well!" He became more serious. "That is a point, actually."

"What is? Surely there is room . . . ?"

"It wasn't the room I was thinking about, more the impracticality of such a collection of people, animals, and baggage going to the barn. The duke will have gone, so I'll have the landau come here after all as soon as we are ready to leave."

"You seem to think it can all be accomplished without even a small hitch, but there's many a slip 'twixt cup and lip, Gareth. So far we can't even find out where Stephen is, let alone plan our en masse escape."

"We'll achieve it all, Susannah, even if I have to coerce the information from one of those damned footmen. In the meantime, although we may not know your brother's whereabouts, we certainly know how to lay our hands upon the original Holland tiara, and I suggest we attend to that without further delay. The duke took it back to its new hiding place directly after dinner, so it's there now. Susannah, is your copy still in that drawer?"

"Yes. Why?"

Gareth went to get it, then gave it to her and gently removed one of her diamond earrings. "There is no need for Exton to realize he no longer has the real tiara. Abbas Ali is something of a jewel expert, and he won't be at all be amused when he perceives that our noble duke has presented him with a fake. You are better acquainted with the original tiara than anyone else, and you know *exactly* what the scratch looks like. Make an identical mark on this copy."

She took the earring from him. "My hand is sure to slip."

"It won't."

With Chatterji leaning over her shoulder to watch, she rested the tiara on her lap and gripped the earring firmly. She had to be accurate, otherwise the duke wouldn't be fooled. Slowly she dragged the diamond over the corner of the tiara. When she had completed the scratch, she inspected it for a moment, then gave the tiara to Gareth with a smile. "There, what do you think?"

He examined her handiwork. "Well, I've only seen the real one briefly, but this looks the same to me," he said, tucking the tiara inside his evening coat. Then he sat down with her and took her hand in his. "I'll make the exchange in a while."

"*We'll* make the exchange in a while," Susannah corrected.

"Oh, no—"

"Yes," she broke in. "You may be right to prevent me from accompanying you tomorrow morning, but tonight *I* am right. Think about it. If you are discovered alone in the conservatory it will look very damning, but if we're both there . . . Well, it would be differently construed. The wife of one of Richard's friends at Chinsura was much given to making love beneath the potted palms on her verandah."

"Was she indeed?" He smiled. "And shall *we* make love beneath the tropical leaves tonight?" he asked lightly.

"No, we will not."

"I'm cut to the quick."

"Sir, I do not mind being caught in a kiss, but I will *not* be caught in flagrante delicto."

"No doubt I will survive the disappointment."

"No doubt."

Gareth's thoughts had already moved on to something else that had been perplexing him. "I wish to God I knew what Mrs. Wilberforce's place is in the scheme of things."

Susannah suddenly realized something so obvious she couldn't believe she hadn't seen it before. "The cloaked woman! Gareth, I believe it could have been Mrs. Wilberforce. The height, size, manner—all are right for her!"

"Where on earth would a housekeeper find the money to pay for a replica tiara? And why? Surely it would be simpler to just take the thing and run."

"I don't know where or why, but the more I think of it, the more sure I become that she was the woman. There's something unpleasant about her, even Jane says so, and she *does* creep about the house."

"Yes, and I am inclined to agree that she is the third thief." Gareth looked at her. "Susannah, one of the things that puzzles me most about this whole 'copy' business is why everyone is so intent upon providing one. Why haven't you all simply decided to steal the wretched tiara and then put as much distance as possible between yourselves and the scene of the crime? Why bother with replicas?"

"Stephen and Jane hoped to avoid charges of theft when they eloped. Mrs. W's reason is a mystery, but I simply wanted the pleasure of deceiving the duke. I imagined his eventual discovery. He wouldn't know when it had been done or who had done it."

"Good enough reasons in anyone's book," Gareth replied and got up to hold a hand out to her. "Now then, since you insist upon coming with me to the conservatory, I suggest we go without further ado."

But as they left, a little brown shadow followed, carefully opening the door and closing it as he had learned. Chatterji wasn't about to be left behind, not when something was going on—*especially* not when it involved his archrival!

When Susannah and Gareth crossed the deserted chapel a few minutes later, Susannah trod on something small and hard that dug into the sole of her light evening slipper. Bending, she picked up the button from the duke's coat. Gareth quickly closed her fingers around it. "We'll find Stephen, *cariad*—on that you have my word."

They entered the conservatory. It was still raining heavily, and the rattle on the glass was deafening. Gareth was uneasy about so much noise, for it meant they wouldn't hear anyone else coming. So he acted swiftly. Hector had described exactly which flagstone to move, and he hauled it swiftly aside. The two blue leather cases lay side by side in the casket, and he soon found the right one. In a trice the tiara had been exchanged for the one Susannah had marked, but as Gareth was hauling the flagstone back over the hole, something suddenly moved in the nearby greenery. Leaves and branches shook violently, as if something were pushing its way through.

Susannah gave a frightened gasp, but then almost laughed aloud as she realized it was only Chatterji leaping from branch to branch. Gareth wished the monkey in Hades. "That damned ape!" he breathed, his words almost lost in the noise of the rain.

There was no time to feel relieved, for candlelight appeared in the chapel. Gareth froze for a second with the tiara in his hand, its rubies winking in the approaching light. Chatterji gave in to temptation and leapt down to snatch it from him, then disappeared into the greenery with his ill-gotten gains.

"Chatterji!" hissed Susannah in dismay.

There was no time to go after the monkey, for the candlelight was almost in the conservatory. Gareth quickly drew Susannah into his arms just as a footman came upon them. The man halted in dismay, unsure what to do, for they had leapt guiltily apart the moment the candlelight shone upon them.

Gareth feigned irritation. "Damn it all, man!"

"I, er, forgive me, sir." The footman hovered. "His Grace has sent me to check that the outer doors are secured, sir."

"Then check!" snapped Gareth.

"Sir." Clearly wishing he was anywhere but in the conservatory, the man stepped past them to test the door. It opened immediately, and in the space of a heartbeat Chatterji slipped outside with his trophy. The footman saw nothing, but Susannah and Gareth witnessed the Holland tiara being borne out into the wet, windswept night, brandished aloft in a victorious monkey paw.

Chapter 32

The plan to lure the Duke of Exton away to London went gratifyingly smoothly. Well wrapped in a cloak, and with one of Hector's hats tugged low over his face, Gareth left the house just before daybreak to hurry through lightly falling drizzle to the barn. A startled Billings helped him with a horse, and he then rode bareback back to Exton Park and knocked frantically on the main doors. When a sleepy footman answered, he thrust a soggy note into his hand, muttering something about Mr. Godber, great urgency, and "must come immediately," then he dashed back to the waiting horse. As he flung it away along the wet drive, the duke was already being roused from his warm bed. Shortly afterward, Gareth and Billings watched from the barn as a gleaming traveling carriage splashed at speed out of the gates and disappeared into the silver predawn light. Gareth smiled with satisfaction. That was His Grace of Exton safely out of the way; he would be at his lawyer's London premises before he knew he had been tricked, and in the meantime, if there was any justice, Stephen would have been found and every last bird would have flown.

As the sound of the carriage died away along the road, which was awash with puddles, Gareth instructed Billings to wait until the sun was well up and then bring the landau back to the house as if from being repaired in Cirencester, for it would not do to alert unnecessary suspicions. Gareth then returned to Exton Park on foot, intending to commence his search of the grounds as soon as it was sensible to do so. The drizzle was gradually ceasing; by the time it stopped, he would have had an early breakfast and then be ready to go out without anyone wondering anything. First of all, however, he would tell Susannah how things had gone. He knew she would still be waiting anxiously for his return, even though she would have guessed that all had

one well because of the duke's departure. As his steps quick-
ned, he heard a distant rumble of thunder from the southwest.

Chatterji did not return until after an hour after sunrise, and
hen empty-handed. If Delavel Harmon was now safely out of
he way, so, unfortunately, was the Holland tiara. Susannah, still
ully dressed in her gown of the night before, with a blanket
laced over her by Anjuli, had fallen asleep on the sofa after
Gareth's dawn visit. The ayah had attended to the packing of
nost of their luggage, which now waited neatly by the door,
eady for the hoped-for swift departure. It was the opening and
losing of that same door that roused Susannah. She sat up in
ime to see the monkey sneaking back toward his muff. His turban was missing, he was soaking wet, there was mud on his
aws and tail, and his little red coat was torn, with what looked
ike wild rose thorns and leaves caught on the sleeve. Cold and
learly miserable, he climbed into the muff, and curled up to go
o sleep.

Susannah was incensed. He had run off with the tiara, left it
vho knew where, and now he thought he could just go to sleep
s if all were well? She would see about *that!* Flinging her blan-
et aside, she got up to confront him, but he was at his most
ired, miserable, and unhelpful. Never had his jaw jutted more,
nd not even a scissors threat made any difference. In the end
he felt a little sorry for him and wiped him dry with a towel,
emoving the mud from his paws and tail.

"Where have you taken it, you tiresome, aggravating, inter-
ering, downright cussed creature?" she murmured cordially. "No
loubt if we could find your turban, we would find the answer."
She allowed him to go to sleep. A little coaxing when he had
lept a while might do the trick, she decided.

As Anjuli hastened down to Gareth's apartment with news of
he monkey's barren return, Susannah went to the open window
o gaze out over the wet park. Everything was very still, the air
ad become humid, and the clouds approaching from the south-
vest were an ominous yellow-gray. Thunder rolled faintly, the
ound seeming to come from nowhere in particular.

When Anjuli returned a few minutes later, she had the morn-
ng tea tray, having intercepted the maid who was bringing it
rom the kitchens. Susannah drank it at the dressing table, while
he ayah unpinned the tousled remains of her evening coiffure
nd began to draw a brush through the tangled tresses. As the

brush went to work, Susannah thought about the park. She wer
over the route she and Gareth had ridden the day before, pic
turing the lakes, the various follies—the temple of Flora, th
rustic cottage, the grotto, the temple, the ruined monastery arc
and the Grecian grove with its statues and fountain—and finall
the disused gates and dilapidated lodge. Suddenly something s
obvious struck her that she couldn't believe she hadn't thoug
of it before. Of course! The duke was quite happy for his gues
to ride anywhere they chose today, *except* the temple!

She turned urgently to Anjuli. "Please hurry down to S
Gareth's apartment again and request him to come here imme
diately!" she cried, taking the remaining hairpins from the sta
tled ayah's hand.

"But Sir Gareth sahib will have gone out by now, memsahib
replied Anjuli. "He requested an early breakfast to be broug
to him, and was about to leave when I went to tell him abou
Chatterji."

"I must ride after him! He'll be wasting his time searchin
anywhere but the temple!" Susannah leapt up and ran to get he
lightest cloak. Anjuli was appalled. "You intend to *ride* in you
evening gown, memsahib?"

"There's no time to change. Every second counts. The soone
we find Stephen, the sooner we can leave this place. Beside
my riding habit has been packed, and my traveling clothes ar
barely more suitable than what I am already wearing." Swing
ing the cloak around herself, Susannah ran out of the apartmen

The head groom was startled when she arrived in the stable
yard. "Why, good morning, ma'am," he said, touching the bri
of his low-crowned hat. "Sir Gareth said you were indispose
and would not be requiring the mare after all."

"I'm feeling much better, thank you."

"As you wish, ma'am."

"Has Sir Gareth been gone long?" she asked as she accom
panied him to her mare's stall.

"Oh, a good ten minutes, ma'am," the groom replied. "Beg
ging your pardon if I speak out of turn, ma'am, but you sai
yesterday you do not like riding. There's a thunderstorm brew
ing, and it is bound to be here before you complete the ride."

"I will take that chance."

"Yes, ma'am." The man peered curiously at the little sati
slippers peeping from beneath her cloak, then glimpsed her o

ge silk gown. Peculiar togs for riding in, he thought, and put down to a lovers' tiff. Why else would such a lady rush off e this after Sir Gareth Carew?

The mare was ready again within two minutes, and Susannah de out of the yard as swiftly as she dared. When she left the avel way and set off down the grassy slope toward the first ke, she realized how very soft and treacherous the ground was er all the overnight rain. The lake was like a mirror as she fol-wed the hoofprints of Gareth's horse along the track, and the aterfowl were oddly quiet. The sky was darker now, and another owl of thunder sounded across the heavens to the southwest. It as nearer, but still quite some distance away. The air was un-easantly warm, and at the edge of the woods she reined in to ke off her cloak. She breathed out with relief, suddenly only o glad she was wearing something as flimsy as a silk evening wn; a riding habit would have been unbearable in this humid-/. After draping the cloak in front of her saddle, she rode on.

The bluebells were very hazy and motionless in the glades, most as if they had been painted, and not a leaf stirred in the es. The heavy clouds burgeoned overhead, and a flicker of ghtning made her glance back. She found herself counting. ne, two, three, four . . . Thunder rolled. The storm was four les away; by superstitious reckoning, anyway.

She reached the temple of Flora and saw the muddle of hoof arks and bootprints where Gareth had dismounted to search in-de. He had clearly found nothing, for the hoofprints led on to-ard the track again, and she urged the mare after them. She und the same marks at the rustic cottage. He had stopped twice w, so surely she must be catching up with him! The second ke and the grotto lay just ahead, and she was convinced that as where she would close his ten-minute lead. She didn't notice s horse's hoofprints veer sharply away into the trees just before e grotto, nor did she hear his low call of warning. It was too te. Suddenly she was face-to-face with a woman who was wait-g on horseback beside the grotto. It was Fleur Fitzgerald.

Chapter 33

Susannah reined in sharply, caught so off guard at being co[n]fronted by Fleur Fitzgerald that she didn't quite know wh[at] to say or do. The actress's face froze the instant she saw he[r] and it was hard to say which woman was more dismayed—S[u]sannah at being caught riding in an evening gown or Fleur b[e]cause she had been expecting to see someone else. Then th[e] actress's withering gaze proceeded to move over the orange si[lk] gown, and Susannah wished with all her heart that she had heed[ed] Anjuli, for at least her riding habit was presentable enough. A[s] it was, she could almost hear the sounds of Calcutta echoi[ng] across the oceans and see the bony little durzi seated cros[s]legged on the floor as he studied the illustration in the out-o[f]date journal she'd given him.

Fleur's gray-gloved fingers tightened over the reins as her ba[y] horse shifted slightly. She, of course, was a very modish pi[c]ture indeed. Her sapphire-blue riding habit seemed molded [to] her voluptuous curves, a starched white gauze scarf floated fro[m] her gray riding hat, and her shining black hair was gathered in[to] a dainty net at the nape of her neck. Sapphire blue. Susann[ah] remembered the tiny piece of cloth Gareth had found caught o[n] the gate.

The moments of stunned surprise were soon over, and the di[slike] like that was kindled at the New Theatre suddenly flared in[to] open flame. Susannah spoke first, determined to fire the ope[n]ing salvo. "Well, what an unexpected honor, Miss Fitzgerald[,]" she said in a tone that conveyed it to be anything but an hon[or.]

"Likewise, Mrs. Leighton," Fleur replied with similar di[s]honesty.

Clearly she had gone to the trouble of finding out whom S[ir] Gareth Carew was suddenly so friendly with, Susannah though[t,] and she could not resist a small prod at the other's perceive[d]

alousy. "So you know who I am? One wonders what Lord Far-
gdon would say if he realized you were so interested in Sir
areth Carew's private life."

Fleur flushed. "Clearly you are equally interested in mine,
Irs. Leighton."

"It is difficult to avoid your private life, Miss Fitzgerald, for
is the subject of common talk. Very common, as it happens.
lay I inquire what are you doing here at Exton Park?" If it was
n account of the tiara, the creature would be disappointed. Per-
aps we both will, come to that, Susannah thought then, for
eaven alone knew where Chatterji had put it.

"My reasons are none of your concern, Mrs. Leighton."

"If you await His Grace of Exton, I fear he will not be com-
g, for he has been called away to London unexpectedly."

"And why would you imagine I am awaiting the duke? Per-
aps it is Sir Gareth I expect. Or had you not considered *that*
ossibility?" The starched scarf on Fleur's hat lifted gently as a
int breath of wind stirred across the lake, the mirrored surface
f which broke up for a moment before settling to glass again.

"Sir Gareth has no interest in you, Miss Fitzgerald, whereas
e duke . . . Well, that is a different matter. You were his mis-
ess for an age, and you are now here on his land. Two and
vo have a habit of making four."

"They do not add up on this occasion, nor will they ever again.
wouldn't arrange a meeting with Delavel Harmon now if he
ere the last man on earth."

"Why? Because he gave you a fake tiara?" Susannah had now
eard Gareth's theory about the ending of the liaison.

Thunder rattled through the clouds. One, two . . . Two miles
ow. Fleur's eyes glittered, almost as if reflecting lightning. "No
oubt it amuses you to laugh at my expense, as no doubt I would
ugh if it were the other way around. I had hoped Delavel would
ot reveal to the world how much of a fool he made of me, but
learly I hoped in vain."

So Gareth was right. "Such hope was a grave error of judg-
ent, if I may say so."

"My entire relationship with the duke him was a grave error
f judgment, Mrs. Leighton, but was entered into for one pur-
ose and one purpose only—to get the tiara, which rightfully be-
ongs to *my* family. It is the Fitzgerald tiara and should no more
ear the odious name of Holland than—than . . ." Words did not

suffice, and Fleur paused before continuing. "As soon as I rea
what the duchess wore to the palace, I guessed which woman ha
been played false! And I was right. I took every jewel he gav
me to be examined, and every last one was paste." She maneu
vered her horse alongside Susannah. "I will not waste furthe
breath upon you, except to warn that if you mention seeing m
here, or what I've said to you, I will make it my business to rui
your reputation in London. I will also see to it that Gareth be
comes a laughingstock because of you, and that is something h
would not like at all. Don't make the mistake of regarding thes
as empty threats, for I know exactly which ears to whisper in."

"No doubt you are well accustomed to whispering in all sort
of ears, Miss Fitzgerald. And in all sorts of beds, but do yo
remember which ear in which bed? It must become difficult afte
a while."

"I fail to see how a woman who rides out like a doxy in jus
a rag of a gown can presume to comment. By the way, wher
was that dreadful garment assembled? A back alley in Calcutta
Yes, by the look of it, I'd say so. You should have stayed i
Bengal, my dear, for it's obviously more your, er, style."

Susannah merely gave her a level smile. "At least my jewel
are real, Miss Fitzgerald."

Fleur flushed angrily. "Don't cross me any more than you al
ready have, because if you do, I—" She broke off as a blind
ing flash of lightning was followed almost instantly by a crasl
of thunder that made the ground tremble. The horses moved un
easily, tossing their heads, and a stir of wind suddenly rustle
through the trees. Susannah shivered in her thin gown.

Fleur caught up her reins and urged her mount away, past th
conifers toward the disused gates, which Susannah now notice
stood sufficiently open to allow a horse through. The actress, n
mean horsewoman, negotiated them with ease and then reine
in, intending to close and padlock them. But more lightning li
the heavens and another thunderclap reverberated above the val
ley, and she rode swiftly away instead.

As the eye-catching sapphire-blue passed out of sight beyon
the boundary wall, Susannah exhaled with relief. She felt sh
had held her own in the encounter, although how she had man
aged it when she looked like *this* she simply did not know!

The wind gusted again, rippling the surface of the lake, an
the first heavy drops of rain began to fall. She didn't hear Garetl

le up behind her; she knew nothing until he had dismounted
d led both horses to the grotto, where he tethered them to the
atue of Venus. Then he lifted her down from the saddle, grabbed
r cloak from over the saddle, and drew her safely down the
otto steps just as the heavens opened.

Three or four blinding flashes of lightning turned everything
dazzling blue, and the accompanying explosions of thunder
reatened to bring the grotto tumbling down—or so Susannah
ought. She screamed and flung herself into Gareth's arms, and
drew her further inside from the shell-studded steps. The hon-
suckle around the entrance trembled as the wind blustered,
d the leaves of the flags at the top of the steps seemed oddly
ight against the leaden skies. There was already a large pud-
e at the foot of the steps, and it began to enlarge visibly as
e torrential downpour splashed into the entrance like a foun-
in, but at the back of the grotto the floor rose slightly, and all
as dry. Gareth led Susannah there and carefully wrapped the
oak around her shivering shoulders, then removed his top hat
d gloves and rested them on a narrow ledge.

More lightning and thunder made everything shake, and the
rses whinnied. Susannah feared they would tear their reins
ee and bolt, but Gareth read her thoughts and took her in his
ms again. "They're tethered firmly enough, so don't fret. It's
nasty squall and will soon be over."

She slipped her arms around his waist and rested her head
ainst his shoulder. She flinched as more lightning lit the skies
tside, but to her relief there was a pause before the crash of
under. Her arms tightened around him, and she stared at the
ater cascading down the steps. Another flash of lightning.
ne . . . Thunder. One mile! She held her breath, her gaze not
avering from the entrance. Seconds passed, then lightning
ain. One, two . . . Two miles. She closed her eyes and began
relax. Gareth's hands were warm through the thin silk of her
wn, and she could feel the beating of his heart, so steady and
assuring when all was chaos outside. Lightning. One, two,
ree . . . Three miles. The wind was dying away, and so—more
owly—was the rain.

She drew back from his embrace, ashamed. "What a feeble
ing you must think me."

"Feeble being? That is the last thing you are, Susannah
ighton."

The storm had temporarily banished Fleur from her mind, bu
no more. "Gareth, do you know whom I've just spoken to?"

"Yes. Fleur Fitzgerald. I saw her tracks and was forewarned
but you rode on. I tried to call you back."

"I didn't hear or see anything until it was too late."

"I know."

"She said—"

"I heard it all," he interrupted quietly and then smiled a lit
tle. "You must not pay heed to her threats. The ears she ha
whispered into will not wish to become involved in her revenge
not even Jerry Faringdon. He's hopelessly in love with her, bu
even he takes everything she says with a pinch of salt. *I* cer
tainly do not care what she says, nor should you."

"I don't."

"Good." He paused. "It was an acrimonious few minutes, t
be sure."

She met his eyes. "I've despised her for a long time."

"With justification."

"Maybe, but the duke treated her very shabbily, don't yo
think?"

"And she didn't do the same to him? They deserved eac
other."

"You're right, I suppose." Then Susannah gave a wicked smile
"Oh, how I wish I could see her right now. She will look lik
a wet sapphire-blue rat, and as for that starched scarf . . . S
much for being the very height of fashionable excellence. Mothe
Nature has an excellent way with her, don't you think?"

"What a very nasty tongue you have, to be sure."

Susannah looked at him. "Who do you think she was expectin
me to be?"

They were both silent for a moment, and they both said th
same name at once. "Mrs. Wilberforce!"

Chapter 34

Susannah put her hands together, and touched her fingertips to her lips. "Of *course!* The housekeeper is Fleur's accomplice! The tiara is common to them both!"

"Very common?" inquired Gareth, a little slyly.

Susannah smiled. "Oh, positively vulgar," she replied, then gasped. "I've just realized what it is about Mrs. Wilberforce that is so familiar. She and Fleur have the same mouth and chin. They're related. Mother and daughter, maybe, or aunt and niece."

He nodded, and ran his fingers incredulously through his hair. "It was quite literally staring us in the face!"

"Just as the duke's key to the old safe stared everyone in the face the night before last. It was a trick of the light that led me to that secret drawer, but the other two—Stephen and Mrs. Wilberforce—were helped by the drawer not closing properly afterward. I'll warrant Mrs. W has been looking everywhere since she came here."

Gareth agreed. "Yes, and then she simply procured another fake. When Hector heard at the conservatory entrance last night, she must have just realized where the duke's new hiding place was. If she takes anything now, she'll think it's bound to be the real tiara. I almost feel sorry for her."

"I don't. Nor do I feel sorry for Fleur, who must have been waiting here today in the hope of at last getting her hands upon *my* family's heirloom." Susannah was heartless.

Gareth glanced toward the grotto entrance, where the light was becoming more translucent. "Well, Mrs. W won't come anywhere near the grotto when she sees our horses."

Susannah gave a sheepish grin. "I don't know why I'm being so smug about Fleur Fitzgerald not receiving the tiara. *I* have failed, too, thanks to Chatterji."

"Maybe the demon monkey will bring it back yet."

"I doubt it, not after all this rain. If you had seen him come in this morning, you'd understand. He absolutely hates getting wet, and he certainly got soaked last night."

"Serves him right," Gareth said unfeelingly.

"Oh, I heartily agree."

Lightning glittered outside, and there was a long pause before a comfortingly distant roll of thunder. The wind had softened to a breeze, and although the rain was still falling quite heavily, the daylight seemed a little brighter. She wondered if Stephen was being kept somewhere dry. Stephen! How could she have forgotten? She looked urgently at Gareth. "I-I haven't told you why I rode after you like a demon in just my gown!"

Gareth smiled. "I seem to recall the word 'doxy,' not 'demon.' Still, an evening gown may be unconventional equestrian gear, but it's infinitely more interesting than a dull old riding habit." He saw the anxiety shadowing her face again and became more serious. "I realize you wouldn't have come out in such a way if it were not important. What has happened?"

"I suddenly realized that Stephen is probably at the temple. It's the one place the duke is anxious we should still not go."

"I've come to the same conclusion, but thought it best to examine every other possibility on the way." Gareth took her chin in his hand and made her look at him. "Susannah, I want you to return to the house as soon as this storm is over."

"Now that I've come this far? No!"

"I am more than capable of looking after myself, but if I have you to consider . . . Let's just say I would feel happier if I knew you were safe."

"Stephen is my brother, and I want to be there when he's found."

"Susannah—"

"No. This time I will not obey you," she said fiercely.

"You are a very mulish woman, Mrs. Leighton."

" 'Mulish' is not a very flattering adjective."

"Would you prefer 'spirited'?"

"Yes."

He smiled and looked at the light outside. "The storm is ending fast now, but there is still time for this . . ." He turned his head back again, and before she knew it he was kissing her. She responded immediately, with an artless candor that told him all he needed to know about her feelings for him. He caught her nto his arms, his kiss becoming more aroused. She couldn't help sinking luxuriously against him, and as their lips moved yearningly together, she felt weak from the wonderful sensations that washed through her. She had never dreamed so much sensuous pleasure could be found in a kiss, never dreamed that she was capable of such fierce and all-consuming desire. Waves of enjoyment swept over her, and she knew that it would always be this way with him, because what she felt for him was complete, unconditional love.

It was he who ended the kiss, and his green eyes were dark with emotion as he took her flushed face in his hands. "You are the sweetest temptation any man could ever encounter, my darling Susannah, but when I make you mine completely, it will be between silk sheets."

Her senses were still sweeping her wildly along, and caution had long since been consigned to the four winds. "I do not want to wait for silk sheets," she whispered.

"We should make love for the first time when all this is over and done with. Fulfillment will be ours for the taking then, ours for the prolonging, ours for the cherishing."

"I want to be yours now, to seal what we feel for each other." She smiled. "But you are right, we must wait."

They both turned as the rain stopped suddenly. It was so abrupt that the ensuing silence seemed almost eerie. The light was hazy now, as if the clouds had thinned and the sun almost broken through. Thunder grumbled somewhere to the northeast, and the birds began to sing. Gareth tugged his top hat on and slipped his hands into his gloves. "Come on, time is marching on and we must investigate that temple," he said and swept her up into his arms to carry her over the now considerable puddle.

At the house, meanwhile, things were progressing in a most startling way. Susannah and Gareth were only too right to suspect Mrs. Wilberforce, for the housekeeper was both Fleur Fitzgerald's lieutenant in crime and her mother, and she would have met her daughter at the grotto had she not been interrupted in the very act of taking the newly marked tiara from the conservatory. She had no idea that the scratch upon it was as fake as the tiara itself—nor did Jane, who was the person who caught her red-handed.

Jane had awakened not long after Susannah, and as the latter rushed out of the house to ride after Gareth, Jane had decided to take Minette for a walk before the approaching storm made such exercise impossible. Wearing a cherry-and-cream-spotted morning gown and matching wide-brimmed hat, she went through the marble hall, intending to leave the house by way of the southern terrace. Minette was not on a lead and kept rushing impatiently ahead, then rushing back again. Then Chatterji materialized as if by magic and bounded onto the poodle's back. This was the signal for Minette's excitement to overflow, and with a delighted yelp, she dashed into the saloon, but when Jane followed, both had vanished. Like Hector the night before, she first examined the library, then the corridor to the guest pavilion, but she encountered Anjuli, who told her the animals had not gone that way.

Realizing they must have gone toward the chapel, Jane caught up her skirt and hastened in that direction. She reached the chapel and saw Minette gazing silently at something in the conservatory. The poodle's ears were pricked and her tail very still, and Chatterji had jumped off her back to clamber up the architrave, from which he too was peering into the conservatory.

Jane paused and then distinctly heard the grating of a flagstone. Puzzled, she crossed the chapel on tiptoe. Minette turned, and her tail began to wag, but the poodle remained quiet as Jane made her stealthy way around the luxuriant plants to see what was going on. Then she halted in appalled amazement as she saw Mrs. Wilberforce on her knees by the square hole beneath the removed flagstone. The housekeeper was sitting back on her heels, with the Holland tiara in her hands. Her face was alight with triumph as she inspected it for the scratch, then pushed it into a soft cloth bag that lay on the floor beside her.

Jane was outraged. "What *precisely* do you think you are doing, Mrs. Wilberforce?" she demanded.

The housekeeper jumped to her feet as if scalded. A medley of horrified expressions crossed her face as she hid the bag behind her back and struggled for something convincing to say. "I-I found the hole like this, Your Grace," she said then.

"And I suppose the tiara *found* its own way into your bag?" Jane inquired icily. The housekeeper's mouth opened and closed like that of a fish as Jane held out a hand. "The bag, if you please."

Mrs. Wilberforce's fingers closed possessively over it, and she backed away. "The tiara doesn't belong to you! It belongs to *us!*" she cried then, her northern accent suddenly returning to her native Irish.

"Us?" Jane repeated.

"The Fitzgeralds. It's always been ours, and neither you nor the Hollands shall have it!"

Jane stared at her. "The Fitzgeralds? You have something to do with Fleur Fitzgerald?"

"I'm her mother!" the woman declared defiantly.

Jane's lips parted as at last she saw the resemblance. "So *that's* why you've come here," she said slowly.

"Your husband tricked her, and now I'm taking back what has belonged to us all along."

"You aren't taking anything," Jane declared with what she hoped was the full authority of her rank.

Suddenly the housekeeper lunged toward her, shoving her backward so ferociously that Jane had no chance of maintaining her balance. She fell so heavily that she was dazed, and Minette immediately surged to the rescue. The poodle tried to seize Mrs. Wilberforce's hem but failed, then Chatterji hurled himself onto her as she ran through the doorway into the chapel. The monkey was intent upon the bag, which he knew contained the tiara. He was furious that somehow *his* trinket had found its way back into the hole in the ground, and this woman had taken it. He sank his teeth into Mrs. Wilberforce's ear, and she screeched with pain. The monkey thought he saw his chance and tried to grab the bag, but the housekeeper held on grimly. There was a tug-of-war until she had the wit to remove the tiara and hurl the empty bag away with Chatterji still clinging to it for all he was worth. The bag struck the pulpit, and the monkey fell heavily to the stone floor.

Minette rushed after Mrs. Wilberforce, barking furiously, and Jane hastened to poor Chatterji, fearing he had been killed, but he was just badly winded. She scooped him up off the floor and cradled him close as she hurried along the corridor toward the main block of the house, where Minette was barking angrily in the marble hall.

But when Jane arrived there was no sign of either Mrs. Wilberforce or the stolen tiara.

Chapter 35

Susannah and Gareth had reached the felled oak tree before they noticed the rain-filled hoofprints and wheel ruts of a pony cart leading out of the trees to their right. They saw there was a little-used way that they hadn't noticed before, and it seemed to come more directly from the direction of the house, whereas the track they had been following was very circuitous in order to take in all the follies. The wheel ruts went around the tree obstacle, then continued along the closed portion of the track toward the temple. Whoever it was must have driven by after the storm, for the marks were very steep and clean-sided; if they had been made during or before the storm they would have been much more flattened, as several others were before them.

Susannah and Gareth reined in. There hadn't been any wheel tracks at all when they rode this way before, and Hector had reported that the duke told his henchmen to take Stephen to his hiding place in the pony cart. Surely this *must* be the way that vehicle had come. Gareth studied the marks. "The cart drove this way last night, presumably with Stephen, and then back again. Now it has come again. It's my guess that someone has gone to see that the captive is all right."

Susannah's lips parted, and she glanced swiftly in the direction of the temple. "That means they are there now!"

"Probably."

"You—you don't think it is the press-gang?"

He smiled. "In a pony cart? I don't think that is the Royal Navy's way. No, it will just be one of the duke's footmen."

They rode on, but much more cautiously, keeping to the grass beside the track in order not to leave a trail of their own. As they neared the temple clearing, they heard the brief whinny of a horse just around a bend ahead. Immediately they turned their mounts into the trees, from which they watched as a pony cart swayed past. It was driven by the pugilist footman named Jones, who was so intent upon trying to keep his damp clay pipe alight that there was no danger of him noticing the watchers among the leaves.

When he had disappeared toward the felled oak, they emerged to ride quickly on to the temple. The clearing was deserted, but the marks of the cart led right up to the temple steps. After dismounting, they ascended to the entrance, where Gareth caught Susannah's hand and led her inside to the inner steps. There he called down. "Stephen? Stephen, can you hear me?" But there was no response, only the steady drip of rainwater after the downpour. He called again; still there was nothing.

Susannah joined him. "Stephen? It's me, Susie. If you can hear me, *please* try to make a sound!"

For a moment it seemed nothing would happen, then suddenly there came a scraping noise. It was so faint that at first they weren't sure they'd heard anything, but then it came a second time, more strongly, and they knew they'd found him. With a glad cry, Susannah gathered her skirts to hasten down into the virtual darkness, but Gareth prevented her. "Care is needed down there. Remember the loose stones and water? Besides you won't see anything without light, and I have brought my lucifers and a candle."

When the candle was lit, he descended first, treading cautiously after the mishaps both he and Minette had met with before. The sound of dripping water grew louder, and Susannah saw the place where Minette had become wedged and the loose stone had caused Gareth a drenching. At the bottom of the steps there was such deep shadow that it was difficult to see anything, but they could hear Stephen more clearly now. He was scuffing his boot heels against something, and trying to call out in spite of the handkerchief the duke had stuffed into his mouth. Gareth moved toward the sound, and suddenly the wavering glimmer of the candle revealed Susannah's imprisoned brother. He was tied hand and foot, and his clothes were in a terrible mess. His cheeks bulged with handkerchief, and his blue eyes were both relieved and urgent as Susannah ran to kneel beside him. "Oh, Stephen! How glad I am to find you!" she cried, pulling the handkerchief out of his mouth and then flinging her arms around his neck.

He had difficulty speaking because his mouth was so dry. "Susie? You should be in Bengal!"

"And you're supposed to be in America," she replied, then sat back on her heels to take the lighted candle Gareth pressed into her hands. She watched as he took a small stiletto from his capacious and resourceful pocket in order to cut the yellow wig ribbon and twine that bound the prisoner.

Stephen sat up painfully and gratefully swallowed some brandy from the tiny silver flask that was also produced from Sir Gareth Carew's amazing pocket. He coughed and spluttered as the fiery liquid coursed down his parched throat, then he closed his eyes as Susannah rubbed his numb wrists and Gareth removed his boots to rub his ankles. After a moment he recovered a little and looked at Susannah again.

"When Jane told me a Mrs. Leighton was her guest here, I didn't for a moment guess it would be you, Susie."

"Nor did I imagine that you were Jane's lover and were trying to steal the Holland tiara," she replied.

"How did you know about me? Did Jane tell you? Is she all right?"

"Yes, and we will soon have the pair of you out of this place," Gareth replied. Then he swiftly explained all that had happened.

Stephen stared, then grinned. "You mean, Exton's on a wild-goose chase to London?"

"I certainly trust so. Can you get up now? We really should be making our getaway."

Stephen took the hand and rose painfully to his feet. He tried to take a step but had to lean back against the wall. Gareth steadied him. "Just give it a minute or so. You haven't been tied up all that long, so it shouldn't last."

Stephen drew a long breath. "Talking of getaways, I'm not leaving without the tiara. It's what started all this, and it's what will finish it."

Gareth sighed. "I've already told you that Susannah's devil of a monkey absconded with it, and if you imagine for a single moment that I'm going to waste precious time combing the park for it, you are gravely mistaken." Stephen gave him a mutinous look that was so like Susannah's that Gareth had to laugh. "By all the saints, if I didn't already know you two were brother and sister, I would certainly know it from *that* expression!"

Stephen smiled again. "We're Hollands through and through,"

he said, taking one of Susannah's hands and drawing the palm to his lips. Then he glanced at Gareth again. "I take your point about the tiara. Other things are far more important."

Susannah squeezed his fingers. "Stephen, I don't want to leave the tiara behind any more than you do, but Chatterji could have left it *anywhere*."

"I can't wait to meet this monstrous monkey." Stephen suddenly noticed the orange silk peeping out of her parted cloak. "Is it nighttime, then? I confess I've lost all track of the hour."

"It's midmorning. I just haven't changed since last night. I'm afraid I rode here like this."

"Life in Bengal has clearly given you a disregard for etiquette," Stephen replied. "What on *earth* does Richard have to say?"

"Richard is dead," she replied quietly.

"Dead? But—"

"It was a riding accident," she explained. There would be time enough to tell him more.

He searched her face in the candlelight. "Should I offer my condolences?" he inquired.

"I am not a grieving widow, if that is what you wonder. We went our separate ways as much as possible."

"I'm sorry, Susie."

"For arranging the match in the first place? Don't be, for I enjoyed Bengal, and now I am now the happiest creature on earth." She glanced at Gareth.

Stephen followed the glance. "So that's the way of it, hmm?"

Gareth laughed. "Should I seek your permission to pay court to your sister?"

"I hardly think so. I was the cause of her first disastrous alliance, so I'm staying well out of things the second time around. As a widow, she is at liberty to please herself. Apart from which, I am not exactly in a position to pass judgment. An affair with a married woman does not adorn my brow with a laurel wreath of moral rectitude. But if you *were* to seek my permission, I would grant it gladly. I recall the favors you tried to do for me that night at the Union Club, and for what it's worth, I appreciate them only too well now, when it's too damned late. I was a blasted idiot that night."

"I won't disagree."

"Well, I certainly had time to repent at leisure."

Gareth glanced at his fob watch. "Time is marching on. Do you think you will be able to walk now, Stephen?"

Stephen nodded. "I would not cut a graceful dash in an Almack's cotillion, but I think I can manage to get out of here."

"Where have you been staying?"

"A posting house just outside Cirencester."

"That is the wrong way, I'm afraid. I trust you don't keep anything too valuable there?"

Stephen shook his head. "Just clothes and so on. I did not bring much from Boston, because I intend to return there. With Jane," he added.

"And we will help you do just that," Gareth promised. "We intend to leave here in my landau to take refuge at Pengower— monkeys, poodles, and all, but I don't want any of Exton's servants recognizing you. So it will be best to collect you from somewhere *outside* the park. Do you know the lodge and disused gates not far from the grotto?"

"Yes, Susannah gave me a key to the gates, and I have been coming and going that way."

"So has Fleur Fitzgerald," Susannah said.

Stephen pulled a face. "The least said about *her,* the better. Anyway, you were talking of the gate and lodge . . . ?"

Gareth nodded. "I want you to take Susannah's horse and leave that way. There's a barn up by the main highway. You are to wait there. My landau will probably have left by now but I want you to stay there anyway."

"Your landau is being kept in a *barn?*" Stephen said incredulously. "Whatever for?"

"It's a long story. Suffice it that at the time it seemed like a wise notion. Now it is more an inconvenience than anything else, but it should not present problems. I want you to wait in the barn, Stephen. We'll pick you up when we leave."

"With all due respect, Carew, my honor demands that I confront Exton first," Stephen replied.

Gareth shook his head. "No one is going to confront him. We're just going to leave while his back's turned."

"But—"

"Do as you're damned well told!" Gareth snapped. "Heroics are apt to get one into unnecessary trouble, and I've long since learned that if one wishes to escape with one's hide intact, one simply gets on with it."

"Nevertheless—"

This time it was Susannah who interrupted. "Do as Gareth says, Stephen. Believe me, he knows what he's talking about."

Stephen gave in unwillingly. "As you wish—but it goes very much against the grain."

Gareth took the candle. "You and Jane will soon be on your way to America, so you can leave Exton to me. I will think of suitable punishment," he said, leading the way back out to the horses. There he removed the sidesaddle from Susannah's mount and concealed it beneath a bush before giving Stephen a leg up.

A moment or so later Susannah's lost-and-found-again brother had disappeared along the track toward the grotto. She turned to Gareth. "What now?"

"We return to the house for Jane, Anjuli, Hector, et al. The quickest way now is to complete the circuit. Come on." He mounted his horse, leaned down to lift her up before him, then kicked his heels.

Chapter 36

Within minutes the Grecian grove appeared ahead, and Su sannah's heartbeats quickened as beyond it she saw th end of the woods, and the open lawns spreading up toward th house.

Gareth would have urged the horse right past the grove if Su sannah had not happened to glance down at the ground, wher she saw Chatterji's missing turban lying in the grass. "Stop Gareth!" she cried.

He reined in immediately, and she slipped down to retrieve th monkey's precious item of clothing. "He must have come all thi way last night," she said, glancing around the grove. The foun tain spilled prettily from Venus's upheld stone urn in the center its dancing water flashing so brilliantly in the sunlight that whe Susannah looked at the goddess's head, she almost thought sh imagined the beam of deep pink shining through the rainbow hued spray. She stared at it, and then went slowly closer.

"What is it?" Gareth asked.

"I've found where my dreadful monkey left the tiara!" sh declared, and pointed to Venus's newly acquired ruby crown.

Gareth laughed and maneuvered the horse closer so that h could reach past the spray of water to remove the tiara. H smiled as he handed it to Susannah. "So, Chatterji *did* think yo and Venus are alike!"

She pushed the tiara into the pocket on the inside of her cloak "Oh, Gareth, I'm so happy we have found it! Stephen will b overjoyed."

He lifted her onto the horse once more. "Mayhap this is good omen, and everything else will go according to plan," h murmured and moved the horse on again.

They emerged from the woods to see a considerable distur bance going on around the house. Small groups of men were searching the gardens, and others were combing the park on horse-back. Wondering what was going on, Gareth urged the horse around the lake and up the slope. They reached the stableyard, where Gareth's landau had already arrived, and soon learned from the rather incredulous head groom that Mrs. Wilberforce had stolen the Holland tiara and run off with it. Susannah and Gareth ex-changed glances, for they knew that the housekeeper had run off with nothing of the sort.

Gareth's postilion had been lingering nearby as they spoke to the head groom, and as they turned to go to the house, he has-tened after them. "Begging your pardon, Sir Gareth."

"Yes, Billings? What is it?"

"It may be nothing, I may even have dreamed it, but . . ."

"Well, spit it out, man!"

"After you'd brought the horse back to the barn this morn-ing, I went to sleep for a while. I-I *had* been up a long time," the man pointed out quickly. "Anyway, I overslept, sir, and the sun was well high when something woke me up all of a start. The horses were a little restless, and the barn door was ajar, al-though I'm *certain* I'd closed it. I went to look out and saw someone riding like the very devil along the road toward Cirencester. It was that big ginger-headed toad of a footman, the one who'd sell his grandmother for a halfpenny. You know the one, sir?"

"Yes. As it happens, he was the one who came to the door when I took the note to the house."

The postilion's face fell. "He was, sir?"

"What are you trying to say, Billings?"

"Well, I don't know for sure, but I'm afraid the fellow may have seen something that aroused his suspicions about the barn. Maybe it was just the hoofprints of your horse where no hoof-prints should be, if you see what I mean. I think he may have come poking around while I was asleep, seen the landau inside, and realized something was going on." The postilion cleared his throat. "Sir, he might also have seen the horse you rode last night. It has a very distinctive broken blaze, which may have been visible even in the rain and darkness. He just might have put two and two together about the note that set the duke driv-ing off like his rear was alight."

Gareth drew a long breath. "If you're right, the duke is going to realize he's been lured away under false pretenses."

"Yes, sir."

"How long ago did you see the man ride off?"

"Long enough for it to be worrisome."

Susannah had listened to everything with increasing dismay. "Gareth, does this mean the duke may return at any moment?"

"I'm afraid it does, *cariad,* but I don't intend to wait around to find out. Billings, get the landau to the front entrance immediately."

"Sir." The postilion turned on his heel to hurry away.

Gareth caught Susannah's hand. "Come on, we'll have to be quick. I only hope Jane doesn't expect to pack an entire wardrobe!" He began to run toward the house, pulling her along with him.

Jane was astonished and overjoyed when she heard what they had to say, and she was not in the least interested in taking a great deal with her. Most of the things she had, she said, would only remind her of Exton Park and its master, both of which she wished to forget. Hector had made some friends in the kitchens, and since the duke's henchmen all happened to be scouring the park for Mrs. Wilberforce, the other servants were willing enough to carry the luggage out to the waiting landau. Soon it was all packed, and Anjuli, Hector, and Jane's maid were squeezed onto the outside seat at the back. Susannah and Gareth waited impatiently in the marble hall for Jane, who had run back to get a book of poems that Stephen had given her.

Minette sat patiently on the floor at Gareth's feet, and Susannah held Chatterji in his muff. The monkey was still feeling bruised and sorry for himself after his ordeal at Mrs. Wilberforce's hands, and he knew how to squeeze the very last drop of sympathy. His wan expression was something to behold, although he brightened considerably when Susannah remembered his turban and returned it to him.

At last Jane returned, and they all hurried toward the entrance, their footsteps echoing among the looming columns. But then they heard the unmistakable rattle of a carriage approaching at speed along the drive.

Gareth halted at the door in dismay. "I'm afraid we're too late. It's the duke!" he breathed, and the sleepless echo picked up his words and tossed them mockingly around the hall. *The duke . . . the duke . . . the duke . . .* For a moment Gareth considered making a run for it anyway. Billings was a deft postilion,

nd the landau could outmaneuver the heavier traveling carriage,
ut the redheaded footman soon put a stop to any such notion.
Ie urged his horse past the duke's carriage, and hurled himself
nto Billings, hauling him down from his horse to the wet gravel.
Then the duke's mud-stained carriage halted directly across the
andau's path, preventing any chance Billings would have had
f driving off, even had he been conscious after the blow to the
hin that the burly footman had dealt him.

The carriage door was immediately flung open, and Delavel Har-
non climbed down. His face was like thunder as he glanced at the
ully laden landau, and a nerve twitched savagely at the side of
is mouth as he indicated that the footman was to precede him
nto the house. The footman drew a double-barreled pistol from
nside his coat and entered the hall, where he found Gareth stand-
ig alone in the center of the floor. Susannah and Jane, together
vith their respective animals, had been ordered to withdraw be-
ind the columns.

The footman cocked the pistol, and the ominous click re-
ounded from the lofty corners of the hall. Minette growled as
ie duke came in, and Jane had to hold tightly to the poodle's
eweled collar. Minette continued to growl, and Chatterji added
is two pennorth by baring his teeth and making his most threat-
ning noises, for any enemy of Minette's was his enemy too.
he echo repeated the sounds until it seemed there were half a
ozen poodles and even more monkeys concealed around the
all.

The duke swaggered forward, only too brave and authorita-
ive when he had the armed footman to back him up. "You're
lever, Carew, I grant you that," he said with grudging admira-
ion. "I should have remembered how inventive you have be-
ome since Hawkesbury took you on. I would certainly be almost
n London by now if it weren't for this stout fellow's sharp
yes." He gestured toward the footman.

"I must remember to congratulate him sometime," Gareth mur-
aured, his green eyes sliding briefly to the smug servant, who
learly saw himself as his master's right-hand man from now
n.

"You aren't going to live that long, Carew," the duke said.

Jane gasped, and Minette's growls erupted into a volley of
ngry barks. Chatterji leapt from his muff to the floor, then ad-
anced a few yards toward the duke, screeching threateningly

with each step. The echo played havoc with all the racket, but Susannah was deaf to it all; she heard only the duke's threat and was frightened for her love.

As the animals quietened again, the duke's cold gaze moved toward his wife. "So you thought to make a deceived husband of me, did you, madam? I confess I'm surprised you found anyone to take you, least of all this pretty fellow, who prides himself on having the pick of London." His eyes slid back to Gareth. "Now, why would you pick the plainest creature in town, I wonder? What's your little game, Carew?"

Gareth was contemptuous. "You really are a fool, Exton," he said quietly. "You see a glove being returned to your wife and believe you are witnessing a tryst. A simple gentlemanly act, and you feel horns sprouting!" He glanced outside, and saw Stephen reining in, having left the barn on seeing the duke return.

The duke leaned across to relieve the footman of the pistol and leveled it at Gareth. "Lying will not get you out of this, Carew!" *Carew, Carew, Carew . . .*

Susannah took an involuntary step forward. "No!" she cried, her blue eyes wide with terror.

The duke turned sharply. "Stay back, madam!"

Gareth nodded at her. "Keep away, my love." Stephen and Hector were creeping up the steps to the door.

The duke's little eyes narrowed. "My love? Well now, Welshman, am I to understand you are stallion enough to service them *both*?"

Gareth laughed at him. "By God, Exton, if horns could penetrate your dense skull, it would be a miracle!"

The duke's lips curled back savagely. "You clearly don't think I am prepared to use this pistol." He took aim at Gareth's heart, but then a shadow moved at the entrance and another voice broke the silence.

"Sir Gareth isn't Jane's lover, Exton, I am!" Stephen said.

The duke was caught completely off guard and whirled about so sharply that his finger tightened involuntarily on the trigger. The pistol went off, and Susannah screamed as the shot whined past her to strike one of the marble columns. It ricocheted across to the other side of the hall, then across again, and Gareth immediately flung himself on the floor as he realized it would continue to bounce from surface to surface. He shouted to the women to get down as well, and Stephen and Hector drew hastily back from the entrance. The redheaded footman hurled himself beneath the candle table, and in a moment only the duke remained standing. They all heard the shot skim from column to wall to column, the pitch of its whine changing with each strike. No one knew where it was, or when it would stop, but suddenly the duke gave a howl of pain, and the pistol clattered to the floor as he clutched his posterior.

Gareth leaned up on his elbows to see what had happened, then burst into peals of laughter. Delavel Harmon, fifth Duke of Exton, had managed to shoot himself in the backside! Susannah sat up as well, and began to giggle, for if ever there was poetic justice, it was this. Stephen rushed across the hall to take Jane in his arms. When he did so, her hold upon Minette's collar loosened, and the poodle immediately dashed over to worry at the duke's ankles.

His Grace of Exton hopped around like a demented morris dancer, trying to shake off the poodle while still clutching his wounded rear, and all eyes were so riveted upon the spectacle that no one noticed the footman beneath the candle table. The dropped pistol had slithered close enough for him to stretch out a hand to it. Being double-barreled, it still had another shot to fire, and if he could reach it . . .

He reckoned without Chatterji, who suddenly darted to the top of the table and seized a candlestick. Clutching it in both paws, the monkey leaned over the edge and hit the man a resounding blow on the top of the head. With a grunt, the footman slumped senseless to the floor, and Hector hobbled quickly over to bind his wrists together with a belt.

Quick as a wink, Chatterji leapt to pick up the pistol and tried to aim it at the duke, but Gareth hastily disarmed him. "Much as I'd like to let you try, we don't want another ricochet, do we?" he said, bending to pat the monkey's turbaned head.

The commotion had by now brought the rest of the household running to see what was happening, and a sea of servants stared openmouthed at the astonishing scene in the marble hall. The footmen who had been responsible for incarcerating Stephen melted discreetly away when they saw their former prisoner only too clearly at liberty. The duke, still beset by Minette, shrieked for some assistance, but no one dared to move while Gareth stood there with the pistol. Jane called Minette off, and the poodle obeyed with great reluctance.

Gareth emptied the pistol, then tossed it away and nodded at the servants. "Attend to your master's backside, and take great care, for it is where he keeps his brains," he said wryly. He turned to Hector. "Go on out and see that Anjuli and the duchess's maid know all is well. And tell Anjuli to attend to poor Billings."

"She already is, sir."

As some of the servants hastened to the duke, who wasn't at all grateful or even civil, Gareth went to Susannah and slid an arm around her waist. "Are you all right, *cariad*?"

"I-I think so," she replied, as Chatterji, as jealous as ever, clambered up to insert himself firmly into her arms.

Gareth grinned at the monkey. "I'm going to win, you know, sirrah, so you might as well get used to it." Chatterji then suffered the double indignity of being ignored *and* slightly squashed as Gareth kissed Susannah tenderly on the lips. The monkey was audibly cross, but he could find nothing handy to bite. Gareth drew away then. "Our business here is finished, *mes amis,* so let's get out of this place, hmm?" he said, steering Susannah toward the door.

"With pleasure," Stephen agreed, ushering Jane out as well.

Gareth's landau bowled away from Exton Park, driven by Hector, whose days at Astley's Amphitheatre had more than equipped him for the art of being a postilion. The unfortunate Billings had taken his place on the rear seat, where he played upon his injuries to win sympathy from Jane's maid, who had been the object of his desire from the moment he saw her.

No one looked back at the house, not even Minette or Chatterji.

A week or so later the Duke of Exton, posterior still very sore, alighted gingerly from his town carriage outside Abbas Ali's house in Park Lane. In his hand he held the blue leather case containing the remaining replica tiara. He knew full well that it was a fake but was banking upon the emissary's not realizing that fact. Delavel Harmon did not need the money from the sale, but he simply could not bring himself to turn away from it. Besides, he had been made a fool of, and someone had to pay; it might as well be Abbas Ali.

The duke was smarting, and not only from the damage to his behind. The story of Jane's departure had reached town with him—he suspected through his servants, who spoke to other ser-

vants, and so on—and his humiliation was now common knowledge. It was bad enough that every drawing room in London
was ringing with laughter about the whole business, but he was
especially crushed to realize that practically the entire member-
ship of the Union Club was cock-a-hoop, having won handsome
wagers on the Duchess of Exton's hoped-for infidelity. Only Bull
Barker had lost, having placed money upon plain Jane's never
straying from her vows. There was another wager, however, upon
which Bull did rather well; he correctly predicted the number of
rude noises his bulldog would make in the course of an hour.

A scowl blotted the duke's already unlovable visage, for there
were no consolations on *his* horizon! He had just driven down
Bond Street and suffered the mortification of seeing a group of
gentlemen laughing delightedly at a cartoon in a printshop window. It was of the fifth Duke of Exton sporting as handsome a
set of antlers as any stag. To make matters worse, he had observed Jerry Faringdon curled up with mirth in the doorway of
the tailor opposite. As soon as the fellow noticed the Exton crest
on the passing carriage, he produced an ace of hearts from his
pocket and waved it mockingly. It was a belittling reminder of
the one and only time the duke had ventured to the Union Club
since arriving. How had he, Delavel Harmon, the scourge of the
green baize, failed to see that cards were slipping from the
scoundrel's cuff? Faringdon had never beaten him before, never
cheated before! And throughout play the fellow's blasted chimpanzee—newly restored because Fleur Fitzgerald had suddenly
broken her contract at Sadler's Wells to return to Dublin—was
also seated at the table, grinning at him like . . . like an *ape!*

His Grace of Exton was still scowling as he entered Abbas
Ali's house. Within minutes, however, he ran out squealing like
a porker, with the emissary's attendants in hot pursuit, scimitars
at the ready. The fake tiara had been rammed onto his head, and
more than one scimitar point had found a mark on his already
damaged rear. He barely managed to fling himself into the carriage, which bowled sharply away, door swinging. The Turks ran
after it for a while, yelling all manner of abuse, then they halted
in the middle of Park Lane, waving their scimitars and invok-
ing a thousand demons upon the evil Exton. They brought the
busy thoroughfare to a standstill, and the commotion attracted a
great deal of attention. Within minutes word of the incident

began to spread, and by nightfall London's drawing rooms rocked with still more amusement.

It was too much, and before the following dawn the duke scuttled back to Exton Park to lick his wounds—metaphorically, of course, for he was not *that* much of a contortionist!

Two months after that, on a fine July morning in Dublin, another carriage drew up at another curb, and Fleur Fitzgerald alighted to enter the city's most exclusive jewelers establishment. She swept inside in a rustle of fine buttercup silk and approached the gleaming oak counter, upon which she placed the tiara her mother had stolen from Exton Park. She demanded a valuation, and the jeweler took his magnifying glass to examine the tiara in detail. Then he looked at her and shook his head. "Madam, if it were real, then—"

Fleur broke in sharply. "What do you mean, if it were real? Of *course* it's real! It's the Fitzgerald tiara."

The jeweler drew a long breath, and his fingers began to drum upon the counter. "As I was saying, madam, if it were real, it would fetch a very handsome price. But this is paste."

Fleur stared at him. "It can't be! It has the scratch. Look!"

He pushed the tiara toward her. "It's a fake," he said flatly.

"But I *know* it's real!" she cried.

"And I know it isn't," he replied.

Fleur gaped at him and then at the tiara. How could it *possibly* be a fake? He was lying! Snatching it up, she hurried out and along the street to another jeweler. But a second opinion was no more encouraging than the first. Nor was the third. Fleur was speechless with bitter disappointment. Her fool of a mother had stolen a replica! Beside herself with fury, the former belle of Drury Lane dashed across the street and hurled the tiara into the Liffey.

One day, one *wonderful* day, she would lay hands upon the real one! Just see if she wouldn't!

That evening, across the Irish Sea in the whitewashed village of Pengower on the shore of Wales, Susannah and Gareth were married in the tiny church. Pengower Castle dominated the village, its towers and battlements still standing foursquare against the elements, as they had done for five hundred years. Inland, the hills said to hold Merlin's cave were purple and crimson in the sunset. The sea was deep turquoise, and gulls soared overhead as the bride and groom emerged from the church porch.

People had come from far and near to see the wedding, and the cheering crowd threw wheat as Sir Gareth Carew led his bride beneath the lych-gate to the waiting landau, which was decked with flowers and ribbons. Anjuli, wearing a pure-white sari and golden bangles, stood hand in hand with Hector, who had a new coat and breeches. The ayah was cradling Chatterji in her arms. The monkey had given up trying to separate Susannah and Gareth and was now doing his best to keep Hector away from Anjuli. His efforts were in vain again, for they ignored him as they smiled boldly at each other. Hector gazed adoringly into the ayah's big dark eyes and thought longingly of the curries that lay ahead.

Minette waited with them, for Jane had decided not to separate her from Chatterji. She was also concerned about Minette's safety on the long voyage to America, for the poodle wasn't exactly renowned for common sense. One of her mad half hours of dashing about would probably end with her going straight over the side into the sea. But though Minette had stayed behind with Susannah and Gareth, Billings the postilion had gone with Stephen and Jane; or rather, he had gone with Jane's maid, with whom his progress was slow but sure. But he reckoned to win her by the time the vessel reached landfall on the other side of the Atlantic.

Gareth paused before assisting the new Lady Carew into the vehicle.

"I love you with all my heart, my lady," he whispered.

"And I love you. Oh, if only Stephen and Jane could marry too." Tears stung her eyes, for her brother and his beloved could not wed because Jane was already a wife.

Gareth smiled. "In America they can call themselves Mr. and Mrs. Holland if they wish. Besides, they're happy, which is all that really counts."

She smiled through her tears. "Yes, I suppose you're right."

"Of course I am." He pulled her close, and to the delight of the onlookers, he kissed her passionately on the lips.

Susannah closed her eyes with happiness, and the rubies of the Holland tiara flashed against her russet hair.

*   *   *

It was Christmas morning in London, and snow was falling outside as Susannah wrote a letter to Stephen and Jane by the fire in the second-floor drawing room of Gareth's town residence in Hanover Square. She was five months with child and still the happiest creature alive. No woman had ever had a finer husband, lover, friend, or confidant than she had in her beloved Gareth, she thought, resting her pen on the portable escritoire on her lap.

Minette was snoring on the floor by the hearth, and Chatterji was on the windowsill, gazing out in fascination at the snowflakes drifting past the window. He had a new blue turban stitched with pearls and a fine little maroon coat made by Gareth's tailor in Bond Street. Nothing could have pandered to the monkey's vanity more than the fittings he had at those superior premises. He had been measured like a fine gentleman, and the coat had been delivered at the door, in a package addressed importantly to "Mr. Chatterji." Needless to say, the monkey was now Gareth's adoring slave and helped him every morning to select which pin to wear in his neckcloth. The monkey had surprisingly discerning taste, and Gareth always wore what he chose.

Gareth had gone out earlier, and Chatterji was waiting for his return. He had never seen snow before and did not know that he cared for it very much. He was about to leave the window for the warmth of the fire, when Gareth's curricle skimmed around the square and drew up outside. Lord Hawkesbury had received a visit from his favorite agent and had been informed that said agent was no longer available for assignments in St. Petersburg—or anywhere else for that matter.

With a screech, Chatterji bounded out of the room and down the stairs to greet Gareth, who moments later came into the drawing room with the monkey in his arms. He came over to Susannah. "I have some news for you, *cariad,*" he said, putting Chatterji aside.

His wife looked at his clothes in surprise. "You haven't taken off your outdoor things!" she said reprovingly, for he had left snowy footprints on the new Axminster.

"I thought my news more important." He took her by the hands.

"What is it?"

"His Grace of Exton is no more."

Susannah stared at him. "No more?" she repeated foolishly.

"He met a rather appropriate end, being shot by one of his own keepers, who mistook him for a poacher." Gareth smiled, and nodded at her unfinished letter. "Now *that* is something I'm sure you'll delight in informing Stephen, mm?"

"Yes! Oh, yes!" She stretched forward to be kissed, and Sir Gareth Carew willingly obliged.